BLACKBERRY
WINTER

SARAH JIO is the #1 international, *New York Times*, and *USA Today* bestselling author of ten novels. She is the host of the Mod About You podcast and also a longtime journalist who has contributed to *Glamour*, *The New York Times*, *Redbook*, *Real Simple*, *O: The Oprah Magazine*, *Bon Appétit*, *Marie Claire*, *Self*, and many other outlets, including NPR's *Morning Edition*. Her books have been published in more than twenty-five countries. She lives in Seattle with her husband, three young boys, and three stepchildren.

sarahjio.com
 sarahjioauthor
 @sarahjio
 @sarahjio

By Sarah Jio

All the Flowers in Paris
Always
The Look of Love
Goodnight June
Morning Glory
The Last Camellia
Blackberry Winter
The Bungalow
The Violets of March

BLACKBERRY WINTER

Sarah Jio

ORION

An Orion paperback

First published in Great Britain in 2019 by Orion Fiction,
an imprint of The Orion Publishing Group Ltd
Carmelite House, 50 Victoria Embankment,
London EC4Y 0DZ

An Hachette UK company

1 3 5 7 9 10 8 6 4 2

A CIP catalogue record for this book is
available from the British Library.

ISBN (Mass Market Paperback) 978 1 4091 9077 6
ISBN (eBook) 978 1 4091 9078 3

Printed and bound in Great Britain by Clays Ltd, Elcograf, S.p.A

www.orionbooks.co.uk

To my sons, Carson, Russell, and Colby, and their assortment of beloved stuffed animals—a ragged teddy bear, three tattered giraffes, and a little striped tiger. Being your mother is my life's greatest joy.

And to mothers everywhere—especially those who have had to say good-bye to a child.

BLACKBERRY
WINTER

Chapter 1

VERA RAY

Seattle, May 1, 1933

An icy wind seeped through the floorboards and I shivered, pulling my gray wool sweater tighter around myself. Just one button remained. At five cents apiece, it seemed frivolous to think of replacing the ones that had gone missing. Besides, spring had come. Or had it? I glanced outside the second-story window, and listened as the wind whistled and howled. An angry wind. The branches of the old cherry tree thrashed against the apartment building with such force, I jumped, worried another blow might break the glass. I couldn't afford a repair bill, not this month. But just then, an unexpected sight spelled me from my worries, momentarily. Light pink blossoms swirled in the air. I sighed, smiling to myself. *Just like snow.*

"Mama?" Daniel squeaked from under the covers. I pulled back the ragged blue quilt, revealing his handsome round face and soft blond hair, which still curled at the ends. *His baby hair.* At three, with plump, rosy cheeks and big eyes a heart-stopping shade of blue, he was somewhere between baby and boy. But when he slept, he appeared exactly the way he had on the day he was born. Sometimes I'd tiptoe into his room in the early morning hours and watch him, clutching his little brown bear, adoringly matted with a torn ear and a threadbare blue velvet bow.

"What is it, love?" I asked, kneeling beside the small pine bed before casting a cautious gaze back toward the window, where the wind raged outside. *What kind of mother am I to leave him here tonight, all alone?* I sighed. *Do I have another choice?* Caroline worked the late shift. And I couldn't bring him to the hotel again, especially after the incident last weekend when Estella found him sleeping in the ninth-floor penthouse suite. She had shooed him out from the warmth of the duvet as if he were a kitchen mouse caught dozing in the flour jar. It had frightened him terribly, and it had almost cost me my job. I took a deep breath. No, he'd be fine here, my precious boy, warm and safe in his bed. I'd lock the door. The walls of the tenement house were thin, but the door, yes, it was strong. Solid mahogany with a fine brass lock.

We both flinched at the sound of a knock at the door, urgent, pounding, insistent. Daniel grimaced. "Is it him again, Mama?" he said, before lowering his voice to a whisper. "The *bad* man?"

I kissed his forehead, attempting to hide the fear rising in my chest. "Don't worry, love," I said before standing. "It's probably just Aunt Caroline. You stay here. I'll go see."

I walked down the stairs and stood in the living room for a moment, frozen, trying to decide what to do. The knocking persisted, louder now, angrier. I knew who it was, and I knew what he wanted. I glanced at my purse, knowing there wasn't more than a dollar, maybe two, inside. Rent was due three weeks ago, and I'd been holding off Mr. Garrison with excuses, but now what? I'd spent my most recent paycheck on groceries and a new pair of shoes for Daniel, poor boy. I couldn't expect him to fit into those baby slippers much longer.

Knock. Knock. Knock.

The pounding mirrored the beat of my heart. I felt frightened, trapped. The apartment took on the feeling of a cage. The walls around me might as well have been rusted wire. *What am I going to do?* Reflexively, I looked down at my wrist. Ever since Daniel's father had presented me with the most exquisite object I'd ever laid eyes on, I'd cherished the gold chain inlaid with three delicate sapphires. That night at the Olympic Hotel I'd been a guest, not a maid wearing a black dress and white apron. As I opened the little blue box and he dangled the bracelet over my wrist, for the first time I felt like someone who was born to wear such finery. It almost seemed silly then, to think I could have, well . . . I closed my eyes tightly as the pounding at the door continued. I began to unhook the clasp, then shook my head. No, I would not hand it over to him. I would not give up that easily. Instead, I pulled the bracelet higher on my forearm, tucking it safely under the sleeve of my dress. I'd find another way.

I took a deep breath and walked slowly to the door, where I unlatched the lock reluctantly. The hinges creaked, revealing Mr. Garrison in the hallway outside. He was a large man, in both stature and girth; it was easy to see why Daniel feared him so. His stern face was all but covered by a gray, unkempt beard. Only ruddy, pockmarked cheeks and dark, unkind eyes shone through. His breath smelled of gin, piney and sour, signaling that he'd come up from the saloon on the floor below. The strict reign of Prohibition hadn't yet ended, but most police looked the other way in this part of town.

"Good evening, Mr. Garrison," I said as sweetly as I could.

He inched closer, wedging his large, steel-toed boot in the doorway. "Save the formalities," he said. "Where's my money?"

"Please—let me apologize, sir," I began in a faltering voice. "I know I've been late on rent. It's been a very hard month for us, and I—"

"You told that story last week," he said without emotion. He pushed past me and made his way into the kitchen, where he helped himself to the small loaf of bread I'd just pulled from the oven. *My dinner.* He opened the icebox and frowned when he didn't find a crock of butter. "I'll ask you once more," he continued, his cheeks stuffed. His eyes narrowed. "Where's my money?"

I clutched the bracelet as my gaze darted past him to the wall, with its scuffed baseboards and peeling paint. *What can I tell him now? What can I do?*

He let out a deep, throaty laugh. "Just as I thought," he said. "A thieving liar."

"Mr. Garrison, I—"

His eyes fixed on me possessively; he moved closer until I could smell the rancidness of his breath and feel the bristle of his beard on my face. He grasped my wrist tightly, just as the bracelet slinked beneath the cuff of my sleeve, hidden from his view. "I thought it might come to this," he said, his fat, rough hand fumbling with my sweater until he pushed it aside and clutched the bodice of my dress. His index finger tugged at a button. "Fortunately for you, I happen to be a generous man, and I'll allow you to pay me in a *different* way."

I took a step back, just as I heard footsteps on the stairs. "Mama?"

"Daniel, go back to bed, love," I said as calmly as I could. "I'll be right there."

"Mama," he said again, beginning to cry.

"Oh, honey," I called out, praying my voice didn't reveal the terror I felt. "Everything's all right. I promise. *Please* go back to bed."

I could not let him see this, or worse, let Mr. Garrison hurt him.

"Mama, I'm scared," he said, his voice muffled through his teddy bear.

Mr. Garrison cleared his throat and straightened his overcoat. "Well, if you can't shut him up," he shouted, regarding Daniel with a sinister grin, "then I'll have to come back. But make no mistake about it, I *will* be back." I didn't like the way he looked at Daniel, as if he were a pet, a nuisance. He turned his gaze back to me, staring at me as if I were a fine flatiron steak sizzling in a skillet. "And I'll get me my payment."

I nodded meekly as he walked out the door. "Yes, Mr. Garrison." I fumbled with the latch as his footsteps pounded down the hall. Before I turned around to face Daniel, I took a deep, reassuring breath and wiped a stray tear from my cheek.

"Oh, Daniel," I said, running to the top of the stairs, cradling him in my arms. "Are you frightened, honey? Don't be frightened. Mama's here. There's nothing to worry about."

"But the man," he sniffled, "he's a bad man. He hurt Mama?"

"No, honey," I said. "Mama wouldn't let that happen."

I reached down to my wrist and unfastened the bracelet, letting it fall into the protective space of my palm.

Daniel looked up at me in confusion, and I studied his big, innocent eyes, wishing things were different for him, for us. "Mama loves her bracelet, dear one. I just want to keep it safe."

He considered the idea for a moment. "So you don't lose it?"

"That's right." I stood up and took his hand. "Will you help Mama put it in the *secret place*?"

Daniel nodded, and we walked to the tiny cupboard below the stairs. He had discovered the space, no bigger than a hatbox, one morning while playing, and we'd decided the special compartment would be our secret from the world. Daniel kept eclectic treasures inside—a bluebird feather he'd found on the street, a sardine can that he'd filled with smooth stones and other odds and ends. A bookmark. A shiny nickel. A clamshell, sun-bleached to a brilliant white. I'd tucked in his birth certificate and other documents in need of safekeeping. And now I placed my bracelet inside.

"There," I said, closing the little door and marveling at the seamless fit. It blended perfectly into the paneling of the staircase. How Daniel had ever discovered it, I'd never know.

He nestled his head against my chest. "Mama sing a song?"

I nodded, smoothing his blond hair against his forehead, marveling at how much he looked like his father. *If only Charles were here.* I quickly dismissed the thought, the fantasy, and began to sing. "Hushaby, don't you cry, go to sleep, little Daniel. When you wake, you shall take, all the pretty little horses." The words passed my lips and soothed us both.

I sang four verses, just enough for Daniel's eyelids to get heavy, before I carried him to his bed, nestling him under the quilt once again.

His face clouded with worry when he eyed my black dress and white pinafore. "Don't go, Mama."

I cupped his chin. "It will only be for a little while, my darling," I said, kissing each of his cheeks, soft and cool on my lips.

Daniel buried his face in his bear, rubbing his nose against its button nose the way he'd done since infancy. "I don't want to." He paused, his three-year-old mind trying hard to summon the right words. "I scared when you go."

"I know, my love," I said, fighting the tears that threatened. "But I have to go. Because *I love you*. You'll understand that someday."

"Mama," Daniel continued, looking to the window, where, behind the glass, the wind gathered strength. "Eva says ghosts come out at night."

My eyes widened. Caroline's daughter possessed an imagination that belied her three-and-a-half years. "What is Eva telling you now, dear?"

Daniel paused, as though contemplating whether to answer. "Well," he said cautiously, "when we're playing, sometimes people look at us. Are they ghosts?"

"Who, dear?"

"The lady."

I knelt down to level my eyes with his. "What lady, Daniel?"

He scrunched his nose. "At the park. I don't like her hat, Mama. It has feathers. Did she hurt a bird? I like birds."

"No, love," I said, vowing to speak to Caroline about Eva's stories. I suspected they were the root of Daniel's nightmares of late.

"Daniel, what did Mama tell you about talking to strangers?"

"But I didn't talk to her," he said, wide-eyed.

I smoothed his hair. "Good boy."

He nodded, nestling his head in his pillow with a sigh. I tucked his bear into the crook of his arm. "See, you're not alone," I said, unable to stop my voice from cracking. I hoped he didn't notice. "Max is here with you."

He pressed the bear to his face again. "Max," he said, smiling.

"Good night, love," I said, turning to the door.

"G'night, Mama."

I closed the door quietly, and then heard a muffled "Wait!"

"Yes, love?" I said, poking my head through the doorway.

"Kiss Max?" he said.

I walked back to the bed and knelt down as Daniel pressed the bear against my lips. "I love you, Max," I whispered as I walked back to the door. "And I love you, Daniel. More than you'll ever know."

I tiptoed downstairs, put another log in the fireplace, said a silent prayer, and walked out the front door, locking it behind me. It was only one shift. I'd be home before sunup. I turned back to the door, then shook my head, reassuring myself. It was the only way. He'd be safe. Safe and sound.

Chapter 2

CLAIRE ALDRIDGE

Seattle, May 2, present day

My eyes shot open and I pressed my hand against my belly. There, that tugging pain in my abdomen again. What had Dr. Jensen called it? Yes, a *phantom pain*—something about my body's memory of the trauma. Phantom or not, I lay there feeling the familiar, lonely ache that had greeted me each morning for the past year. I paused to acknowledge the memory, wondering, the way I did every day when the alarm clock sounded, how I could bring myself to get up, to get dressed—to act like a normal human being, when I only wanted to curl up into a ball and take Tylenol PM to obliterate all feeling.

I rubbed my eyes and squinted at the clock: 5:14 a.m. I lay still and listened as the wind unleashed its rage against the exterior of our fourteenth-floor apartment. I shivered and pulled the duvet up around my neck. Even Siberian down couldn't cut the chill. *Why is it so cold?* Ethan must have turned down the thermostat—again.

"Ethan?" I whispered, reaching my arm out to his side of the king-size bed, but the sheets were cold and stiff. He'd gone to work early, again.

I stood up and retrieved my robe from the upholstered blue-and-white-striped chair next to the bed. The phone rang persistently, and I made my way out to the living room. The apartment's wraparound windows provided views of Seattle's Pike Place Market below, and of Elliott Bay, with its steady stream of incoming and outgoing ferries. The day we toured the apartment, four years ago, I'd told Ethan it felt like we were floating in the air. "Your castle in the sky," he had said three weeks later, handing me a shiny silver key.

But it wasn't the familiar view that captivated me that morning. In fact, there *was* no view. It was all . . . *white.* I rubbed my eyes to get a closer look at the scene outside the double-paned glass. *Snow.* And not just a few flurries—a genuine blizzard. I looked at the calendar on the wall near my desk, shaking my head in confusion. A snowstorm on May 2? *Unbelievable.*

"Hello," I muttered into the phone, finally silencing its ring.

"Claire!"

"Frank." My boss at the newspaper, yes, but at this early hour, my greeting lacked polite professionalism.

"Are you looking out your window?" A dedicated editor, Frank was often at his desk before sunrise, while I usually stumbled into the office around nine. And that was on a good day. The features department didn't foster the same sense of urgency that the news desk did, and yet Frank behaved as if profiles of local gardeners and reviews of children's theater productions were pressing, vital matters. His staff, including me, could hardly object. Frank's wife had died three years ago, and ever since, he'd thrown himself into his work with such intensity, I sometimes suspected that he slept in his office.

"You mean the snow, right?"

"Yes, *the snow*! Can you believe this?"

"I know," I said, examining the balcony, where the wrought-iron table and chairs were dusted in white. "I guess the forecasters missed this one."

"They sure did," Frank said. I could hear him thumbing through papers on his desk. "Here it is—the forecast, as printed in today's paper: 'Cloudy, high of fifty-nine, chance of light rain.'"

I shook my head. "How can this even happen? It's almost summer—at least, last I checked it was."

"I'm not a meteorologist, but I know it's rare. We've got to cover it." Frank's voice had all the hallmarks of an editor hot on the trail of a story.

I yawned. "Don't you think it's more of news's beat? Wait, unless you want me to do a piece on the city's snowmen."

"No, no," Frank continued. "It's a much bigger story. Claire, I've been going through old files, and you'll never believe what I found."

"Frank," I said, fumbling with the thermostat. I turned it up to seventy-five. Ethan hated wasting energy. "It's not even six a.m. How long have you been in the office?"

He ignored my question. "This isn't the first time Seattle's seen a storm like this."

I rolled my eyes. "Right, it snowed in January, didn't it?"

"Claire," he continued, "no, listen. A late-season snowstorm hit on this very same date in 1933." I heard more paper shuffling. "The timing is uncanny. Some eighty years ago, an identical storm—a massive blizzard—completely shut down the city."

"It's interesting," I said, feeling the urge to make a cup of hot cocoa and head back to bed. "But I still don't understand why this is a feature story. Shouldn't Debbie in news be covering this? Remember, she covered last year's freak tornado in South Seattle?"

"Because it's *bigger* than that," he said. "Think about it. Two snowstorms, sharing one calendar date, separated by nearly a century? If you don't call that feature-worthy, I don't know what is, Claire."

I could detect the boss tone creeping into his voice, so I relented. "Word count and deadline?"

"You're right about news," he said. "They'll tackle today and tomorrow, but I'd like a bigger piece, an exposé of the storm then and now. We'll devote the entire section to it. I can give you six thousand words, and I'd like it by Friday."

"Friday?" I protested.

"You won't have to look hard for sources," he continued. "I'm sure there's a trove of material in the archives. Your angle can be: 'The storm's great return.'"

I smirked. "You make it sound like it's a living thing."

"Who knows?" Frank said. "Maybe it's a prompt to look back in time. To see what we missed. . . ." His voice trailed off.

"Frank," I said, sighing, "your sentimentality about weather is adorable, but don't get too excited. I'm still wondering how I'm going to write six thousand words on snowmen."

"Blackberry winter," he muttered.

"I'm sorry?"

"The storm," he continued. "It's called a blackberry winter. It's what meteorologists call a late-season cold snap. Interesting, isn't it?"

"I guess," I said, flipping the wall switch to the gas fireplace. Frank's weather lesson had me craving a slice of warm blackberry pie. "If nothing else, we'll have a great headline."

"And hopefully a great story, too," he said. "See you in the office."

"Frank, wait—have you seen Ethan this morning?" My husband, the paper's managing editor, beat me to work most days, but he had been starting his mornings progressively earlier.

"Not yet," he said. "It's just me here, and a few folks in news. Why?"

"Oh, nothing," I said, trying to hide the emotion I felt. "I was just worried about him getting in all right, with the snow and all."

"Well, you be careful out there," he said. "Fifth Avenue is an ice skating rink."

I hung up the phone and looked down to the street below, squinting to make out two figures, a father and his young child, engaged in a snowball fight.

I pressed my nose against the window, feeling the cold glass against my skin. I smiled, taking in the scene before my breath fogged up the pane. *A blackberry winter.*

Chapter 3

VERA

"You're late," Estella said, eyeing me from behind her gray steel desk when I walked into the maids' quarters at the Olympic. A single lightbulb dangled from a wire in the dimly lit basement room. She nodded toward a mound of freshly laundered white linens in urgent need of folding.

"I know," I said apologetically. "I'm so sorry. The streetcar was late, and just before I left I had a confrontation with my—"

"I'm not interested in your excuses!" she barked. "The fifth-floor suites need cleaning, and quick. We have a group checking in tonight. Dignitaries. The work must be done fast and with attention to detail. And watch your corners on the beds. Yesterday they were sloppy, and I had to send Wilma in to remake them all." She sighed and returned to the paperwork in front of her.

"I'm sorry, ma'am," I said, stowing my purse in a cabinet and tightening my apron before heading to the service elevator. "I'll do better."

"And Vera," Estella said, "you didn't bring *the boy* again, did you?" She craned her neck as if she expected to find him hiding under my skirt.

"No, ma'am," I muttered, suddenly wondering if I'd left a water glass out for Daniel. *Did I? Will he be thirsty?* I repressed the thought as Estella's eyes bore into me.

"Good," she said. "Because if you mistake Seattle's finest hotel for a nursery school again, I'm afraid I'll be forced to give your job to any number of women who would love to have it. You ought to be grateful to be gainfully employed when so many people aren't."

"Yes, ma'am," I said. "I *am* very grateful. It won't happen again."

"Very well," she said, gesturing toward a silver tray that held two enormous slices of chocolate cake and a champagne bottle. *If only Daniel could have a slice of chocolate cake.* I made a mental note to scrape together tip money to make him one. Every child deserved a taste of cake, even poor children. "Take that up to room 503," she said. "Manuel's out on another delivery. It's for an *important* guest, so look smart about it, won't you?"

"Yes, ma'am," I said, wheeling the cart out the door.

As the service elevator pushed upward, I studied the cake— dark chocolate, with fudge wedged between each layer—and the bottle of French bubbly, its label printed with exotic words I did not understand. I felt a pang of hunger, but willed myself to look away from the cake. With any luck, I'd come across a bit of cheese or a dinner roll in one of the rooms I cleaned that night. Last week I found a steak sandwich. It had been nibbled at the edge, but I didn't mind, having not eaten at all that day.

I steadied the cart when the elevator came to an abrupt stop, wincing as the champagne flutes clinked together, narrowly avoiding toppling to the ground. *What would Estella say if I broke them?* I pushed the car out into the hallway, nodding at a fashionable couple walking by. They ignored me. *Where are they going? To the theater? The opera?* It was easy to get lost in fanciful dreams working at a hotel, and to pass the time, I permitted myself to think about what it might be like to lie in a bed of freshly pressed linens and fluffed pillows. While dusting the golden trim, I'd peek into closets and admire the couture clothing hanging within, the jewels spread across dresser tops, the perfume bottles that cost as much as six months' rent. I once dabbed a little on my wrist, breathing in the exotic floral scent of wealth and luxury, until I thought of Estella, then quickly scrubbed with soap and water.

As I made my way through each suite, I'd dream up stories about the lives of the guests, always wondering what it would be like for me, for *Daniel*, if our circumstances were different.

I stopped at room 503 and knocked. Music played inside. Jazz, maybe. "Just a minute," a female voice called out, followed by the sound of giggling.

Moments later the door opened and a beautiful woman appeared, about my age. Her breasts brimmed over the edge of a pale pink lace nightgown cinched tightly around her waist. Her short hair, dyed to a striking yellow blond, curled slightly at the ends, just like in the advertisements. When she looked down at the cart, I could see the dark of her natural color peeking through the roots. "Oh, goody," she squealed, running her index finger along the edge of the cake and then licking it, ignoring my presence entirely. "Lon," she cooed into the room, "you devil, you. You know champagne and chocolate is my weakness."

I followed her inside. The air smelled of musky cologne, and my cheeks burned red when I noticed a half-clothed man lying in the bed. With the coverlet draped at his waist, he looked like a king propped up against a bevy of pillows. "Just set it over here by me, doll," he said kindly, looking straight into my eyes. I turned away, embarrassed at the sight of his bare chest, tan and dewy, like he'd just exerted himself.

"Oh," he said, grinning, beckoning me to hold eye contact with him. "Don't be shy, sweetheart. Are you new here?"

"No, sir," I said. "I mean, well, yes, sir. Just six months."

The woman looked very annoyed by our exchange. "Lonnie," she whined, "let me feed you some cake."

"In a minute, Susie," he said without taking his eyes off me. "I'm Lon Edwards. I don't believe I've had the pleasure of meeting you." He extended his hand. The woman brooded.

I took it awkwardly, unsure of what to say, so I squeaked, "I'm Vera. Vera Ray."

"Pleased to meet you, dear," he said, tucking a crisp one-dollar bill into my apron pocket.

I stood back and curtsied. "Thank you, sir, er, Lon; I mean, Mr. Edwards."

"I hope to see you again," he said, grinning, before turning his gaze back to Susie, who appeared starved for his attention—and the chocolate cake.

"Yes, sir," I stammered. "Thank you, sir. Good night."

As the door clicked closed behind me, I exhaled, just as I saw Gwen waiting for me in the hallway. Short, plump, with an unfortunate scar on her left cheek, she rarely frowned or complained, which is why I had taken to her immediately.

"Estella sent me up to help you with this floor," she chirped. "Big group coming in. We have to work fast." She grinned. "I see you've met Lon."

I shrugged, patting my pocket. "He tips well."

Gwen grinned. "He also has a thing for maids."

"Gwen!" I puffed. "You're not saying that I would—"

"No, no," she said, poking my side playfully with the edge of her feather duster. "It's just that the woman with him now—Susie—she used to work in housekeeping, before you started."

"You mean, she was . . . ?"

Gwen nodded. "Just like us. And now he keeps her in his suite, all fancy and made up, at his beck and call."

My cheeks flushed at the thought. "How perfectly terrible."

Gwen shrugged. "Susie doesn't seem to think so. He gives her a hundred dollars a week, and access to his car and driver. Sure beats scrubbing the floors."

"A hundred dollars a week?"

Gwen looked wistful. "A fortune."

"Well," I said, taking a deep breath and then exhaling away the thought. "I'd never put myself up for sale like that."

Gwen shrugged. "Never say never," she said as we keyed into the first of the eleven rooms that needed cleaning. "These are frightening times. So many people are hard on their luck. My eldest sister lives in Kansas. Her husband is out of work, and they have eight children. *Eight* mouths to feed. Imagine what she'd do to feed her family. I'm just grateful I only have my own piehole to look after."

I thought of Daniel and the predicament I faced with the rent payment. I couldn't string Mr. Garrison along very much longer. We'd be out on the streets in a few days, maybe a week if we were lucky.

"Gwen," I muttered, "you don't happen to have twenty dollars I can borrow, do you? It's for my rent payment. I'm in a terrible bind."

"I wish I did, honey," she said, her kind eyes sparkling with compassion. I felt a pang of guilt. *How can I expect her to bail me out when I know she's in the same boat?* "Here," she said, handing me two crumpled bills. "My last two dollars."

"I promise, I'll pay you back," I said.

"Don't worry about it," she replied, pointing to the bed. "Let's get started on stripping down these sheets. I'll even let you have all the tip money we find in the rooms. Maybe we'll get lucky."

"Maybe," I said.

By five a.m., we'd finished the floor, even the enormous penthouse suite, and I had raw, cracked hands to show for it. Gwen yawned, handing me a bottle of discarded face cream she'd pilfered from an empty room. "Put some of this on," she said. "It'll help."

I smiled at the kind gesture.

"Want to stop at the diner before heading home?"

"I can't," I said. "I have to get back before Daniel wakes."

Gwen put her hand on my arm. "It's hard to leave him, isn't it?"

I nodded, aware of every second wasted. Daniel was waiting. "It's unbearable, actually." My eyes stung a little and I looked away.

"This isn't forever, you know," she said. "You'll find your way. You'll meet someone. Someone wonderful."

I wanted to say, *But I already did, and look what happened*, but instead I nodded. "Yes," I said. "My ship has to come in one of these days, right? And yours, too."

Gwen winked. "That's right, honey," she said, giving me a squeeze. "Now, how'd you make out with tips?"

I shrugged. "Four dollars."

Gwen smiled. "Combine that with my two and Lon's tip and you have—"

"Not enough to pay rent," I said, defeated.

Gwen sighed. "Well, it's a start. Give that handsome boy a kiss for me."

"I will," I said, opening the door to the street. A cold wind hit my cheeks, pushing its tendrils into the cracks of my sweater and sending chills through my tired body. As I stepped onto the sidewalk, I gasped when my feet sank into at least four inches of fresh, white snow. *Good heavens, snow? In May?* The weather matched the uncertainty, the cruelness of the world. I sighed. *How will I get home now? The streetcar can't be running—not in this weather.*

I knew I'd have to walk, and fast. The apartment wasn't far, but in snow, and with a hole in the sole of my right shoe, it might as well have been miles. But it didn't matter; Daniel was my destination. I trudged along, steadfast, but a half hour later my feet ached, and I winced in pain at the stinging intensity of the exposed patch of flesh. I hobbled into an alley, tore the lining of my dress free from its seam, and wrapped it around my foot. A man with a sooty face hovered near a trash can. He tended a small fire under a makeshift shelter, poking the embers with a stick. My hands felt icy and I longed for warmth, but his unwelcome gaze told me to press on. Besides, there wasn't time to stop; Daniel waited. I climbed one hill and then a second. The swath of linen only dulled my frost-kissed skin for a moment before the sting returned, throbbing with fierce pangs. *Two more hills. Keep going.* I could be home by sunrise, to greet him with a kiss the moment he opened his eyes. I owed him that.

By the time I reached the apartment building, I could no longer feel my feet. Even so, I hurried inside, dragging my numb limbs up the stairs. Though unheated, the stairwell's ten-degree rise in temperature warmed me.

"Well, hello there, good-looking," a man called to me from the hallway. I hated living above the saloon. It meant pushing past a half-dozen drunkards—some unconscious in the hallway; others angry, looking for a fight; and still more looking for a woman. A bold one reached out and grabbed my hand, but I broke free long enough to make my way up the stairs and barricade myself inside the apartment. As I locked the door, I panicked for a moment. In my state of exhaustion, I couldn't remember if I'd let myself in with a key or if the door had been unlocked. *Surely I locked it before leaving for work last night?* Fatigue was playing tricks on me.

The fire I'd lit in the fireplace the night before had long since died out. The air felt cold. Bitter cold. *Poor Daniel, with only a thin quilt to warm him. Was he chilled last night?* I shuddered at the thought of the city's wealthy—warm and comfortable under millions of down feathers, eating cake at midnight—while my son shivered in his bed in an apartment above a rowdy saloon, alone. *What's wrong with this world?* I set my purse down and peeled off my snow-covered sweater, dotted with bits of ice that sparkled in the morning light. I walked to the compartment under the stairs and pried open the little door, pulling out my bracelet from its secret hiding spot. Daniel loved running his little fingers along the gold chain. I fastened the clasp, knowing how happy he'd be to see it on my wrist again.

I suppressed a yawn as I climbed the stairs to Daniel's room, but my exhaustion was unmatched by the excitement I felt to see my little boy. He'd be giddy about the snow, of course. We'd make snowmen, and then cuddle up together by the fire. I'd get an hour of sleep in the afternoon while he napped. A perfect day.

I opened the door to his room. "Daniel, Mommy's home!"

I knelt down by his little bed and pulled back the quilt, revealing only crumpled sheets. My eyes searched the room, under the bed, behind the door. *Where is he?* "Daniel, are you hiding from Mama, love?"

Silence.

I ran to the washroom, and then downstairs to the kitchen.

"Daniel!" I screamed. "Daniel, where are you hiding? Come out, right this minute!"

My heart pounded in my chest with such intensity it muted the sound of the men engaged in a fistfight on the floor below. My eyes scoured every inch of the apartment, and I prayed it was only one of his little jokes. Surely, in a moment, he'd pop out from behind the pantry door and say, "Surprise!" the way he did when we played games together?

"Daniel?" I called once more, but only my voice echoed back to me in the cold, lonely air.

I pushed through the apartment door and ran down the stairs. I hadn't stopped to put on a wrap, but it didn't matter. I didn't feel the cold; only terror. *He has to be close by. Maybe he woke and saw the snow and decided to go out to play.*

I ran past the men loitering around the saloon, and out to the street. "Daniel!" I screamed into the cold air, my voice immediately muffled into a hush by the thick layer of snow. "Daniel!" I called out again, this time louder. I might as well have been screaming through a muzzle of cotton balls. A suffocating silence hovered. I looked right, then left.

"Have you seen my son?" I pleaded with a businessman in an overcoat and top hat. "He's three, about this tall." I held my hand to the place on my leg where Daniel's head hit. "He was wearing blue plaid pajamas. He has a teddy bear with a—"

The man frowned and pushed past me. "Some mother you are, letting a three-year-old out in *this* weather," he muttered as he walked away.

His words stung, but I kept on, running toward another person on the sidewalk. "Ma'am!" I cried to a woman shepherding her young daughter along the sidewalk. Both wore matching wool coats with smart gray hats. My heart sank. *Daniel doesn't even have a warm coat. If he's out in this weather* ... I looked directly at the woman, my eyes pleading, mother to mother. "Have you seen a little boy wandering around here, by chance? His name is Daniel." I barely recognized my own voice. Desperate. High-pitched.

She eyed me suspiciously. "No," she said without emotion. "I haven't." She pulled her daughter closer as they walked away.

"Daniel!" I screamed again, this time down an alley, where I sometimes let him play hopscotch or jacks with the other children while I knitted in the afternoon. *No answer.* Then it occurred to me to look for footprints in the snow. His feet were small enough that I could distinguish their impressions. But after searching for a few minutes, I realized my efforts were futile. The snow, falling so hard now, covered any trace of his tracks with its cruel blanket of white.

I walked a few steps farther, and this time, toward the back of the alley, a fleck of blue caught my eye. I ran to it and fell to my knees, sobbing, shaking my head violently. *No. No God, no!* Daniel's precious bear, Max, lay facedown in the snow. I picked it up and held it to my chest, rocking back and forth the way I might have comforted Daniel after a nightmare. I trembled from a place deep inside. My little boy was *gone*.

Chapter 4

CLAIRE

We all behave differently in the face of trauma and anguish, or so says my therapist, Margaret. Some people act out; others act *in*—bottling up their pain and holding it deep inside, letting it brew and fester, which had been my way since the horror of last May. Ethan, on the other hand, seemed to deal with his grief by acting *out*. Throwing himself into his work. Drinking copious amounts of scotch. Staying out late with friends—friends, I might add, who had meant nothing to him last year. Even the red BMW he'd bought on a whim in March. It was all tied to his pain, Margaret said. When I'd seen him stepping into the convertible outside the office, my eyes had welled up with tears. It wasn't the expense that bothered me, but the choice. Ethan wasn't a flashy red BMW sort of guy.

I'd tried to get him to go with me to my weekly appointments. I thought that if we could talk about the past together, we both might stop pretending it had never happened and learn to face the new normal, whatever that was. But he had shaken his head. "I don't do shrinks," he said. And so our paths had diverged. Love still lingered—I felt it in the unspoken moments, the way he'd leave the floss out on the bathroom counter in the mornings because he knew I had a habit of forgetting; or the way his eyes would linger on mine every time I said good night. But the emptiness grew like a cancer, and I feared it had spread too far to control. Our marriage, it seemed, was verging on a terminal diagnosis.

"Morning, Claire," chirped Gene, our building's doorman, as I stepped off the elevator. "Can you believe this weather?"

I cinched the belt of my lightweight trench coat tighter, considering whether to return upstairs for a wardrobe change. Gloves and a scarf, for starters, and—I looked down at my calf-high leather boots—maybe a pair of snow boots. I should have opted for something with a little more traction, but I couldn't bear to lace up my tennis shoes. I hadn't worn them since *the accident*, and I didn't have the confidence to put them on again. Not yet, anyway. "A blizzard in May," I said to Gene, shaking my head in disbelief as I looked out the building's double doors. "Why do I live here again?"

Gene grinned. "Do you think you're dressed warmly enough?" He pointed toward the street. "That's arctic air out there." Ever since *the incident*, he, and everyone else, it seemed, looked after me like a lost little bird. *Are you too cold? Too hot? Will you be safe walking out to the corner market after dark?*

I appreciated his concern, but it annoyed me just the same. *Do I have an enormous sign attached to my back stating,* ATTENTION: I'M PHYSICALLY AND MENTALLY UNABLE TO CARE FOR MYSELF. HELP ME, PLEASE?

Still, I didn't fault Gene. "I'll be fine," I said confidently, revealing a strained smile. "I may be a California transplant, but I've been through enough Northwest winters to avoid frostbite on my way to the office."

"Just the same," he said, pulling a pair of mittens from his pocket, "wear these. Your hands will freeze without them."

I hesitated, then accepted the scraggly marriage of blue and white yarn. "Thank you," I said, putting them on only to please him.

"Good," he said. "Now you can throw a proper snowball."

I walked out the door, sinking my feet into a good three inches of snow. My toes instantly felt the cold. *Why didn't I wear wool socks?* The streets were vacant except for a group of young boys hard at work on a snowman. *Will Café Lavanto be open?* I hated the thought of hiking up several hilly blocks to my favorite café, but hot cocoa smothered in whipped cream would be worth the effort, I reasoned. Besides, I didn't feel like going into the office just yet, and I could pass the trip off as research. Storm-story research.

Twenty minutes later, when I found the door to the café locked, I cursed my decision, and my boots, which were sopping wet and on the verge of freezing my feet into two boot-shaped blocks of ice.

"Claire?"

I turned to see Dominic, Café Lavanto's owner, walking toward me. Tall with sandy brown hair and a kind smile, he had always struck me as out of place behind the coffee counter. It was one of those pairings that didn't quite add up, like my college English lit professor who'd moonlighted as a tattoo artist.

"Thank goodness," I said, leaning against the doors. "I made the mistake of walking up here in these." I pointed to my shoes. "And now I'm afraid my toes are too frozen to get back down. Mind if I defrost in here for a bit?" I regarded the quiet storefronts, which would normally be buzzing with people by this hour of the morning. "I guess I didn't expect the city to completely shut down."

"You know Seattle," Dominic said with a grin. "A few flakes

and it's mass pandemonium." He reached into a black leather messenger bag to retrieve the key to the café. "I'm the only one who could make it in. The buses aren't running and cars are skidding out all over the place. Did you see the pileup on Second Avenue?"

I shook my head and thought of Ethan.

He pushed the key into the lock. "Come in, let's get you warmed up."

"Thank goodness you're open," I said, following him inside. "Seattle's a ghost town right now."

He shook his head, locking the door from the inside. "No, I don't think I'll open today. I could use a day off, anyway. But someone had to check on Pascal."

"Pascal?"

"The cat," he said.

"You mean, I've been coming here for six years and didn't know about the resident feline?"

Dominic grinned. "He's a grumpy old man. But he has a thing for brunettes."

I felt my cheeks tingle as they began to defrost in the warmth of the café.

"He spends most of his time upstairs in the loft, anyway," he continued.

"The loft?"

"It's not much, just a storeroom where we keep supplies. Mario, the former owner, kept his desk up there. I'm thinking about turning it into a studio apartment—live above the shop."

"Sounds like a nice life," I said, detecting the vibration of my cell phone inside my purse. I ignored it. "So I hear you recently bought the café, is that right?

Dominic nodded. "I did. And I'll be in debt until I'm one

hundred and five. The gamble is worth it, though. I love the old place. I'm going to be making some changes, though. Starting with a real awning, a lunch menu. And a new name."

"Oh? What's wrong with Café Lavanto?"

"Nothing, really," he said. "It's just that it has no ties to here—to history."

"And you'd change it to . . . ?"

He poured milk into a steel pitcher and inched it under the espresso machine's frother wand. "I'm not sure," he said. "Maybe you can help me think of something good." He winked. "You're a writer, aren't you? A wordsmith?" Bubbles erupted in the pitcher as the steam hissed.

"You remember?"

"Sure. The *Herald*, right?"

"That's right. But if you ask my mother, who sent me through four years of Yale expecting me to emerge as a staff editor at *The New Yorker*, I'm a hack." I rubbed my hands together to warm them.

"Oh, come on," Dominic said, grinning. "Don't you think you're being a little too hard on yourself? Surely your parents are proud?"

I shrugged. "I write fluff for the local newspaper—which is what I'm doing today, in fact, reporting on the snowstorm. Not exactly what you'd call substance."

"Well, I, for one, think your work sounds very interesting, and worthy," he said, leaning against the counter. "Certainly better than a thirty-five-year-old barista. Imagine the comments I get every year at Thanksgiving."

I liked his humility. "What did you do before this?"

He looked up from the coffee grinder, which he had just filled with espresso beans, shiny and slick-looking under the café lights. "Just one false start after another," he replied.

"Failure builds character," I said.

He didn't respond right away, and I worried I had offended him. "Sorry," I said. "I didn't mean to imply that *you* are . . ." *Why did I open my mouth?*

"That I'm hopelessly unsuccessful?" he said. "Fine with me. This place wasn't exactly the wisest business decision."

I bit my lip. *At least he's smiling.*

"But even if I go bankrupt in a year, I won't regret it," he continued, gazing around the café with pride. "Sometimes you just have to take chances, especially when it makes you happy." He sighed. "When I came to work here three years ago, I'd just been laid off from the accounting firm that hired me straight out of college. I had a lot going for me then—a decent salary, a fiancée, an apartment, and a pug named Scruffles."

I stifled a laugh. "Scruffles?"

"Don't ask," he said with a pained smile. "Her dog."

I nodded knowingly.

"When I lost my job, she left."

"And she took the dog?"

"She took the dog," he said, polishing the chrome of the espresso machine with a white cloth.

I half-smiled. "So you got a job here?"

"Yeah, as a barista," he said. "It was only going to be temporary. Then I realized how much I loved the gig—getting my hands gritty and stained from coffee grounds, pouring perfect foam into ceramic cups. I didn't miss the long hours at the firm or the number crunching or any of it. Making coffee was cathartic somehow. It sounds weird, but I *needed* it. And when Mario offered to sell the business, I jumped at the chance, even though my family warned against it."

I smiled. "Well then, you're lucky. Do you know how many people hate their jobs?"

He hopped over the counter with a box of dry cat food in his hands, pouring a generous portion into a white dish on the floor near the door. "Pascal," he called. "Here, kitty."

Moments later an overweight black-and-white cat appeared, eyeing me cautiously before settling in for his meal.

"Can I make you something?" Dominic asked, turning to the enormous espresso machine. It felt funny being the sole customer at the café, sort of like being backstage at a theater before curtain time.

"Oh, you don't have to make anything for me," I said.

He turned on the coffee grinder and its hum filled the air with a comforting lull. "I insist."

I grinned. "Well . . ."

"It's no trouble," he said. "I'm making myself a cappuccino. You like hot chocolate, right?"

"You remember?"

"Of course I remember," he said. "And I always see you sprinkling cinnamon on top. Would you like me to mix some spices into the cocoa? I could make a Mexican hot chocolate. You'd really like it."

"Yes, thank you."

He spun around to retrieve a canister of cocoa powder. "I don't mean to pry," he said, "but why is it that your husband . . ." He paused. "He is your husband, right?"

"Yes," I said.

"Right," he continued. "Why does he always give you a hard time about ordering hot chocolate?"

I smirked. "So you've heard him tease me, I take it?"

Dominic nodded.

I shrugged. "I'm married to Seattle's biggest coffee snob."

Ethan had lived in Seattle his entire life, born and bred. He'd grown up with the espresso culture and was suspicious of any-one who didn't share his love of fine coffee, or worse, anyone who pronounced espresso "expresso." Our kitchen was home to eleven French presses, a percolator from nineteenth-century Italy, two tra-ditional coffeemakers, and an espresso machine that cost more than most people's cars.

"So he's tried to convert you?"

"Yes," I said. "Ethan just doesn't understand why I can't get into coffee."

He handed me a brimming mug, artfully swirled with cinnamon-dusted whipped cream. "For you," he said, grinning. "And for the record, I don't think there's anything shameful about being a connoisseur of hot cocoa."

I smiled, slurping a generous mouthful of whipped cream. "I like the way you put that," I said. "'Connoisseur of cocoa.'"

Pascal purred at my feet before sauntering back upstairs. I eyed the old brick fireplace across the room. The mortar crumbled in places, but a painted tile just above the hearth caught my eye. I squinted to get a better look, but couldn't make out the scene painted on the ivory-colored placard. Funny, all the times I'd visited the café, I'd never noticed it. I made a note to inspect it more closely on my next visit.

"So what if it's not a good business venture?" I said. "It's the coolest café in town."

Dominic gazed around the little room and nodded. "It is a special building, isn't it?" he said, grinning. "It's actually kind of shocking that someone didn't gut the place and turn it into a Starbucks."

I smiled, glancing at my watch. "Well," I said, "look at me, keeping you like this. I better get back out there and brave the weather. I have an editor who needs a story."

"Where are you headed?"

"To the *Herald* building on Alaskan Way," I said. "If I can get there."

"Let me walk you," he offered, a little self-consciously. "At least until you find a cab."

"I'd love that," I said, and together we made our way out to the snowy streets.

Despite the blizzard churning outside, the newsroom bustled as if the thermometer registered a balmy seventy degrees. It didn't surprise me, though. Newspaper reporters rarely play hooky. Dedication is in their blood, which is why I wondered if I was really cut out for the job. So much had changed since last May, since . . . I wondered if I still had what it took.

"There you are!" I turned to find Abby approaching my cubicle. The paper's research editor, she had a sense of humor I'd warmed to immediately. On my very first day at the *Herald*, she had walked up to my desk after my first staff meeting, looked me in the eye, and said, "I like you. You don't wear pointy shoes." She then inhaled the air around my desk. "But do you smoke?"

"No," I said, a little stunned.

"Good," she replied. Her face told me I passed her friendship test. "I'm Abby." At that moment, I knew we'd be instant friends.

Abby had a knack for finding obscure facts about anything or anyone. The color of the former mayor's daughter's hair, for instance, or the soup served at a now-defunct restaurant on Marion Street in 1983—you name it, she could find it. She had come to my rescue more than a few times in the past few months when I was on deadline but lacked the material I needed to pull together a decent story. "Frank's looking for you," she said with a knowing smile.

I rubbed my forehead. "Is he chewing on his pencil?"

"Yes," Abby replied. "Sound the alarms. I believe I saw pencil chewing."

"Great," I said, shrinking lower into my chair to avoid being seen above my cubicle walls. Abby and I both knew not to cross Frank when he chewed his pencil. It signaled a fire-breathing editor on the loose.

"Do you know what he wants?" Abby asked, sinking into my guest chair.

I turned on my computer and watched as my monitor slowly lit up, illuminating a photo of Ethan and me in Mexico three years earlier. *How happy we looked.* I sighed and turned back to Abby. "Frank wants me to write about the storm."

She shrugged. "So? Doesn't seem like such a big deal to me."

"That's just it," I said. "There's nothing *big* about it. You can't write a story about weather—a good one, anyway." I collected some loose papers on my desk and straightened them into a neat stack, shaking my head. "I don't know, Abs. Maybe it's me. I can't seem to get excited about *any* story these days."

"Honey, then take yourself off the piece," she said. "Do you want me to talk to Frank about giving you some days off? You know, you never really stopped to rest after"—she paused to search my face, for permission, perhaps to say what came next—"after your hospital stay. Besides, unlike me, you, my dear, have job security. You're a Kensington, after all. You can call the shots."

I wadded up a press release on my desk and tossed it in Abby's direction with a grin. "Very cute," I said. "I may have married a Kensington, but I am *not* a Kensington."

Ethan's family owned the newspaper, one of the last family-owned dailies in the country. I'd been writing under my given name, Claire Aldridge, before I met him, so it didn't make sense professionally to change it. Besides, I rather liked the statement it made to his very traditional parents, Glenda and Edward Kensington. Both shareholders in the newspaper, they managed the business from afar, leaving Ethan to run the day-to-day affairs, since his sister, Leslie, had no interest in holding down a real job, with her schedule studded with society events and salon appointments. His grandfather, Warren, the paper's patriarchal editor in chief, checked in less now that he was in his eighties and in ailing health, but his name remained at the top of the masthead.

The newspaper, founded by Ethan's great-grandfather at the turn of the century, was a family institution, one all Kensingtons, including our future children, if we had them, were expected to participate in.

"Well," Abby continued, "I still think you should play the Kensington card and get some R and R. It's been a tough year. Why not give yourself some time to regroup, rest?"

While I was quick to change the subject when others brought up the past, it didn't bother me when Abby did. "Thanks," I said, nodding. "But I'm fine. Really."

I looked up to see Frank's face peeking over the top of my cubicle, pencil firmly planted in mouth. "There you are," he said. I could hear the urgency in his voice. "Anything to report?"

I cocked my head to the right, wondering if pencils still contained the type of lead that causes poisoning. Perhaps that could explain Frank's slightly neurotic behavior. "Report?"

"On the *story.*"

"Oh, yes," I said. "I was just, uh, talking to Abby about that."

"Good," he said, tucking the pencil behind his ear. "Get me an update by this afternoon, if you can."

"Will do," I replied, nodding as Frank spun around and walked back to his office.

I turned to Abby. "Help."

She clasped her hands in her lap. "So, a story about a snow-storm."

"Yup."

"Remember what I said about taking some time off?"

"Not going to do it."

She nodded. "All right, then, let's get to work. Have you started interviewing?"

I shook my head.

"What's your angle?"

"I don't have one." I sighed in defeat, before remembering what Frank had said about the storm in 1933. "Frank wants to title the piece 'Blackberry Winter.'"

"Blackberry what?"

I tried to focus. "Winter. It's what forecasters call a late-season cold-weather event, I guess. Frank said something about a similar storm happening on the same day in 1933. It practically crippled the city."

Abby sat up straighter in her chair. "You're kidding."

I shrugged. "Frank has this crazy idea that the storm has returned in some significant way. He wants me to do a then-and-now exposé. Can you believe that? A feature on *weather*. I can't think of a more dull assignment."

Abby shook her head. "Dull? Claire, you can't be serious. This is good stuff. Have you even started looking into what went on in that snowstorm in 1933?"

I shook my head. "Honestly, Abby, I think I'd rather go clean the toilet than start researching this story. I'm in trouble."

"All right," she said. "Give me an hour, and I'll find you something good. You know I love an excuse to search the archives." She looked wistful. "The 1930s and the Great Depression—I'm sure I'll find something good."

I shrugged. "I hope so."

Abby stood up and nodded with assurance. "Order Thai. I'll be back at noon."

"I'll try," I said, poking my head out into the hallway. "Not sure if any delivery guys will be driving in this weather."

"Tell them you'll tip forty percent," she said. "Good research requires pad Thai."

Ethan's office, on the other side of the newsroom, was locked when I walked over to see him a half hour later. As I knocked on his door, it occurred to me that I had begun to feel more like his employee than his wife. In the past few months, we'd shared a bed, but little else.

"Hi, Claire," Ethan's assistant, Tracy, said from her desk a few feet away. She gestured to Ethan's door. "You just missed him, sorry. He had a meeting, then he's off to a lunch meeting."

"Oh," I said, forcing a smile. "With who?"

Tracy paused for an uncomfortable few seconds. "Um, I think he said he was joining Cassandra at that new Italian place down the street."

"In this weather? They're open?"

"They opened especially for her," Tracy said, her tone indicating slight annoyance. "She's doing a review, you know."

I helped myself to a piece of butterscotch from Tracy's candy dish, tossing the wrapper into a nearby trash can. "And Ethan is moonlighting as an assistant food critic?"

Tracy shrugged. "She said something about gnocchi."

"Gnocchi."

She nodded.

"He hates gnocchi."

Tracy gave me a sympathetic look.

On paper, it made perfect sense that the managing editor of the paper would join the food critic for a tasting event. But Tracy and I both knew the truth: At that very moment, my husband was having lunch with his ex. "Thanks," I said, collecting myself. "I'll catch him later."

Up until recently, it hadn't bothered me that Cassandra, the paper's food critic and Ethan's former girlfriend, worked three doors down, and that she seemed to delight in including him on her frequent lunch and dinner outings. But lately, well, I couldn't help but worry. Cassandra, tall, blond—everything I wasn't—hadn't dated anyone seriously since they broke up, just a few months before Ethan and I had met. And the rumor among newspaper staff was that she had never got over him. I walked past her desk, also empty, and nervously tugged at my wedding ring.

Lunch arrived at noon, and I tucked a twenty-dollar bill into the hand of the deliveryman, whose hat was covered in a fresh dusting of snow. "Thanks, ma'am," he said, nearly bumping into Abby on his way out the door.

"I smell Thai!" she exclaimed, clutching a thick file folder.

I opened up a box of noodles smothered in peanut sauce, and the sweet scent wafted in the air. "One spring roll or two?"

"Two," Abby said, taking a seat on the floor, where she opened up the file folder and began spreading papers on the carpet. "Research makes me hungry. And just wait until you see what I found."

I handed a plate to her and took a seat beside her on the floor. "So?"

"So," she said, handing me a photocopied newspaper clipping dated May 7, 1933, "read this."

I scanned the first few paragraphs of the story, but nothing jumped out at me. "It's just a roundup of the police blotter for the week," I said. "Transients arrested, petty theft—am I missing something?"

"Yes," Abby said, before taking a bite of noodles. She pointed to a paragraph halfway down and I redirected my eyes. "Snow halts visit from Prince George."

"Really? You're getting excited about a visit from a dull British monarch?"

"Well, it's the backstory that's fascinating," she said, handing me another news clipping. "Apparently, he was courting a Seattle woman. If it weren't for the storm, Seattle may have had its very first princess."

I frowned.

"No love for royals?"

"Abs, I didn't even have *Diana* fever when everyone had Diana fever," I said, setting my half-eaten plate on my desk with a sigh. "There's got to be something else."

I picked up the news clipping again and read it halfheartedly, hoping to find something, anything—and then my eyes stopped.

"'Three-year-old Seattle boy, Daniel Ray, reported missing on the morning of May 2, from his home in Seattle. Suspected runaway.'"

"Sad," Abby said. "Lost the day of the snowstorm."

I nodded. "My sister has a three-year-old. They don't run away at that age."

"So you think he was abducted?" Abby asked, leaning in for a closer look at the article.

"Well, it's the only thing that really makes sense," I said, standing up and taking a seat at my desk. "But let's see what we can find out. I keyed the boy's name into a library database and several results popped up. I clicked on the first, and scanned the page to find more details from the police. The boy's mother was Vera Ray. I read quickly before turning to Abby. "She came home from work, and he had disappeared," I said. "She found his teddy bear in the snow." I placed my hand on my heart. "My God, how heartbreaking."

Abby nodded. "Do you think they ever found him?"

"I don't know," I said, clicking through the remaining articles. "There doesn't seem to be any conclusion here."

Abby leaned back against the wall near my file cabinet. "What about the mother?"

I searched for her name, and clicked on the first result that came up. "Look," I said. "Her name is in several police reports." I selected all and sent them to the printer down the hall.

I keyed in the boy's name again, and studied one of the article clippings more closely. "This is all from the *Seattle Post-Intelligencer*, not the *Herald*. Did we not report on it?"

Abby eyed the list of articles. "Oddly, it looks like we didn't," she said. "The *Herald* must have missed the story entirely.

I clicked on another link, this one returning an article with a photograph of the young boy with light hair and plump cheeks. His big, round eyes stared back at me. I clutched my belly, feeling the familiar ache, and closed my eyes tightly.

"Claire," Abby whispered, "are you OK?"

"I will be when I figure out what happened to this boy," I said. I couldn't explain it to her, or even to myself, but there was something about this child, little Daniel Ray from 1933, that spoke to my heart.

Abby grinned. "So I take it you found your story?"

"Yes," I said without taking my eyes off the screen.

Chapter 5

VERA

"There, now," said someone hovering overhead. "Take a drink. It will do you good."

Where am I? Whose voice is that? I opened my eyes and the hazy scene slowly came into focus. *Caroline.* Tawny flames flickered in the fireplace. A scratchy wool blanket clung to my lap.

"Auntie Vera, are you awake?" Little Eva, Caroline's daughter, pressed her cheek against my chest. Not much older than Daniel, she possessed a level of maturity beyond her years.

My eyes burned and my head ached. I clutched my feet in agony. They stung and throbbed like no other pain I'd felt.

"Frostbite," Caroline said softly. "You're lucky we found you when we did. I've been bringing them back to room temperature for the last hour. I think we saved your toe."

She inspected my right foot, then placed a glass of water in my hands. "Drink."

I buried my face in the pillow on the sofa, but Caroline gently tilted my chin forward, pressing the glass to my lips. I let the fluid seep into my mouth, choking a little as the cool water washed down my parched throat.

"We found you out on the street an hour ago," she continued. "You were delirious, honey, before you fainted. Mr. Ivanoff was kind enough to help carry you up."

Mr. Ivanoff, a mason who hailed from Russia, had always been good to us. Last month he saw Daniel in the lobby of the apartment building and smiled benevolently. "Boy has no father?" he asked, his accent thick.

"No, he doesn't," I said quietly, as Daniel marveled at Mr. Ivanoff's tools.

The man nodded. "Then I let him help me with my work today. You don't mind, do you?"

I smiled at the kind gesture.

"Please, Mama?" Daniel chirped.

"Of course, dear," I said.

I had pulled out my knitting needles and settled into a chair in the corner as Daniel and his new friend set out to repair the mortar on the saloon's fireplace.

I sat up suddenly, looking around Caroline's apartment frantically. *Daniel.* The fog had lifted to reveal the terror I had felt earlier. *My son. Gone.*

I stood up, setting the glass down with an unsteady hand. It fell to the floor and shattered, water splattering onto the shabby blue rug. "I have to find him!" I cried. "We have to do something. Somebody took him. Somebody took Daniel!"

Caroline rushed to my side. "Now, now," she said. "You've been out in the snow all morning. Your feet must be frozen solid. You can't go back out there. I won't let you."

I pushed her arms away and took a step toward the door, but my legs gave out under me. As Caroline lifted my head onto her lap, my heart beat so loudly, it was all I could hear. *How much time has passed?* Darkness lingered outside Caroline's window. "He must be hungry and cold," I whimpered, trying unsuccessfully to stand again before giving in to Caroline's pleas.

She helped me to the sofa and stroked my hair until my sobbing subsided. "We'll find him," she said quietly.

Little Eva, Daniel's best friend, sat next to her mother with a frightened look on her face. "Aunt Vera?" she whispered, peeking her head over my shoulder.

"Don't bother Aunt Vera right now, dear," Caroline said. "She needs to rest."

"But Mama," Eva replied, "I'm afraid. Did the bird lady take Daniel?"

I opened my eyes. "The bird lady? Eva, what do you mean?"

"The bad lady who kills birds," she continued.

"Eva!" Caroline barked. "Hush. You run upstairs and find your doll."

The child nodded obediently and left the room.

"Don't listen to her," Caroline said. "She doesn't know what she's saying."

I buried my face in my trembling hands. "But, I—" My voice cracked as I began to weep, this time without tears. I had none left. "Oh, Caroline," I cried. "We have to find him. Please help me find him. Please God, please let him come home to me."

"I will help, honey," she said softly. "Just as soon as I take care of you."

An hour later, Caroline went to the corner market for firewood, and I sat up and clutched my head. It pounded violently, but I stood up anyway. My knees wobbled and I quickly steadied myself on the arm of the sofa. *I have to get out of here. I have to find him. I must get back to the apartment.*

"You stay here, dear," I whispered to Eva. "Your mama will be back soon. Tell her I had to go find Daniel. Tell her I'm sorry. She'll understand."

Eva nodded as I walked out the door. I couldn't waste another second. My feet throbbed beneath me. I clutched the railing, hobbling down each step, until I reached the street, where a chilling wind blew into my face so forcibly, it took my breath away. But I pressed on, limping along the sidewalk, willing the pain away. I had to stay strong. But my feet ached so terribly, and the snow beneath them felt like acid on a wound. *Keep walking. He might be waiting.* The scene ahead came in and out of focus. My strength was failing me, I knew. *Stay strong. Keep walking.* A figure approached. Large, shadowy, pounding one fist into his palm. I fixed my eyes on his face; it sent a shiver through my body. *Oh God, Mr. Garrison.*

"Look who we have here," he said, the corners of his mouth forming a sick smile. "Ran out before you paid your rent, did you?" He placed a bold hand on my forearm, yanking me toward him.

"Please!" I screamed. "My son has gone missing. I have to find him!"

"Too late," he said without emotion. I could see the dried crust of frothy ale on his mustache. "No rent, no home."

"But, I . . ." Before I could finish the sentence, I started to sway; then my vision went black.

I don't know how much time passed, but when I opened my eyes I felt an icy wind at my neck. Blood trickled from my lip.

Mr. Garrison hovered over me, his hot, sour breath in my face. "You're coming with me," he said, lifting me in his arms.

"Stop!" Caroline screamed. "Let her go!"

An older man came running from across the street. "Is there a problem here?"

"This man," Caroline cried, pointing at Mr. Garrison, "he's done something to my friend."

The older man puffed his chest. "Where is your sense of decency?" he shouted. Mr. Garrison released his hold on me and I slid back to the ground, into the wet snow. "Leave the poor woman alone!"

Mr. Garrison sneered at the man, then slunk back into the pub, muttering under his breath.

"Can I help you get her home, miss?" the man said to Caroline.

She lifted my arm over her shoulder and helped me to my feet. "No," she said, "but thank you. I live just a few blocks away. I can manage."

"I won't stop looking for him," I said in a weak voice.

"I know, dear," she said. "But I won't let you die trying. When we get back, I'll get you settled; then I'll go to the police."

"You will?"

"Of course I will," she said, squeezing my shoulder tighter. "We'll file a report. They'll start looking for him." The certainty in her voice soothed me.

Back at her apartment, she tucked a blanket around me, then put on her sweater and went out to the street to flag down a police officer. Eva lay her head on my chest as I waited, listening to the old cuckoo clock tick on the wall above, aware of every second passing. I sat up when I heard footsteps in the hallway outside the apartment. The door opened and Caroline walked through the doorway with a police officer. He held a black baton and eyed the percolator on the stove, then looked at Caroline.

"I don't suppose you have a cup of coffee for an officer who's been in the cold all day, miss?"

She obliged, dashing to the kitchen to light the stove before emptying the last dusting of grounds from the coffee can into the percolator.

"It'll just take a minute, officer," she said. "Vera's over here. As I said downstairs, her son is missing."

The officer looked disinterested. "Miss Ray?"

"Yes," I said. "Thank you ever so much for—"

"I don't have much time," he barked. "Be brief."

"Of course," I said, adjusting the blanket over my legs. "This morning, when I came home from work, my son, Daniel, had vanished."

The officer raised his eyelids and took a sip of coffee from the mug Caroline had just tucked into his hands. "So you're saying he was home by himself? How old is the boy?"

"Three," I said. The officer's eyes bore into me.

"She works at the Olympic Hotel," Caroline said, jumping in to fill the silence. "She works hard to support him. I watch him as often as I can, but last night I was working too, and he—"

"He had to stay home by himself," I said. There was no way around the truth. "I took him to work last week and my supervisor said she'd can me if I brought him again. Officer, with so many people out of work these days, I can't bear to lose—"

"I don't need a lesson on employment conditions in this city, miss," he said, eyeing me with suspicion. "Where's the boy's father?"

"Daniel doesn't have a father," I said. "At least not one who's a part of his life."

The officer smirked. "I see."

I showed him Daniel's little bear. "I found this in the snow. It belongs to my son."

The man pulled out a notebook and scribbled a few words

onto the tablet, nodding to himself. "A runaway," he finally said. "He'll probably come home. They always do."

My stomach churned. "No, no," I said. "You have it all wrong. Daniel would never run away. He had to be taken. I'm sure of it."

The officer continued to smirk. "Were there any signs of breaking and entering? Was a window broken? A door? Valuables stolen?"

I stared at him blankly. "No, not that I could tell."

He set the empty coffee cup down, then closed his notebook with a hasty flick of his wrist. "Exactly as I suspected. The boy'll be back." He paused to let out a raspy chuckle. "When he's hungry enough."

The door closed with a thud, and I buried my face in my hands. "I have to go back to the apartment," I sobbed. "I have to go back. In case he comes home."

Caroline shook her head. "Not with that tyrant of a landlord lurking. You're staying here. We can ask Mr. Ivanoff to escort us over there in the morning. For now, you need to rest."

Eva reappeared at the foot of the stairs, where Caroline was standing. "Mama!" she cried. "Did Daniel remember to button his coat? He always forgets to, and I tell him—" Caroline rushed her hand to Eva's mouth to silence her.

Outside, the snow swirled in the air, frigid and unrelenting, and I didn't even know if my little boy had his coat on.

Chapter 6

CLAIRE

"I love it!" Frank exclaimed after I'd told him about my angle for the feature. "Little boy lost in a snowstorm. That will tug at every reader's heart. How much time do you need to write it?"

"At least a week," I said. "I'd like to really dive into this one—see if I can find any relatives, friends to interview."

Frank nodded. "I can give you the time. Keep me posted."

Later that evening, I found Ethan in the kitchen, staring into the bare refrigerator.

"Hi," I said, setting my keys on the table. The sound echoed into every crevice of the apartment, amplifying the pervasive silence, thick and uncomfortable.

"Hi," he said, without turning around. "Crazy storm today, huh? Hey, didn't we have a leftover burrito in here somewhere?"

"I threw it away," I said.

Ethan turned around and frowned, as if throwing away take-out was a betrayal—no, a veritable act of war. "Why would you do that?" he asked, wounded.

"Because it was two weeks old and covered in green slime."

"Oh," he said, before heading to the couch. "Has it been that long?"

"Yep," I said, realizing then that it might have also been two weeks since we'd had a real conversation.

"Your doctor's office called."

I tried to busy myself with the mail.

"You really should go in for that appointment, Claire."

I felt anger well up inside, for the tone of his voice—distant, unfeeling—for the lunch with Cassandra today, but mostly for the pain of the past. "Don't tell me what I need to do, Ethan," I snapped.

He shrugged and reached for the remote control, muttering something under his breath.

I opened a box of raisin bran, poured some haphazardly into a bowl, and topped it with soy milk before retreating to the bedroom. I didn't bother to wipe up the liquid splatter on the granite countertop.

How can he be so insensitive? So blasé? He knew how I felt about going back to the clinic, seeing my doctor's face, *reliving* it all. *Why did he bring it up? Does he* want *to hurt me?* I took a bite and let the crunch of the cereal drown out thoughts of Ethan, of the past. Instead, I thought about little Daniel Ray. *What became of him and his mother? Were they ever reunited? Did the snowstorm play a role in the tragedy?*

On a Christmas trip to visit my grandparents in Maine as a child, it had snowed a foot. My little brother and I, two California kids, were wild-eyed by the sight, and we spent the week building snowmen, making snow angels, and catching snowflakes on our tongues. Pure joy. I longed to feel that way again, to mend the pain in my heart, the hole. *Did Daniel play in the snow the morning of his disappearance? Did he feel the same joy?*

I sat on the bed and reached for the phone, wishing for the

confidence to make the call. At the hospital, my doctor had given me her personal cell phone number and encouraged me to contact her. I dialed the number, letting the phone ring for a frighteningly long second, then hung it up quickly. *No. Not yet.*

Instead, I pulled back the quilt on the bed and hid under its warmth. An hour later, I heard Ethan come in. His keys jingled in his hand, and I turned to watch him pull a sweater from the closet, robotically, and walk out. The door to the apartment closed with an uncaring slam.

The next morning, snow still blanketed the streets, and forecasters warned that more could be coming. I made the hike up to Café Lavanto, this time in more suitable footwear. I had agreed to meet Abby there at nine, and she waited at a table by the fireplace, which I was happy to see stoked and roaring.

"Morning," she said, sipping her trademark triple Americano.

"Hi," I said, sliding into a chair next to her.

She frowned. "What's with the sad face?"

I set my bag down dejectedly. "Ethan."

"Sorry, hon," she said. "What's the latest?"

I sighed. "Oh, Abs, I don't even know where to begin. It's that bad."

"Well," she said, "you two have been through something major. You don't come through that unchanged." Even though unmarried herself, Abby was the best marriage counselor I knew.

"You're right," I replied. "I don't want to lose him, but I don't know how to fix things, either." I paused and looked around the café, noticing Dominic behind the espresso bar. "Ethan had lunch with Cassandra again."

Abby frowned. "That woman's toxic, I tell you."

"You're telling me," I said, noticing the faint ring of my phone in my bag. "Sorry," I said. "I better get this."

I didn't recognize the number. "Hello?"

"Ms. Aldridge?"

"Yes?"

"This is Jerry from Elliott Bay Jewelers. Your watch is ready for pickup—the special order came in from New York this morning," a man said. I'd almost forgotten about the watch I'd ordered for Ethan on a whim a month ago. He'd been wanting a Hugo Allen for at least a year. It had a stopwatch feature, which he'd said would come in handy for kids' games and sports. For a daddy. Father's Day was approaching, and I'd felt that a gift on the third Sunday in June might make him smile. It was going to be an olive branch.

"Oh, yes," I said, half-wishing I'd never ordered it in the first place. "I'll . . . come in to pick it up."

"Did you want us to engrave something on the inside?"

"Engrave something?"

"Well, you certainly don't have to," he said. "But a lot of our customers like to personalize their gifts. It just makes it more special."

"Oh," I said. "Right."

"So what would you like the engraving to say?"

What would I like to say? To my husband. The man who is slipping away from me. The man I worry I no longer know. I shook my head. *How do you sum up your heart in a single sentence?*

He obviously recognized my apprehension. "Do you want to think it over and then call us back when you decide?" Jewelers have a sixth sense about love.

"Yes, that would be helpful," I said. "Thank you."

I ended the call and looked at Abby. "I couldn't do it."

She shrugged. "What?"

"That was the jeweler. I bought Ethan a watch," I said. "It's this stupid overpriced watch that he saw somewhere. I was going to give it to him on Father's Day." I tugged at my sleeve, feeling the heat from the fireplace in full effect. "They asked me what I wanted the engraving to say, and I totally blanked. I couldn't think of anything, Abby."

She opened another packet of sugar and swirled it into her cup. "Can I tell you something?"

"OK."

"I don't think he has any interest in Cassandra," she said. "I think he wants you."

"He *has* me." I smirked.

"No, honey, he doesn't. Not the girl he married. She's been gone for a long time now, drowning in grief."

I studied my hands in my lap and the diamond solitaire on my finger. She was right. I was a lemming heading for the cliff, unable to stop myself.

"Listen," she continued. "Yesterday at the office, I saw something in your eyes I hadn't seen in a long time. For a moment, you were back again. You were excited about *something*. God, Claire, I haven't seen you excited about anything for a long time."

I nodded, feeling a flicker of emotion inside before it fizzled out.

"I think this story, this little boy, is resonating with you," she continued. She took a sip of her coffee. "What was his name again?"

"Daniel," I said, staring at the flames in the fireplace. "Daniel Ray."

I felt a tap on my shoulder and turned around to find Dominic standing at the table. "Morning," he said cheerfully. "Hope I'm not interrupting." He set a mug in front of me, topped high with whipped cream. "Thought you'd like your hot chocolate."

My cheeks burned. I had to be blushing, but I hoped they wouldn't notice. "Thank you," I said, gesturing to Abby. "Have you two met?"

He shook his head.

"Abby, Dominic. Dominic, Abby."

"Nice to meet you," Abby said, grinning more at me than at him.

Dominic knelt down and put another log in the old fireplace. "I hope it doesn't get too warm for you," he said.

"It's great," I assured him, slipping off my sweater. I studied the brickwork on the hearth, remembering the tile I'd seen from across the room the day before. I looked at it more closely now. The text read, "Lander's Pub House." "That tile," I said to Dominic, "what does it mean?"

"Oh," he replied, glancing at the ceramic. "This place used to be a pub—or a saloon; whatever they called those places back then. It survived Prohibition, too." He pointed to a dent in the floorboards that had apparently escaped repair. "It's where the town drunkards congregated. The police just sent them over here. It was a rowdy place back in the day. We still have a couple antique beer barrels and a stein or two up in the loft." He ran his hand along the fireplace, pulling a wedge of loose gray mortar free. "But this," he continued, "this is special. See the initials here?" He pointed to the edge of the tile, signed "S. W. Ivanoff." "One of Seattle's most famous masons. The man did the majority of the decorative hearths in the old Olympic Hotel and other landmarks in the city. A true artisan.

Of course, his work was never truly recognized until after his death."

I pulled out my notebook and scrawled the name down. "Who knows?" I said. "The architecture section might be interested in profiling his work."

"Well," Dominic said, the bell on the door alerting us to an incoming customer. I felt a blast of icy air on my cheeks, which tempered the warmth of the blazing fire. "Good to see you again," he said, looking directly at me.

"You too," I replied, as he turned and walked back to the bar.

"*Someone* has a little crush on you," Abby said in a singsong whisper.

I looked away. "Oh, stop."

"All right, all right," she conceded. "But, hey, at least you *have* an admirer."

"So do you," I added. "Do I need to bring up Rick in news?"

We both burst into laughter. Rick—sweet, yes, with a full mullet—had a long-suffering crush on Abby. Sadly, he had the charm of a red-foot tortoise—and lived with his parents.

Abby took a final sip of her coffee, then reached for her white puffy down thigh-length North Face coat. She zipped it up and grinned. "Does this thing make me look like the Michelin Man?"

"Do you want the truth?" I asked, trying to stifle a laugh.

She nodded.

"Sorta," I said, letting a giggle slip through. "But at least you're warm."

She grinned. "Well, I better get this Michelin Man butt of mine into the office. Frank's got me working on a stack of research for the Sunday paper, and you wouldn't believe the requests Cassandra threw at me last night."

Cassandra. I cringed. Her name had a prickly feel to it. I wanted to say *ouch* when anyone said it aloud.

"The woman wants an entire tome on the city's Italian restaurants in the 1980s and 90s," Abby continued. "Food critics take themselves a *leetle* too seriously. Anyway, the only thing I've come up with thus far is a killer craving for baked ziti."

I smiled. "Good luck with that."

Abby glanced at Dominic across the room. "You staying here to work?"

"Nah," I said, standing up. My eyes met Dominic's. I quickly looked away. "I'll head in with you. We can share a cab."

"Knock, knock."

I looked up from my computer to see Ethan standing in the doorway. "Hello, stranger," he said stiffly, handing me an enormous bouquet of tulips, pink, white, orange, and yellow. Wrapped in brown butcher paper and tied with twine, they bore the telltale signs of the Pike Place Market.

I blinked hard, taking in a whiff of the pastel petals, letting their lemony sweetness momentarily intoxicate me. "They're beautiful," I said, coming to my senses again. "Thank you."

"I was just passing through the Market, and I thought of you," Ethan said, sliding into the guest chair. Tall, with broad shoulders, chestnut-brown hair, and a knee-weakening grin, he didn't have to try to be charming. He just was. The grandson of the newspaper's patriarch, Ethan had cut his teeth at a big newspaper back east, and when he walked into the *Herald* building so many years ago, the newly minted managing editor, I was attracted to him immediately. And I still was. But things were different now. We were once two people madly in love. And now? Well, I couldn't even remember the last time we'd been intimate.

"That was sweet of you," I said in a tone I normally used with coworkers. I heard the chime of an incoming e-mail and turned back to my computer.

"Oh," he said, "are you on deadline?"

"No," I said. "Well, yes, actually, sort of. Frank's got me on a goose chase of a story, and I think I'm finally making headway on an angle that's worth researching."

Ethan stood up abruptly. "Well, I won't keep you, then. I guess I'll see you tonight at the gala?"

"The gala?"

"You didn't forget, did you?"

"I'm sorry," I said, confused. "I guess I did."

Ethan frowned. "The Ronald McDonald House Charities gala," he said. "The one my parents are chairing? My grandfather is being honored with the Lifetime Achievement Award tonight." He sighed. "Claire, you've known about this for months."

I *had* known about it for months. Hazily. I recalled talk of the event, and mostly fuss from Ethan's mother, Glenda, about how I'd need to find a suitable, formal floor-length gown. I don't do floor length, but my meek protest had been no match for Ethan's mother.

"Oh, yeah," I said blankly.

"Did you find a dress?"

"No," I replied.

"Can you wear something you already have?"

How insensitive, especially after everything I've been through. "You know I can't fit into any dress in my closet!" I said a little more loudly than I'd anticipated. I looked at my feet and dug my toe into the carpet. I regretted snapping at him. After all, he was only try-ing to help. "Sorry," I said. "Your mother's going to hate me for forgetting."

Ethan crossed his arms. "Claire, she's not going to *hate* you."

"Don't worry," I said in more of a huff than I intended. "I'll be there. And not in a paper bag. I'll stop by Nordstrom on the way home."

Ethan's eyes looked tender for a moment. "Claire," he said, softly, "I've been thinking, and I . . ."

I sat up straighter in my chair. "What?"

"Nothing," he said, his voice quickly switching back to the businesslike tone we typically used at work. "It's nothing." He gave me a forced grin before heading out the door.

I spent the morning researching, and quickly realized that locating a lost boy from 1933 is no easy feat. The receptionist on the phone at the police department made that much clear.

"You're looking for *who*?"

"A little boy," I said. "He vanished in May of 1933. As far as I know, he was never found."

"Ma'am," the woman said, smacking her gum, "what is it that you want me to do? Are you calling to file a report?" I could imag-ine the exasperated look on her face.

"No, no," I said. "I'm just hoping that you can check your records for a Daniel or Vera Ray. I'm working on a story, for the newspaper."

She sighed, clearly unimpressed. "Our records don't date back *that* far."

"Oh," I said, sinking back into my chair.

"Listen," the woman finally said after a long moment of silence. "If you want to do a little heavy lifting, come on down to the police headquarters. I can show you to our archives, and you're welcome to take a look. You have press credentials, right? You're from a newspaper?"

"Yes," I said. "The *Seattle Herald*."

"All right," she said. "Just don't make the department look bad in your story. The chief hates it when that happens."

"I'll do my best," I said, hanging up the phone and simultaneously reaching for my coat.

"I'm surprised you made it over here," said a junior police officer. He escorted me down the long corridor that led to the basement archives, home to police records from decades past. "The forecasters are calling for at least another two inches this afternoon."

I pointed to my boots, still caked in white, and smiled. "I almost didn't make it."

The officer grinned. "Guess you have a pretty important story, then?"

I nodded. "Yes. At least, I think I do."

"It's so weird, this storm," he continued. "One of the officers got a call from his mother. She lives here in town, and she says that a storm just like this one hit in May back in the thirties."

"I know," I said.

"Oh, you got a relative who remembered it?"

"No," I said. "But I'm writing about a little boy who went missing the day of that snowstorm."

"I got three boys of my own," he said. "Five, three, and one." He shook his head regretfully. "Can't imagine losing a child. But what it would do to my wife, that's what I worry about most. She'd never get over it, I can tell you that."

I nodded. "No mother should ever lose a child," I said, staring at the door ahead. "I think it's why this story is so important to me. As far as I can tell, this little boy was never reunited with his mother. I want to know what happened."

We walked into a dark room, and the officer turned on the light switch. Fluorescent bulbs flicked and hissed overhead. "What year was he taken?" His voice echoed against the gray concrete walls.

I pulled my notebook from my bag, scanning my notes. "Nineteen thirty-three."

"Right this way," he said. "Homicides are down this aisle, and you can find everything else over by the wall."

Homicides.

I eyed the shelves stacked with boxes, trying not to imagine the grim artifacts they might hold. *Bloodstained clothing. Murder weapons. Bones.* I shuddered. "Thank you," I said, walking toward a shelf labeled MISSING PERSONS.

"I'll be down the hall if you need anything," the officer said, turning to the door. But a moment later he looked back at me. "You're a good person to try to find that kid."

I shrugged. "I'm just doing my job."

With the assistance of a nearby ladder, I pulled a few boxes down from the shelf and thumbed through their files until I reached the R section. A thorough look produced nothing, and I climbed down the ladder disheartened. *How could he just vanish without a single record?*

I eyed the top shelf. Had I missed something? I ascended the ladder again, scanning the shelf carefully for a box of importance. I shook my head. They were all alphabetical, and there was just one box for the letter R. *What if one was mislabeled?* I opened up the next box, labeled S. Nothing. Then I tried the box with a Q on it. At the very back, two R records waited. *They must have been misfiled.* I pulled out the first, read it, then set it aside. But my fingers froze when, on the second record, I came across the typewritten name of little Daniel Ray.

```
Vera Ray, of Seattle, reports that her
son, Daniel Ray, disappeared. He was
last seen at the residence of 4395 Fifth
Avenue, #2. Suspected runaway.
```

How could they be so quick to write him off as a runaway? Children don't run away at age three. He was only a baby. No, there had to be another explanation.

I wrote down the address, then riffled through the file, eager to find more information, but after an hour, nothing turned up. I walked back out to the hallway, where the officer walked me upstairs. "Find anything?" he asked.

"Yeah," I said, looking out the doors to the snowy street. "An address." I could only imagine what might wait there.

I arrived back at the office at two, hoping to grab my laptop and make a few phone calls before visiting the former home of Daniel and Vera Ray. Before I could set my bag down, I nearly bumped into Cassandra.

"Oh hi," she said, standing in the doorway of my cubicle. She wore a silk top, and the lace of her black camisole protruded through an unfastened button.

"Hi," I said, wondering what she was doing there, but more

important, why she always looked so fresh-faced and perfect. I'd stolen a look at myself in the bathroom mirror earlier and had gasped at the dark shadows under my eyes.

"Ethan and I just got back from lunch at Giancarlo's, and we brought you back a doggie bag," she said.

Ethan and I.

I stared at the little brown paper sack dangling from her manicured hand.

She set the bag on my desk, then noticed the vase of tulips from Ethan. "Oh, aren't those just gorgeous? We passed them at the Market, and I told Ethan he absolutely had to get them for you."

My heart sank. *So the flowers were her idea.*

"Sometimes men just need a little encouragement," she said, twirling a strand of her long hair around her finger. "Well, I'll see you tonight, then? At the gala?"

"Right," I said blankly. "See you tonight."

"Claire," she said, turning back to me. "You really should try that asparagus risotto. It was amazing."

I nodded without turning around, tossing the bag into the wastebasket under my desk as soon as I heard her footsteps receding.

I had two hours before I needed to be dressed for the gala, so I hurried outside and tracked down a cab. I rattled off the address to the driver, wondering what I'd find when I got there. An old apartment building? Perhaps, if I was lucky, there could be an elderly resident with a memory of the storm—of little Daniel, even.

The cab skidded to a stop, and I was too distracted digging through my purse for a ten-dollar bill to notice where we were, until I reached for the door handle and looked up. "I'm sorry,"

I said, confused, staring out the window at Café Lavanto, its green awning dusted with snow. "I must have given you the wrong address. This can't be right."

"Forty-three ninety-five Fifth Avenue, right?" he said, looking up at the address placard on the café's window.

I glanced at my notebook, shaking my head. "Well, that's what I wrote down, anyway." I paid the fare and stepped out onto the sidewalk. My breath turned to steam as soon as it hit the icy air.

The café was quiet, with just a single customer in an upholstered chair by the fireplace. I found Dominic at the bar. He wiped the counter with a dishcloth and flung it over his shoulder. "Late afternoon cocoa craving?"

I shook my head. "If I told you, you'd never believe me."

"Try me."

I pulled out the file folder in my bag and set it down on the counter, opening it up to a photocopied news clipping from 1933, with Daniel Ray's haunting face in blurred black and white. "This little boy," I said. "He used to live here."

"Here?"

I looked up at the ceiling, imagining the building's layout overhead. "Well, upstairs, probably. The apartments must have been built early in the last century, possibly even before that."

"Makes sense," Dominic said, having a closer look at the news story. "The floors above the loft are empty, just storage, but I think they used to be apartments at one point. Most of the buildings on this street were old tenement houses. Almost all have been converted into office space, or luxury condos." He looked around the café with admiration. "I could never sell this building."

I smiled. "You really love this place, don't you?"

"I do," he said simply. "It saved me, in a sense. I came to work here when I thought I'd lost everything, when I didn't know how to move forward. And now I'm the owner. I feel pretty lucky."

I smiled, pointing to the door that led to the upper story. "The loft you told me about yesterday," I said. "Would you mind letting me have a look? I wonder if that was the apartment Daniel and his mother might have shared?"

"Sure," he said, leading me down the hallway and to the base of a little flight of stairs much too narrow to satisfy current building codes. I nodded, following him up, stairs creaking underfoot, into what might have been a small living room decades ago. It connected to a tiny, primitive kitchen in disrepair. The ivory cupboards looked tired, and cracks zigzagged through the old porcelain sink, yellowed from years of wear with rust spots near the drain.

I noticed another small staircase to the right. I looked at Dominic. "What's up there?"

"Just a little room," he said. "An attic, really. We keep boxes of paperwork there. It might have been a bedroom, I suppose."

"Do you mind if I have a look?"

"Not at all," he said.

The staircase seemed to bow with each step, and I felt Dominic's hand on my back, steadying me just before I nearly slipped on the second-to-last step. Since the hospital stay, my balance had been off, and the deficiency made me feel like a little old lady at times.

"Thanks," I said a little nervously.

I walked into the room and crossed my arms for warmth.

"Sorry," Dominic said. "I don't keep this floor heated. Got to save money where we can these days. Besides, the old owner put in baseboards and they're energy hogs."

I walked over to an old single-paned window, which looked out over the alley and a large tree stump below, then turned back to Dominic and took a deep breath. "Do you ever get a *feeling* about a place? A certain vibe?"

He nodded. "To be honest," he said, "this room has always given me the creeps."

I studied the walls, with layers of peeling paint and remnants of wallpaper from decades past. "You can almost feel it," I said.

"Feel what?"

I pulled the news clipping out of the folder again and stared at the little boy on the page. "You can almost feel the sadness. Something bad happened here."

He nodded. "What do you think *happened*?"

I pointed to the page in my hand. "I think this little boy was abducted here in 1933."

"Did they ever find him?"

"No," I said. "I mean, not that I can tell."

Dominic smiled. "And you, Sherlock, intend to find him?"

"Well," I said, "I intend to find out what happened to him, anyway." I looked at my watch. Half past four. "The gala!" I nearly screamed. "I have an hour to buy a dress and get somewhere very important."

"I've known a lot of women," he said with a grin, "and never have I met one who could shop and dress in under an hour."

Flustered, I stuffed the file folder back in my bag. "Well, I'm not your everyday woman."

"Can I help you?" he asked once downstairs again.

"Help me? Unless you can sew me a dress, I—"

"I'll drive you," he said, handing me a motorcycle helmet. "Put it on. I'll close early today. I can get you to Nordstrom quicker than a cab."

"But in the snow?"

"Trust me," he said, strapping on another helmet, "I've driven my bike in worse conditions. Plus, the roads are sanded now. We'll be fine."

"All right," I said hesitantly, following him to the back door.

Even at a slow speed, the cold wind whizzed through my coat, and I instinctively wrapped my arms more tightly around Dominic. "Too cold?" he asked, straining his voice to be heard over the motorcycle's engine, which was roaring and popping so loudly that children looked up, startled, from their sidewalk snowmen.

"I'm OK," I replied. Though I didn't share my true thoughts. *What if Ethan sees me? What would he say? Since when do I, a married woman, hop on the back of a motorcycle with a guy I hardly know? Then again, who gave him permission to start lunching with his ex? Even.*

Dominic pulled the bike into a parking spot in front of Nordstrom and we both stepped off, stowing the helmets on top of the seat with a bungee cord. "Could you use a second pair of eyes?"

I smiled. "Really? You'd actually go dress shopping with me? I think my husband would rather gouge his eyes out than do that."

"I have four sisters," he said. "I can hold my own at Nordstrom."

I glanced at the window display, a mannequin in a silver gown, and felt my heart flutter with fear. *Why am I having such a hard time with this? It's only shopping, for crying out loud. Why is the idea of trying on a dress giving me such anxiety?* I looked into Dominic's kind eyes and appreciated him being there. Even more, I *wanted* him to be there. "Yes," I said, returning his smile. "I would love your help. I have zero fashion sense—and a mother-in-law who will peck me to pieces if I don't find suitable attire."

"Leave it to me," he said, chivalrously holding the door.

Together we rode the escalator up to the second-floor dress section and combed the aisles for an appropriate gown.

"How about this one?" Dominic held up a black sequined floor-length dress.

"Too fitted," I said, shaking my head in disapproval. "I'd look like a sausage in it."

He refocused his efforts and plucked a blue gown from a nearby rack. "This," he said, "is very nice."

I nodded. "It is."

"Blue's your color."

I held up my bracelet. The gold chain with its three blue sapphires sparkled under the department store lights. Ethan had given it to me on my thirtieth birthday. I would never forget the way he had beamed with pride when he clasped it on my wrist.

"A perfect match," Dominic said. "Here, go try it on."

I grabbed the hanger and walked quickly to the dressing room. I caught a glimpse of my bare body in the mirror before I slipped the gown over my head. I looked away quickly. *My God, how did I forget? Today is May 3. The anniversary of it all.*

I felt the sudden urge to put my clothes back on, run out of the dressing room, and keep running until I was safe inside the apartment. I'd curl up in bed. A sleeping pill could numb the pain. I still had a few left in the prescription bottle in my medicine cabinet. They always helped, for a time. But the sapphires on my wrist sparkled again, the jewels reflecting their brightness in my tears. I thought of Ethan and the promise I had made to him. I zipped up the dress, smoothing it where it wrinkled a bit at the sides. *I can do this.*

I hardly recognized the woman staring back at me in the mirror, perhaps because my uniform for the past year had consisted of baggy, drab clothing. I'd almost forgotten that I had a *shape*. I opened the fitting room door and walked out.

"You look . . . stunning," Dominic said, waiting patiently in the hallway. "It's the one."

"It better be, because I have to be at the Olympic Hotel in fifteen minutes."

"Wear it out," he said. "They can cut the tags off at the counter."

I smiled, pointing at my tan boots. "Guess I'd better pick up some shoes, too."

"Yeah," he said, smiling.

I said good-bye to Dominic and hailed a cab to the Olympic Hotel, where I found Ethan waiting for me in the lobby, pacing. An elaborate vintage chandelier dangled overhead. I read the look on his face instantly: irritation.

"There you are," he said, glancing at his watch. "Do you realize that you're a half hour late?"

"Nice to see you, too," I said sarcastically, running my hand along the edge of my dress to be sure the tags were gone.

Ethan frowned. "Why do you have to be so . . ."

I folded my arms. "So *what*?"

"So defensive," he said. "So angry all the time."

I sighed.

"Claire," he continued, "it's been a long day. Can we just go in and sit down? Can we pretend to get along? Just for tonight?"

I felt a lump in my throat. "You don't remember, do you?"

"What?"

"Today," I said, searching his eyes. "You don't remember what today is."

He looked toward the ballroom, then back at me, annoyed. "I don't know what you're talking about, but if we don't get inside, we're going to miss—"

"A year ago today . . ." I said in almost a whisper, the memory too sacred to let a passing stranger overhear.

His face changed then. The rigidness softened. He took a step toward me. "Oh, honey, I'm so sorry." He put his hand on my back. "I can't believe I forgot."

"Well," I said, wiping a tear from my eye, "maybe you were too busy lunching with Cassandra."

Ethan stiffened. "Claire, don't be ridiculous. Listen, let's go inside and sit down. We can talk later."

I hated the tone in his voice, just as much as I hated the tone in mine. Cold. Unfeeling. *Who is this bickering couple we've become?* I looked at the black heels Dominic had helped me select mere minutes ago, then up at Ethan again. *What if I just embraced him? Would he hold me in his arms the way he used to?* I felt a rush of sadness.

"You blame me," I said under my breath. "For what happened." *There, I said it.*

"Oh, come on, Claire. You can't be serious."

"Don't pretend like you don't resent me," I continued. "I know you think it was my fault. I see it in your eyes every damn time I look at you."

"Claire," Ethan said, "that's unfair."

"Well, you're not denying it."

He stared at his feet. "I—"

We both looked up when we heard footsteps behind us.

"Oh, there you are, Ethan," Cassandra said, holding two glasses of champagne. Her gold sequin dress clung to her body, flattering her curves in a way that no dress could do for mine. "Everything all right out here?" she asked. "Your mother asked me to see if I could find you. Your grandfather's about to take the stage."

Ethan nodded. "Thanks Cassandra, I—"

"I was just leaving," I said, tugging at my bracelet as I made my way back out to the sidewalk. I hailed an approaching cab and climbed into the backseat, quickly turning away from the window. I couldn't let them see my tears.

Chapter 7

VERA

Charles.

It took little effort to recall his face, even if it had been four years since I'd taken in those kind eyes, that strong chin, the smile that had charmed me in an instant.

I almost didn't meet him. I shouldn't have met him, really. Charles was too good for me. High society. Everyone knew that. Everyone, perhaps, but him. He came from wealth, from privilege, too big a catch for a girl from the poor side of town, the daughter of a fisherman. But Caroline convinced me to join her that night for the opening of the fanciest hotel Seattle had ever seen, and there, beyond the polished double doors, he stood in the hotel's grand foyer under the crystal chandelier, smoking a cigar as servants bustled, balancing heavy, hors d'oeuvres–filled trays aloft. Plenty of beautiful women fluttered in his sight, primped, curled, and powdered. And, yet, for a reason I still can't understand, he looked only at me.

"Come on," Caroline whispered.

I deflected his gaze, feeling foolish.

"Let's sneak in."

I frowned. "You know they'll take one look at us and give us the boot."

"Nonsense," she said. "Look at you in that gorgeous dress." True, we were wearing our finest, and if you squinted, you might mistake our handmade dresses, perfect flapper attire, for a Chanel creation, but upon close inspection, the truth would shine through: two destitute nineteen-year-olds with little more than two pennies to pinch together.

I sighed. "All right," I finally conceded. "As long as you don't think we'll get into any trouble."

"Of course we won't," she said a little too confidently, reaching for my hand and dragging me toward the entrance.

A doorman eyed us suspiciously. "And you are?"

"I'm Miss Ella Wentworth and this is my debutante cousin, Gilda, from Atlanta," Caroline said.

I batted my eyes, playing along, trying to suppress a laugh. *Did she have to use the word* debutante?

The man eyed his notebook. "I'm afraid I don't see you on the list," he said.

"Oh, that's a shame," Caroline cooed. "Daddy will be very upset to hear. You do know who my father is, don't you?"

The man shook his head.

"Alexander Wentworth," she said. "Of Wentworth *Real Estate*." Caroline looked up at the tall building. "He invested so much in this property. It's a pity the guest list didn't get sorted out properly." She sighed, tugging at the gold chain around her neck. "I'll have to talk to Daddy about that."

"Wait—wait," the man stammered. "I'm sure it's only a misunderstanding. Please, come in, Miss Wentworth. And give our sincerest apologies to your father."

"I will," Caroline said, nodding regally, as we passed through the entrance and into the sparkling party. She swiped a flute of punch off a waiter's tray and handed it to me before taking one for herself. "That," she said, taking a sip, "is how it's done."

"Caroline," I whispered, "you're out of your mind."

She giggled from behind her glass. "Oh come on—have a little fun."

I shook my head. "I think we should go."

She looked at me and threw back her head with a laugh. "And miss the best party of the season? I think not."

I eyed the women around us, their collective finery. I wished I'd sewn an extra piece of fringe around the hem of my dress. It looked so plain next to yards of satin and lace. "We don't belong here," I whispered to her.

"Sure we do," she said, unaffected by my insecurities. "And look over there." She pointed to two men standing straight ahead, and I saw, again, the man who had made eye contact with me moments before. He gazed at me with a beckoning grin and I turned away quickly. "Should we go talk to them?" she continued, bobbing a curl flirtatiously with her hand.

"Caroline!" I pulled her arm and whisked her into the room to our left, where people hovered around a grand piano. "What has gotten into you?"

She grinned. "Look, let's just have a little fun. Besides, I rather fancy the idea of spending the evening in the company of *rich* men."

I shook my head. "I won't stand here and—" I paused when I felt a tapping on my shoulder, only to discover the two men from the foyer.

The one in the gray suit smiled. "You won't stand here and . . . ? Do tell."

I blushed. "Oh, nothing," I muttered, sending Caroline a look of panic, but her eyes had already been swallowed up by the man's friend.

"I'm Charles," the taller of the two said, holding his hand out to me. I took it dutifully, but found that once our palms touched, I didn't want to let go. "And you are?"

"Vera," I said, looking away so as not to be hypnotized by his gaze. "Vera Ray."

He gestured to a pair of wingback chairs near a crackling fireplace to our right. "Care to sit down?"

I looked at Caroline for approval, but she was too consumed in conversation with Charles's friend to notice. "Of course," I said nervously. The only men I'd associated with were of the working-class variety. This man's suit and unmarred hands told me he was of an entirely different breed. I worried that upon close inspection he'd find me unsuitable. I appreciated the dimly lit room, where the shabbiness of my dress and the scuffs on my shoes weren't as obvious.

"Some party," he said, looking around the room.

"Yes, indeed," I replied, clutching my purse tightly.

He peered at me for an uncomfortably long moment. "You know," he said, "I don't think I've seen you around before. You weren't at the art museum event last month, were you?"

"No," I said nervously.

Charles looked satisfied. "Well, you didn't miss much. It was quite dull." He leaned in closer to me. "Can you keep a secret?"

I nodded hesitantly.

"I hate these functions. My father insisted that I attend."

"My friend insisted that *I* attend," I said with a smile.

Charles sank his chin in his hand and grinned. "Well, aren't we a pair?"

My cheeks warmed.

He pushed a lock of hair from his forehead. "Truth is, I'd rather be anywhere but here." He pointed to a man about his age wiping a table in the distance. "I envy him."

I gave him a disbelieving look. "Why?"

"Because he's free," he said simply.

"And you're not?"

Charles tugged on the collar of his crisply pressed shirt as if it were a manacle. "Not really. I'm expected to play a role."

"Well," I said, "with all due respect, a lot of people would kill to be in your position."

"And they'd soon realize it's not all it's cracked up to be." He sighed. "I'd rather be a farmer."

"You? A farmer?"

His eyes brightened. "I'd grow corn, so I could get lost in it. Did you know that in California they grow corn mazes—big stalks as tall as me spread out as far as the eye can see?"

I shook my head.

"Well, that's what I'd do, anyway," he said, "if I could choose another life. And you?" His eyes sparkled with sincerity. "Are you happy?"

I smoothed my dress self-consciously. *Can he see through me? Does he know I don't belong here?* "Why wouldn't I be?" I said a little more defensively that I'd intended.

A band began playing soft music, and a few couples rose from their chairs and began walking to the dance floor. He looked at me shyly. "Let's dance."

My heart raced. *Dance? Me?* I shook my head. "I'm sorry, I'm afraid not."

"Oh," Charles replied, injured. "I promise, I won't bite."

I looked away, trying to think of an excuse. "No, no, it's just that, well . . ."

"Tell me," he said tenderly. "What are you afraid of? No, let me guess. You're engaged to be married?" He placed his hand on his heart dramatically, as if Cupid had just shot an arrow right through the lapel of his suit jacket.

"No," I said, smiling despite myself. "It's just that I . . . can't."

"You can't what?"

"I can't *dance*," I whispered.

Charles looked amused. "Oh, is that all?" He reached for my hand. "Come on. I'll teach you."

My heart raced as he led me to the freshly waxed parquet floor. I looked around at the couples moving graciously, elegantly around us. I could jitterbug, but this? I was out of my element.

Charles placed my left hand on his shoulder and took my right hand in his, positioning my body so close to his that I felt the warmth radiating from his suit jacket. "This is a waltz," he said. "It's easy. Just follow me."

In minutes, I caught on, and I followed Charles's lead around the dance floor. He guided me with such precision, he made up for my lack of dancing prowess.

"You're a natural," he said, smiling at me with his warm green eyes.

I grinned, looking away. "Well, I have you to thank for that."

He eyed me curiously, determined to continue the conversation. "Tell me, Miss Ray, who are your family? I don't recognize the Ray name. Is your father in real estate?"

I freed my hand from his and suddenly stopped dancing. "I really must go."

"I'm sorry," he said. "Did I say something wrong?"

I glanced over to where I thought Caroline was, but couldn't see her in the dim, smoky air. *What am I doing here? This isn't a place for me.* "I'm very sorry," I said, turning toward the door. "Good night."

I ran through the throng of people, pushing my way into the foyer, frantically looking for Caroline. Perhaps she could mingle with the rich without batting an eye, but I couldn't pretend. It wasn't in me.

"Excuse me," I mumbled, pushing past a group of men smoking cigars. I took a step farther and collided with a hotel maid I recognized instantly. "Gwen?"

She looked at me with confusion. "Vera? What are *you* doing here?"

I shook my head. "Caroline talked the doorman into letting us in."

Gwen raised one eyebrow. "She could talk a mink into giving up its fur, that one."

I sighed. "This is beautiful and all, but . . . I just can't pretend to be"—I looked back toward the party—"one of them. I don't belong here."

"Maybe not," Gwen said, "but you seem to have an admirer."

I turned around to see Charles approaching. "Quick," I said, "help me hide."

Gwen shrugged and led me down a hallway, where we both jumped inside a maid's closet. I pushed a mop aside to make more room. "All right," she said once the door was safely closed behind us. "Why is it that you're hiding from Seattle's most eligible bachelor?"

"Charles?"

"Yes, dummy," she said with a sigh. "His father owns half of Seattle. This hotel, too."

"Well," I said, "then I'll save him the disappointment when he finds out I'm not a society girl."

"Honey," Gwen snorted, "I'm sorry to put it so bluntly—I'm sure he already knows you're not a society girl."

The unforgiving light in the closet did nothing to conceal the hole beginning to form on the toe of my right shoe. "Oh."

"He clearly doesn't care," she continued. "Maybe he likes you for . . . you."

"Gwen," I said, "you're very sweet, but I think you're out of your mind." I squeezed her hand. "I'm going home. Is there a back entrance I can use?"

"Yes," she said, opening the door and pointing down the hall. "Right that way."

"Thanks. And if you see Caroline, can you let her know? Discreetly?"

"I will," she replied. "I'll pass her a note in the caviar." She snickered.

I walked down the hallway and opened the door, which deposited me in the alley. I took two steps, then jumped when I heard shuffling behind me. I turned around to see Charles leaning against the building with a shy smile.

"There you are," he said. "I thought you were running away from me."

"I was," I said honestly.

He took a step closer. "I have to know," he said. "What did I say that has you so spooked? Did I do something to upset you?"

"Listen," I replied, "you have the wrong idea about me. I'm not a debutante. I didn't go to finishing school. And I wasn't even invited to this event."

Charles shrugged. "And you think I care about all that?"

I paused, studying his face—honest, kind. "You don't?"

"I can't stand those kinds of girls," he said, gesturing toward the party. "They're all the same. If you'll let me, I'd love to get to know *you*. Can we start over?"

I smiled, extending my hand. "I'm Vera Ray; so nice to meet you."

Chapter 8

§

CLAIRE

The cab pulled in front of the apartment building and skidded for a moment on the icy streets until it came to a jarring stop. The streetlights made the sequins on my dress shimmer. I sighed, longing to be in sweats and a T-shirt.

"He's a lucky man," the driver quipped, eyeing my dress.

"I'm sorry?"

"Your date tonight," he continued.

"Oh," I said. I guess he didn't notice my red eyes and tear-stained cheeks. "Yes." I shrugged and handed him a twenty before stepping out onto the sidewalk. "He doesn't know I exist anymore," I whispered to myself after the cab drove away.

Gene opened the door for me, and I gathered the hem of my dress before it caught on the hinge. "Home early tonight? I thought you and Ethan were at the—"

"You know I don't like all that glitz and glamour," I said, before he could press further. "Besides, this dress is itchy."

Gene looked at me for a long moment. "Claire, how are you doing?" he asked, his eyes big and kind and filled with so much goodness. "Since the accident," he said, faltering, "you haven't been the same."

I nodded. "You're right," I said. "I haven't."

He wrapped his strong arm around my shoulder, and it gave me permission, somehow, to feel the feelings that hovered inside, the ones I'd tried so hard to keep hidden, to not feel. "Today's the anniversary, isn't it?"

"Oh, Gene," I cried. "Sometimes I feel as if my heart is going to burst."

"Then let it," he said, stroking my hair the way my father used to when I was a little girl. "You've been carrying this burden too long. Let it out. Let it all out, dear."

I closed my eyes, letting the memories pour out like a mudslide, destroying the stiff little world I'd created for myself, the emotional armor that protected me from feeling the pain of the past. I closed my eyes. And I remembered.

One year ago

"Pink or blue?" Ethan asked, nuzzling my neck from behind.

I turned to face him, and he held in each hand a tiny outfit— one, a dusty blue sweater with light blue leggings; the other, a pink dress with white tights and ruffles on the bottom. My heart melted. "Either way, this baby is going to be well dressed."

Ethan eyed the pink outfit, smiling to himself. "I think she's going to be a girl."

I shook my head. "A boy."

He pulled me close, rubbing his hand lovingly across my enormous belly. We'd decided to be surprised by the baby's gender, despite considerable protest from our families, most notably Ethan's. "Do you know how much I love you?" he whispered into my ear.

I grinned, planting a firm kiss on his cheek, noticing my running shoes by the door. "I'm going to sneak out for a quick jog before dinner."

Ethan frowned. "Claire, I wish you wouldn't. You're pushing yourself too hard."

I admit, the sight of me in all my eight-months-pregnant enormity jogging down the streets of Seattle had elicited some shocked stares, but I'd researched running during pregnancy, and everything I'd read on the topic indicated that it was generally safe. And while my doctor wasn't thrilled with the idea of me continuing my four-mile jogs into my third trimester, she didn't forbid them either. I stopped when I was overly winded and stayed adequately hydrated. Besides, as a lifelong runner, for me, giving up jogging would have been like giving up breathing.

"Ethan," I protested, "you know that Dr. Jensen says running is perfectly fine during pregnancy."

"Yeah, maybe in early pregnancy," he said. "But it can't be a good idea now."

"The baby's not going to *fall out*," I said, laughing. I rubbed his arm. "Honey, everything's going to be fine."

I reached for my iPod, pushing the earbuds into my ears. "I'll be back in a half hour," I said before he could say another word.

I waved to Gene as I made my way out to the sidewalk. The May sun beamed down. The mild air hit my cheeks as I turned the volume up and began to pick up my pace. I felt the baby kick inside as I bounded past James Street, and I wondered what it would be like to push a jogger stroller. Like anything else, I knew I'd get used to it. I imagined my mornings with my baby in tow. I'd tuck him into his seat and we'd go jogging together.

Him.

My little boy. Or maybe little girl, as Ethan had predicted. My heart raced, too fast now, so I slowed my pace and took in a long breath of the sea air wafting up from Elliott Bay, salty and crisp. I turned the music up louder, then regained my pace, just as something appeared in my peripheral vision. A car. Red. Coming close. Too close. The music blasted in my ears as I lunged left, my left shoe catching on a large crack in the sidewalk. For a moment, it felt as if I was flying, gliding weightlessly through the air, until the fender hit my body. I didn't feel the impact, not really. My body's shock response blunted the pain. There was only pressure and what felt like a pop deep inside. And then everything went black.

I opened my eyes and squinted. The overhead light, piercingly bright, made my weak eyes flutter. Ethan hovered to my right; Mother to my left. Both wore blue surgical gowns and caps. The room blurred, and I closed my eyes tightly, opening them a moment later with greater focus. *Why can't I feel my legs?*

"Ethan," I whispered, "what happened? My legs—they're numb. What's going on? I was running..." The memory came slowly at first, and then it hit just as vividly as the moment the car had struck. "A—a car," I stammered. "A car hit me. Ethan ... the baby!" I glanced down at my belly. It appeared smaller. I panicked, placing my hands on my stomach. It felt soft, mushy, empty. I screamed. "Where's my baby? Where's my baby? Where did they take the baby? Bring him to me!" I sat up, and even though my legs lay lifeless and numb, I lunged toward the edge of the bed, determined to get up, to find my child.

Ethan jumped forward, pulling my arms gently back to the

bed. "No, Claire," he said softly. I detected defeat in his voice, grief. "The baby—"

"Stop!" my mother cried. I turned to face her, but she looked only at Ethan. "She's not ready yet. Give her more time."

Ethan shook his head. "She should know." He turned back to me and looked at me with a face that broke my heart. He didn't have to tell me. I already knew. I stared at the wall as the words passed his lips, the words that would change my life forever. "The baby didn't make it."

The room began to spin.

He sat down in a chair by my bed. "I held—"

"No!" I screamed. "Don't. Don't tell me."

Ethan looked at me through tear-flooded eyes. "Why? Don't you want to know whether we had a boy or a girl? Don't you want to know that I held our child in my arms for a brief moment before—"

"Don't," I sobbed, burying my face in the pillow to my right.

"They brought the baby to you," Ethan said, wiping a tear from his cheeks. "You were unconscious, but you—"

"Stop," I cried. "I can't bear it."

I looked down at the bloodstain on my chest, and I began to tremble so violently that a nurse rushed over and injected a needle into my arm, letting the cool contents of the syringe seep into my vein. As my body went limp, I lay trapped inside my mind, haunted by the baby I would never know and the husband who I feared blamed me for it.

Chapter 9

VERA

It had been six days since he'd vanished, six days since the heavens had draped the city in a veil of white and changed my world forever. I searched the streets by day and held vigil in Caroline's tiny apartment by night, praying, hoping.

"Eva!" Caroline barked as she walked through the door shortly before seven a.m. She looked tired, ashen. Twelve-hour night shifts in the factory without a single break. "Go get Mama a wedge of cheese from the icebox," she said, setting her purse down before slumping onto the floor by the fireplace. I inched my legs up to make room for her on the sofa, but she didn't notice, or maybe she was simply too fatigued to pick herself up again.

"But Mama." Eva looked at me nervously, and then back at her mother.

"Eva, what did I say? Bring me the cheese." Caroline turned to me and extended her right hand. It trembled so violently I shuddered. "Payday's not till tomorrow. I haven't eaten since yesterday." She pointed to the window. "If that damn snow would just stop, already."

"But Mama," Eva squeaked. "Aunt Vera . . . *ate* the cheese."

"I'm so sorry," I said to Caroline before she could respond. "There wasn't anything left. I gave Eva most of it. There was only a bite, and I . . ."

Caroline tucked her knees to her chest and buried her face in her hands. "It's OK. It's OK." A dry, lonely sob seeped through the cracks in her fingers. "I don't know how much longer we can go on like this. The rent. The food. I'll have to go knocking on Mrs. Harris's door again. You should have seen the way she looked at me last week when I asked to borrow a few slices of bread. I haven't been able to get milk for months. Eva deserves milk." She looked up suddenly, and wiped her tears with her sleeve. "Look at me, blubbering on like this when you've lost . . ."

I knelt down by my old friend. She was gaunt, with hollow cheeks and a distant gaze—such a contrast to the woman I'd known just four years prior, the woman who'd had the world in the palm of her hand. No, I couldn't stay. Not any longer. The last thing Caroline needed was another mouth to feed.

"It's time I go," I said, reaching for my sweater hanging on a rusty nail in the wall.

"No!" Caroline cried, standing up quickly. She grabbed my arm, urging me back to the couch. "I won't hear of it. You have nowhere else to go. You're staying put."

I shook my head. "Listen, you can barely feed Eva, let alone me. Besides, I need to go back."

"What about your landlord?"

"I'll figure something out," I said vaguely. "I need to be there for Daniel when he comes home." My heart lightened when I said the words. *Of course he'll come home.* I imagined my little boy walking through the door, smiling in the way that revealed the tiny dimple on his chin. He'd run to me, and I'd press my nose against his forehead, his soft blond curls soaking up my tears. It was all a big mix-up, he'd explain. He'd seen the snow, he'd tell me, and gotten lost. A kind family had taken him in until the storm passed. They'd been good to him, given him a warm bed. And hot chocolate. I smiled to myself.

"Oh, honey," Caroline cried. "I want to believe that Daniel is coming home; Lord knows I do. But at some point you're going to have to—"

"No!" I snapped, closing my eyes tightly. I took a deep, calming breath. "He will come home. I *know* it."

I walked to the door and grasped the doorknob. Just before I stepped outside, I felt a soft tug at my dress.

"Aunt Vera?" Eva whispered, her eyes big and cautious.

I knelt down to her. "Yes, honey?"

She handed me a piece of paper. "I made this for you."

A bold tear rolled down my cheek and nestled into the crease of my mouth, salty and bitter. "Why, it's just . . . beautiful, dear," I said, looking over the drawing she'd made for me.

"That's Daniel, there," she said, pointing to a stick figure holding a stuffed bear. "And that's me," she added.

A third figure hovered over the crudely drawn children. A woman, perhaps? The elaborate hat she wore resembled a peacock. "Who's that, Eva?"

The girl scrunched her nose. "No one."

"She must be *someone*," I said. "You drew her here behind you and Daniel. Who is she, honey?"

"Just a lady, that's all."

I nodded. "Well," I said, standing up again, "I love it. Thank you. I shall treasure it, always."

"You know you can come back," Caroline said before I turned to leave. "You're always welcome here."

I answered with an air of finality I could no longer repress. "Thank you, dear friend, for everything."

I walked the familiar route back to the apartment, but I didn't feel my feet touch the ground. I merely floated. Like a ghost, invisible in my grief. People passed, but no one looked at me. *Do they see me?*

I pushed past a crowd of angry men lingering near the saloon. The air reeked of ale, skunky tobacco, and sweaty skin from the night before. "Excuse me," I said to a reasonable-looking man near the doorway. "Have you seen Mr. Ivanoff?" He'd been working in the saloon the morning of the storm. Maybe he'd seen something, someone.

The man's smile morphed into a sneer, and I regretted the question immediately. "Ivanoff, the mason?"

"Yes," I said, inching toward the stairs.

The man rubbed the stubble on his chin and took a step closer. "What do you want with him?"

"I want to speak to him," I said.

"Well, then you'll need to go down to the jail," he said with an amused look on his face. "He was arrested last night."

"Arrested?"

"That's right," he said. "Slapped around his missus. Hurt her pretty bad. Doc had to stitch her up."

My heart raced. I remembered how gentle Mr. Ivanoff had been with Daniel, how softly he'd spoken to him. Like a father. I shivered. *How did I not see that he had a violent streak?*

The man edged closer. "If you're looking for someone else to show you a good time, I—"

"Good day," I said, pushing past him.

I picked up my skirt and ran to the stairs, nearly tripping on an old bearded man passed out on the landing as I made my way up to the second floor. I pulled the key from my pocket, and a vein in my hand pulsed as I jammed it into the lock.

My heart swelled. *Maybe Daniel is here. Maybe he climbed the cherry tree and pushed through the little window. Maybe he's waiting inside.*

I turned the key, but it stuck. I tried again, turning it right and left, with no luck. *My God. Mr. Garrison. He must have changed the lock.*

"No!" I cried, pressing my cheek against the door. I heard footsteps inside. "Hello?" I pounded on the door. "Hello? Who's in there?"

I jumped back when the doorknob began to turn. The confused face of a girl, no older than eleven, appeared in the doorway. "Can I help you?" she asked.

I pushed past her. "What are you doing here, in my home? Where is Daniel?" I ran to the stairs. "Daniel! It's Mama. Mama is home."

A man in a wrinkled white shirt, yellowed and stained around the collar, walked out of the kitchen, suspenders dangling from his pants. "Jane, who is this?"

The girl shrugged. "I don't know, Papa. She says it's her apartment."

"It—it *is* my apartment," I stammered. "Why are you here? Where is my son? Daniel!"

"There must be some mistake," the man said. "We moved in three days ago. The landlord said the previous owner died. Told us she had no kin, so he sold us the furniture for five dollars."

"Died?"

The man shrugged.

"Do I appear dead to you?"

I looked at the remnants of my home, my life—the little coffee table with its carved oak flowers at the edges. My father had made it, before he died. The two chairs, threadbare but comfortable. The white vase on the table where I'd display the wildflowers Daniel picked for me on walks along Fourth Avenue. My things. My life. *Taken.*

Disinterested, the girl reached for her doll on the sofa and climbed the stairs. "Wait right there," the man said to me, clearly annoyed. "Dinner's boiling over on the stove."

As soon as he left, I walked a few steps to the base of the stairs. A small chest of drawers had been wedged up against the wall, and I strained, attempting to move it forward until I found the secret compartment. I opened it and sighed. Daniel's feather, shells. Memories wafted into the room and I wanted to linger in them, but I knew there wasn't time. I reached into my bag and pulled out Max. I straightened the little bear's blue bow and tucked him inside the space behind the wall. He belonged here. And Daniel would find him again. My heart told me that.

I heard footsteps behind me, and I closed the little door quickly, dropping my purse. I picked it up swiftly.

"What do you think you're doing, miss?" the man said suspiciously.

"I was just—"

He frowned. "I'm going to have to ask you to leave now."

"Please," I said, "if you see a little boy—"

"If I see *you* again, I'm going to report you to the police."

The girl appeared in the room again and looked at me with sympathetic eyes before her father pushed me out into the hallway and closed the door with a loud thud.

Outside on the street, I surveyed my purse, grateful that my pocketbook, meager as it was, remained inside. Eva's little drawing, however, hadn't met such a fortunate fate. *It must have fallen out.*

I walked numbly out to the sidewalk. Children bundled in warm coats played hopscotch on the street as mothers looked on. "Daniel!" I called out in vain. Seagulls flew overhead, swooping and squawking in a mocking manner. The world, and every creature in it, seemed cruel and uncaring.

"Vera, is that you?" a familiar voice called out from the sidewalk up ahead.

"Gwen?"

"Oh, honey," she said. "I've been so worried about you. I just saw Caroline. She told me what happened. I'm so sorry."

"He's gone," I said. The words sounded foreign as they crossed my lips, as if someone else had uttered them.

"What do you mean, *gone?*"

"When I came home from work, he wasn't there," I said, feeling the tears sting my eyes. "The police won't do anything because they think he ran away, but Gwen, he would have never run away."

She put her arm around my shoulder, pulling me close. "Look at you," she said. "You're a skeleton. Have you eaten?"

I shook my head.

She patted my arm. "There's no sense crying out here in the cold. And you look like you haven't eaten in days. Let me buy you a hot meal."

My stomach growled. I hated that I had to stop to deal with hunger during a time like this, but I knew I'd be useless to Daniel passed out from weakness, so I obliged. "All right," I said meekly.

Gwen and I walked to Lindgren's, a little café in the Market where we used to dine, in happier times. "Two ham-and-gravy sandwiches," she said to the waitress behind the counter.

When our food arrived, I ate absently, without tasting the flavors in my mouth. Experiencing pleasure felt wrong, somehow. Instead I took comfort in the numbness.

"Are you coming back to work?" Gwen asked cautiously.

I sighed. "I guess I'll have to. That is, if I have a job waiting for me. I must have missed a half dozen shifts since . . ."

"Estella will understand."

I shook my head. "Do you really think so?"

"I'll talk to her for you," she said, doling out an assortment of change from her pocketbook and setting it atop the bill. "Come down to the hotel with me. I'll do the explaining."

The radiator crackled and hissed in its usual fashion inside the servants' quarters of the hotel. Linen rested in huge piles, waiting to be pressed. Estella sat at her old desk, just as she always did. And yet, everything seemed different. The axis of the world had shifted since Daniel's disappearance, changing everything forever.

"Well, there you are," Estella greeted me sarcastically.

Gwen jumped to my defense. "You won't believe what she's gone through, Estella," she said. "Her son has been abducted. She's been out searching for him day and night."

Estella's eyes narrowed, and I detected a flash of pity on her face. "Well," she said, eyeing a piece of paper in front of her distractedly, "that *is* very sad."

"So you'll let her come back to work?" Gwen continued.

Estella sighed, folding the paper and tucking it into an envelope. "I wish I could," she said. "But I've already hired another girl."

"You what?" Gwen raged. "How could you? Look, this poor woman needs a job more than ever. She's here to work even despite her missing son. Surely you have a place for her."

Estella shook her head. "I'm afraid I don't. She didn't show up for work, so I was forced to hire a replacement. No hard feelings." She straightened the spectacles on her nose. "This discussion has ended. Gwen, the sixth-floor suite needs cleaning. Look smart about it."

"Yes, ma'am," Gwen grunted.

Together we walked out to the hallway. My head felt heavy. "Gwen, you did your best. I'll be all right."

"I'll give you all my tip money," she said, "until you can get back on your feet again."

"You most certainly will not," I said. "But that's very kind of you anyway."

She followed me out to the lobby. "How will you get by, then?"

"I'll find a way," I replied. "I always have. Now, you'd better get up to the sixth floor before Estella finds you."

Gwen nodded. "All right. Take care of yourself, Vera."

"I will."

She disappeared into the corridor that led to the servants' elevator, and I stood for a moment, stunned, unsure of where to go or what to do. I walked a few paces and then sat down in an overstuffed chair in the lobby, teal with white satin stripes. It felt good to rest in a seat designated for wealthy patrons of the hotel. My feet ached, and a large blister had formed near the hole in my shoe. I closed my eyes.

"Excuse me." A voice interrupted my reverie. "I'm going to have to ask you to leave."

I opened my eyes to find the front desk manager, an aging woman named Martha, standing before me. "You know as well as anyone that the lobby is only a place for guests of the Olympic."

I nodded, rising to my feet. "I'm sorry," I said, limping toward the door.

"She's a guest," a deep, male voice said from behind me.

I turned around to see Lon Edwards, the man I'd met in the penthouse suite last week. Today he was fully clothed.

"She's *my* guest," he said to Martha with authority.

Martha lowered her eyes in submission, ignoring the look of confusion on my face. "Why, yes, Mr. Edwards," she said with a saccharine smile. "Of course."

After Martha scurried back to the front desk, Lon smiled at me. "It's Vera, right?"

"Yes," I said. "It was awfully nice of you to do that for me, but I really didn't need any help, Mr. Edwards."

"Just the same," he said, "I'd like to take you to dinner."

I shook my head adamantly. "I can't."

"Oh, come now, Miss Ray, it's only dinner," he said playfully. "Surely I can find a way to talk you into it?" He snapped his fingers and a man about half his age and height approached.

"Yes, sir?" he said.

"Andrew, this is Miss Ray. Take her to the salon, and to Frederick and Nelson. See to it that she gets anything she wants."

The man nodded. "Miss, when you're ready, the car's just outside."

"No," I said suddenly. "No. I can't. I mean, it's kind of you to take an interest in me, Lon—I mean, Mr. Edwards—but you don't understand. It's my son. My son has vanished. He's been taken. I can't have dinner with you because I have to find *him*." Sympathy appeared in Lon's eyes, and when I saw it, I felt hungry for it. *Starved.* My knees weakened.

"You poor thing," he said. "Have you gone to the police?"

"Yes," I replied. "But they aren't doing anything. They think he ran away."

"I'll make some phone calls. I know the chief of police."

My heart lightened. "You do?"

His face looked authoritative and sure. "Certainly," he said. "We went to school together. You just leave it to me." He paused and winked. "Maybe we can discuss the details over dinner?"

I took a deep breath. For a moment, I felt new hope. Lon knew what to do. He was a powerful man. He could help bring Daniel back to me.

"Are you ready now, Miss Ray?" Lon's assistant said.

Where else am I going to go, without a job, without a home, without my son? Why shouldn't I step inside Lon Edwards's town car, especially if he might help me find Daniel?

"Yes," I said quietly, with a defeated sigh. "I'm ready."

Chapter 10

CLAIRE

Ethan didn't come home the night of the gala, didn't even call. And as I cracked an egg into the frying pan the next morning, watching the white firm up around the edges and being careful to keep the yolk intact, I hated that I missed him. I longed to slide the egg—over easy, his favorite—onto a piece of whole wheat toast, sprinkle it with sea salt and a ridiculous amount of cracked pepper, just the way he liked it, and bring it to him. I missed the old ebb and flow of our mornings. Most of all, I longed to see him smile again, a smile unclouded by the past or uncertainty about the future.

I eyed the egg sizzling in the pan. *He's probably at his parents' house, that's all.* Ethan sometimes stayed there when we fought, or when he was working late and needed a distraction-free environment. After we lost the baby, he'd spent a great deal of time at their home, a few miles outside the city. I tilted the pan at an angle over the plate, but breakfast slid into a defeated heap on the tile floor. *Splat.* I stared at the mess of runny yolk as the memory of last night came into focus like a slap to the face.

Cassandra. I felt a bitter taste on my tongue before dismissing the thought. *No, he wouldn't.* But the clock ticked on the wall above. Eleven a.m. And I had no idea where my husband was.

My heart beat faster when the phone rang. There he was. Calling to apologize, no doubt. "Ethan?" I felt hopeful to hear his voice, and yet my tone sounded angry and jaded.

But the person on the other end of the line wasn't my husband. Familiar, male, yet not Ethan. "Claire, it's Dominic."

"Dominic?"

"From the café," he said a little shyly. I could hear the bustle of the morning crowd at Café Lavanto in the background: an espresso steamer hissing; the buzz of conversation; a cash register drawer opening and closing in the distance. "I'm so sorry to bother you, to, uh, call you at home. Your number was in the phone book, and . . ." He sounded flustered. "Listen, I don't want you to think I'm a stalker or anything. It's just that I found something, for your article. You're going to want to see this."

"Really?" I caught a glimpse of my reflection in the window and grimaced. Last night's eye makeup appeared in alarming, tear-smeared streaks down my cheeks.

"I've got to run," Dominic continued. "It's crazy here today, and one of our baristas called in sick. But do you think you can drop by the café this morning?"

"Yes," I said, glancing outside at the remnants of the week's snowstorm. With the snow finally melting a bit, the sidewalks were studded with mud and dirt and had taken on a gray, sludgy color. Dirty snow. "I can be there in a half hour."

I walked into Café Lavanto with new eyes that morning, knowing that Vera and Daniel had lived here—well, upstairs, anyway. I glanced around the café, where college students sat propped in front of laptops and happy couples gazed at each other sleepily over cups of frothy foam. *Were Vera and Daniel happy here?*

Dominic waved to me from behind the counter, his white shirt stained at the pocket with a dusting of coffee grounds. "You came," he said, grinning. He motioned to a barista to take over at the espresso machine before he walked toward me.

"Thanks for calling," I said.

"How did the gala go?"

I shrugged. "Not well."

"Sorry," he said, untying his apron and hanging it on a hook on the wall. "Do you want to talk about it?"

I shook my head, letting my eyes wander the pastry case in front of me. "What I really want is to stuff my face with one of those raspberry scones."

Dominic smiled conspiratorially. "Then let's get you one." He reached for the tongs on the counter and walked back around the bar to extract an enormous scone from the case. "Eat up," he said, handing me the plate.

I took a bite, letting the crumbs fall from my mouth, un-ashamed. It felt good to eat, to sink my teeth into the thick, buttery scone. "So, what is this thing you found?"

Dominic nodded. "Come with me."

We walked into the back room, and he indicated a file cabinet against the wall. "I was going through some paperwork last night, and I found this." He produced an envelope, yellowed and wrinkled, with a torn edge.

I popped another piece of scone in my mouth and set the plate down. "What is it?"

He leaned against the wall. "Why don't you see for yourself?"

I carefully lifted the edge of the flap and peered inside, pulling out a folded scrap of paper and a black-and-white photograph. I set the brittle paper aside and held the photo up to the light. Worn, its scalloped edges tattered, it depicted a woman and a man lost in a romantic embrace. The woman, beautiful in a shy sort of way, with cropped hair that curled at the edges and a simple dress belted at the waist, stared lovingly up at the man in his smart suit. He smiled back at her with adoration. Clearly, they were in love, this couple. Anyone could see that. *Could this be Vera and her husband? Daniel's father?* I turned the photograph over to find a caption on the reverse. "Vera and Charles, March, 1929, Seattle Dance Marathon."

I grinned. "Dance marathon?" The words sounded foreign on my tongue. "Do you have any idea what that is?"

Dominic scratched his head. "Wait a sec, do you remember that scene from *It's a Wonderful Life*? The one when they're dancing and—"

I instantly appreciated that he knew the movie, one of my favorites. "Yes!" I said. "They fall into the pool underneath the dance floor."

"Yeah," he said. "I think that's a dance marathon. I read about one in a novel. People would try to dance until they were too exhausted to keep going. They'd dance for prizes—cash, free stuff, whatever. Sometimes they'd go on for days."

"Days?"

"Yeah, I remember the character in the book I read had bloody feet at the end."

I looked at the photo of the young couple again and wondered what had happened on the night of the dance marathon. It had been taken before Daniel's birth. *Was Vera happy then? And who was this man, this Charles? How was the photo left here?*

I ran my finger along its scalloped edges and remembered the box of family photos I'd rescued from my grandmother's home before she moved to the retirement center. Aunt Beth had left them by the garbage can. "Just old black-and-whites," she had said, flicking her wrist in the way one might dismiss a pile of junk mail. "Relatives nobody remembers."

"No," I said, running to the box. "Don't throw them out. I'll keep them." I may not have known the names of the majority of the ancestors pictured inside, but it felt like a betrayal to send their memories to the landfill. I couldn't bear the thought.

I tucked the photo safely inside the envelope and picked up the yellowed paper once again, unfolding it carefully so as not to tear it.

"Look," I said to Dominic. "It's a drawing." The stick figure on the page was the work of a child—that was certain. I squinted to make out the faded pen-and-ink scene. "It's a drawing of"—I held it closer—"two children, and a woman, I think. See, look at the hat. The women all wore big, beautiful hats back then. I think those are feathers, or maybe it's a bow. I can't tell."

"You're good," Dominic said.

I smiled to myself. "I have a three-year-old niece who sends me new drawings in the mail every few weeks. I'm a bit of a pro at this."

Dominic moved nearer, studying the page in my hands. "So do you think the little boy drew it? Could it be his?" His arm brushed my hand. My skin felt dry and taut. Tired. I wished I'd taken the time to shower instead of opting to run a brush through my hair and throw on a baseball cap.

"Sorry," he said.

I shook my head, dismissing any lingering awkwardness. "No, I don't think this is his."

"Why?"

I pointed to the far right corner of the page. "See the heart?"

Dominic nodded.

"Boys don't draw hearts."

"Aha," he said. "Good sleuthing. But it's too bad. I thought this might be something Daniel made. I hoped it would be a clue for your story."

I flipped the page over and noticed two words scrawled on the back. I studied the crude letters carefully. "Oh, this is a clue, all right," I said. "See this? It's a name. I think it says . . ." I paused. "Eva. Eva Morelandsteed."

"Do you think she's any relation to the little boy who was abducted?"

"Maybe," I said, folding the paper back into its tidy square and nestling it inside the envelope. "Mind if I keep this for a while?"

"It's yours," Dominic said.

"Thanks." I turned to the door, then looked back at him. "Hey, what are you doing today?"

A smile erupted on his face. "Nothing, why?"

"If you can sneak away, want to grab lunch somewhere?" If Ethan could lunch with Cassandra, I could lunch with Dominic.

"I'd love that," he said, reaching for his jacket. "How about that little place in the market, the Italian bistro that just opened?"

I smiled to myself. "I hear the asparagus risotto is really something."

"Great," he said, zipping up his jacket. "The sun's out. Let's walk."

"Sounds perfect," I replied. The cool wind stung my tired skin, but my heart, at that moment, felt very warm.

Cassandra's glowing review of Giancarlo's had rendered getting a table impossible. The line out front told us to make other plans.

"I know of a little place downstairs, at the bottom of the Market," Dominic suggested. "It's been around forever. It's nothing fancy—just diner fare. But you haven't lived until you've tasted their ham-and-gravy sandwiches."

"I'm in."

We descended the stairs into the bowels of the Market, where the scent of curry and allspice wafted on the damp air.

"I love it down here," Dominic said quietly, as if we'd stepped into sacred space. "Up there, that's for tourists. This is the *soul* of the Market."

I looked around in awe. "I can't believe I've been in Seattle this long and haven't been down here," I said. "I didn't even know there was a lower floor. I'm embarrassed."

Dominic pointed to a shop on our right. "There, that's where you can find some of the most exotic spices in the world."

"I can smell them," I said, taking in a breath of the aromatic air.

"And you have to try Al's beignets." He nodded a hello to an older man who stood behind a small food cart. "We'll take four, extra powdered sugar," he said, the scent of fried dough swirling. Dominic handed the man five dollars, then tucked a steaming hot bag into my hand. "For dessert."

We walked a few paces farther and arrived at the restaurant. Just as Dominic had said, it was nothing fancy, just a few booths against the walls and scattered tables and chairs set with nothing more than napkin dispensers and Heinz ketchup bottles that looked like they needed a good wipe-down. A few men sat at the bar on stools with squeaky hinges and torn vinyl seats. A simple green sign that read LINDGREN's hung over the entryway.

A gum-smacking waitress approached us, offering me a grease-stained menu before handing one to Dominic. "How've you been, sugar?"

"Pretty well, thanks." He turned to me. "Claire, this is Donna. Donna, Claire."

"Nice to meet you, sweetie," the older woman said in a smoky voice before turning back to Dominic. "Haven't seen you around in a while. Funny thing, just this morning there were some men in suits in here, talking about your—"

"Ah, yes, I've been busy," he said uncomfortably, cutting off whatever else it was she was about to say. He gave me a nervous, apologetic smile.

Donna shrugged. "All right, you two. Let's get you seated."

He pointed to the far corner of the restaurant. "Do you mind if we grab that table over there by the windows?"

"Sure, hon," she said, winking. "It's got your name on it."

My curiosity persisted as I took a seat in a wobbly chair. "Men in suits? What's that all about?"

He pulled a napkin out of the old steel dispenser and began folding it into small squares. "Oh, who knows," he said, feigning an unconvincing air of disinterest. "Maybe they were complaining about the slow service at the café. Some businessmen just don't realize that it takes time to make a good cappuccino." His voice sounded strangely distant for a moment before he snapped back to his cheerful self. "Sorry, I don't mean to complain," he said. "Maybe it's a sign that I should take that vacation I'm always talking about going on."

A seagull squawked from its perch outside, prompting a glance out the old casement windows. Single-paned and drafty, they kept a watchful eye on the ferries filing in and out of Elliott Bay. I had a feeling that he wasn't giving me the whole story and was making an effort to change the topic, but I didn't mind, really. "Where would you go?" I asked, resting my chin in my hand, elbow firmly planted on the table. "On this vacation?"

Dominic's eyes lit up. "Oh, well, Australia first," he said, tracing a spot on the table as if it were a map of the world laid out before him. "I've always wanted to see the reef. Then New Zealand, and maybe Fiji."

I imagined him snorkeling through blue water, his golden skin darkened even more by the sun. "Sounds amazing," I said. "So why haven't you made the trip yet?"

"Well, I—"

Donna returned to take our order. "What will it be? The usual?"

Dominic looked at me. "I always get the ham-and-gravy sandwich."

"We've been making it since the Great Depression," Donna chimed in. "Back then coffee gravy was the poor-man's staple. Now it's high class. One of those gourmet magazines wrote it up last year. They sent a photographer out from New York City to take pictures." She pointed to a frame on the wall.

"I'm sorry," I said, a little confused. "Did you say *coffee* gravy?"

She nodded. "The ham is seared in the pan, and when the fat is rendered, we pour in some coffee and let it reduce down to a nice thick sauce. It's how people stretched the dollar back then."

"Well, I'm not much of a coffee drinker," I said, "but I think I'll try it anyway."

"Good," Donna said. "You won't be disappointed. Folks have been eating this dish for almost a century now. It's a classic. Side of mashed potatoes to go with?"

Dominic and I both nodded.

"So, how's your article coming?"

"Well, I'm not really sure if it's going anywhere. My editor is expecting copy tomorrow, and I don't have a single word written." I frowned. "I can't stop thinking about that little boy."

"Don't lose heart," he said. "The hardest things always turn out to be the most rewarding."

Dominic's words rang true. I thought of the first and only marathon I'd run, shortly after Ethan and I got married. I trained for nine months and barreled across the finish line with a bloody toe and cramped muscles, but I'd never felt so proud of myself, so self-assured. When Ethan scooped me into his arms and nuzzled his face against mine, sweaty and red, I felt a sense of peace I'd never felt before.

I looked out the window, squinting into the distance.

"What are you looking for out there?" Dominic asked.

"Bainbridge Island," I said, turning back to him. "I'm taking the ferry over to visit an old friend tomorrow."

He nodded. "Ah," he said, as if reminiscing. "It's a beautiful place. I'd love to live there someday."

"Why don't you? You could commute. It's only a half-hour ferry."

He looked at his hands in his lap. "I can't," he said. "At least not right now. Real estate is pricey on the island, and every extra dollar I make I send home."

"Home?"

"My mom's sick," he replied. "No health insurance. The medication she takes is costly, but it keeps her alive."

"Wow. I'm so sorry. So you're supporting her?"

He nodded. "You'd love her."

My cheeks flushed.

I heard my phone ringing in my bag, but I ignored it. "She must really love you," I said. "There's something special about a mother's relationship with her son." I refolded the napkin in my lap and rested my chin in my palm. "I can't stop thinking of Vera and Daniel. Just knowing that they once made their home at the café." I sighed again. "It's haunting."

Dominic grinned. "I always thought we had ghosts."

A few moments later, Donna returned with two plates. True to its description, the ham sandwich oozed with dark brown gravy. I sank my teeth in unabashedly.

"What do you think?" Dominic asked.

"Wow," I said. "This is *good*."

He smiled proudly. "I knew you'd like it."

I heard my phone ringing again. This time I reached down, reluctantly, and fished it out of my bag, immediately seeing Ethan's number on the screen.

"Sorry," I said to Dominic. "Will you excuse me for a minute?"

"No problem."

"Hello," I answered, walking quickly outside the restaurant.

"Claire, I've been trying to get ahold of you all morning."

I smirked. "To explain why you didn't come home last night?"

"Claire, I've been at the hospital all night."

I gasped. "Are you all right?"

"Yes, I'm fine. It's my grandfather. He had a heart attack. Right after he accepted the award last night at the gala. I've been by his bedside since he came out of surgery."

"Oh no," I said. "Is he going to be OK?"

"We're not sure yet," he said. "Time will tell. I tried to call you last night but you must have turned your phone off. And there was no answer at the apartment this morning." He paused, detecting the noise around me. A man who appeared hard on his luck had begun playing a banjo a few steps away. "Where are you?"

I looked inside the restaurant at Dominic and I felt a pang of guilt. "I'm having lunch at the Market. With a friend."

Warren was the grandfather I'd never had. Mine had both passed away before I was born, and when I married into the

Kensington family, Grandpa Warren had welcomed me with open arms. I'd bonded with him the moment we met, in fact. He challenged me to a game of hearts, and I won. "She's a keeper, this one," he had said to Ethan. "Any woman who can beat a man at a game of cards is a woman you can spend a lifetime with." I knew he wasn't talking about me, not really. His late wife, Ethan's grandmother, had passed away years before I came into the family. But I didn't have to meet her to know that she and Warren had shared a deep love. You could see it in the pictures of their life together, but mostly you could see it in his eyes. More than fifteen years after her death, he still got teary talking about her.

"I'll be over as soon as I can," I said. "Tell him I'm coming."

I ran back to the table, reaching for my bag on the chair. "I'm so sorry, Dominic, but there's been an emergency. My husband's grandfather is in the hospital. He's had a heart attack. I need to go."

"Oh, I'm so sorry," he said, standing up. "Can I help?"

"No, no," I stammered, suddenly feeling the guilt I'd pushed aside earlier. "I'll just catch a cab from here. I'll . . . I'll call you." I looked down at my half-eaten lunch before I ran out the door.

Warren managed a weak smile as I walked in the room. His arms lay limp at his side in the gray hospital bed. "Look at you," I whispered. "You know you can't go and have a heart attack without giving me some advance warning." I heard Ethan enter; I didn't turn around to greet him.

Warren winked. "Sorry, honey; this old ticker has a mind of its own, I guess."

"Well," I said, forcing the tears back, "you have many good years left. We need to get you well."

The old man nodded. "If you say so, dear. But if it's all the same to you, I'd rather leave now and go see my sweetheart. I miss her."

"I know you do, Warren," I said. "But *we* love you too, don't forget."

I felt the warmth of Ethan's body near. "He needs to rest," he whispered to me. "Let's sit down."

I didn't like his know-it-all tone, but I agreed that Warren looked tired, so I followed him outside the room, where we sat down on a bench in the hallway. Nurses bustled around us. The air smelled of beef stroganoff and disinfectant.

"They think he's going to recover," he said. "For now."

"That's a relief," I replied, rubbing my hands together nervously.

I looked up to see Ethan's parents, Glenda and Edward, walking toward us.

"How is he this afternoon?" Glenda asked Ethan. She ignored my presence.

Ethan shrugged. "The same. The doctor says his heart's weak. He's not going to be able to keep the same schedule he did. We have to help him manage his stress. It's finally time he slowed down."

Glenda looked at Edward and then at me. "Claire, darling," she said.

I gulped. She only addressed me as *darling* when a favor or a directive was imminent.

She gave Ethan a knowing look. "Claire, we think you should probably curtail your weekly visits to Warren for the time being."

"I'm sorry?" I said, a little stunned. "What do you mean?" I'd been visiting Warren at his home once a week for the past two years. We played hearts, watched old films, or just read together, he with his war novels, and I with my romance novels.

"It's his heart, dear," she continued. "You heard Ethan. The doctor says it's been weakened. With all of your . . . well, it's just that Warren doesn't need any extra . . . drama right now."

"Extra *drama*?" My cheeks burned. "You think my visiting him is bad for his health?" I looked at Ethan for backup.

"Well of course we don't mean *that*, darling," Glenda said, patting my back ceremoniously. I hated the patronizing tone in her voice. "We're just looking out for his best interest, as he makes his recovery—"

"Mom," Ethan said, holding out his hand in protest. "Grandfather *loves* Claire. She's one of the few people who make him happy." He squeezed my hand in solidarity, but I was too shell-shocked to squeeze it back.

I felt Glenda's stone-cold gaze on my face when I turned to Ethan. Rogue tears welled up in my eyes, and I couldn't bear to let his parents see them brim over my lids, yet I knew I couldn't stop them. "Thank you," I whispered to my husband, before releasing his hand and turning to the elevator.

"Claire, please," Ethan said, after his parents had walked farther down the hallway. He pulled me close to him and kissed my forehead lightly. "Don't listen to my mom."

I nodded as the elevator opened. A nurse in blue scrubs eyed the sign ahead. "Oops, wrong floor," she said. In a wheelchair near her was a woman in a hospital gown who clutched a tightly swaddled newborn to her breast, his face red and puffy. The new mother smiled, a tired, satisfied smile, as her proud husband hovered over them. Love oozed from their every fingertip. The elevator door closed.

"I'm sorry, Ethan," I said in a voice that quivered. "I can't stay here. I have to go."

I waited for the elevator to open again and then stepped inside. When the doors closed, I buried my face in my hands and wept.

Chapter 11

§

VERA

The plump female shopkeeper at Frederick and Nelson eyed me disapprovingly before looking up at Lon's assistant and letting out an annoyed sigh. "Another one?"

Andrew pointed to a rack of formal dresses in the distance. "She'll need an array of gowns," he said. "Mr. Edwards prefers red, but throw in some other colors—for variety. And she'll need *other* garments too." He gave the woman a knowing look, before checking his watch. "Charge it to Mr. Edwards's account, as usual."

"All right," the woman said, raising an eyebrow. "We have work to do."

"Good," Andrew said. "Please see to it that she arrives at the hairdresser by four. Mr. Edwards will be meeting her for dinner at five, and not a minute later." I felt like goods on a delivery truck.

I followed her into a changing room and stood numbly in front of a mirror as she pried off my clothing. My dress fell to the floor in disgrace, a crumpled pile of dark blue frayed fabric.

Another woman walked in the room, this one younger.

"Melinda!" the older woman barked. "Get rid of this dress. She won't be needing it anymore."

I felt a surge of sadness as I watched the sales assistant pick up the dress and carry it away. The pocket was torn and the hem ragged. And yet, I had worn it the last time I'd cradled Daniel in my arms. It felt, in some way, as if I were discarding a part of him. A part of us.

"Please," I begged. "May I keep it?"

The woman let out a dry cackle. "That old rag?"

I stared at my bare feet, trying with all my might to keep the tears from coming.

"Fortunately for you, Mr. Edwards has taken a liking to you," the woman continued. "You can wear nicer things now."

I closed my eyes tightly as she tugged at my undergarments. I half-listened as she measured my bust. "He typically prefers a rounder figure," she said, staring at my breasts with a scrutinizing expression. "It would do you good to eat more."

I grimaced as she unhooked my corset, exposing my body completely. The cold air felt cruel against my bare skin. The mirror's reflection revealed a stomach that sagged at its center, where I'd carried Daniel just three years prior. I had birthed him at home, alone. Caroline had been there at the end; she'd patted my face with a cool cloth and sung to me. Labor had been long and painful. But when I'd held him in my arms, none of that had mattered. I'd have done it all over again for him. *My Daniel.* I felt the tears welling up again. *I will not cry. I will not let this woman see me cry.*

"I see you've had children," the woman said disapprovingly, strapping a beige corset around my ribs.

I nodded. "Yes," I said quietly. "Just one. A wonderful little boy who—"

"It's good you gave him up," she said. "No sense raising a bastard child."

"How dare you?" I said, taking a step back.

The woman shrugged. "I didn't mean to offend you," she said, perhaps more worried about losing the commission from Lon's account than hurting my feelings. "I only meant that it's hard to raise a child these days in any circumstance, let alone *out of wedlock*."

She stepped closer and pulled a white silk slip over my head, inching it snugly over my body. She folded her arms as she gave me the once-over. "You do know what happened to the last one, don't you?"

I shook my head. "The last what?"

"Mr. Edwards's last girl."

I shook my head, remembering Susie, the former maid.

"She got pregnant," she said. "The little fool. He was forced to let her go."

I didn't want to share Lon's bed any more than I wanted to share his dinner table. But I would do anything to find my son. Lon was well connected. Gwen had seen him lunching with a senator. If anyone could get the police to search for Daniel, he could.

"Pull in your stomach," the woman said. "This corset needs tightening if we're going to get you into a gown tonight. Mr. Edwards will want you to look stunning on the dance floor."

I took a deep breath and sucked in my stomach. I closed my eyes and thought of the last time I'd gone dancing. With Charles. I let the memory comfort me like a warm blanket.

Four Years Prior

A horn sounded outside. Caroline squealed. "*Charles* is here!"

I smoothed my hair before running to the window of the

apartment I shared with three friends. I looked out to the street, where he sat in the front seat of his shiny gray Buick, dark hair slicked back, a quiet smile on his face. Dashing. It had been a month and a half since we'd met at the hotel. He'd walked me home that night and promised to call after his holiday in Europe. I thought about him often, despite my attempts to purge his memory from my mind—and my heart. He was wonderful, yes, but he belonged with the type of women I'd seen at the hotel—refined, dripping in jewels—not with someone who had a hole in her shoe and nary a nickel to her name. And yet when he phoned the apartment the week before, I couldn't help but wonder, despite what he'd said at the Olympic Hotel, could a man from privilege really love a woman from poverty?

Georgia folded her arms. "It's not fair," she whined. "Does he have a brother?"

"Don't distract her, Georgia," Caroline snapped. "She has to get ready!"

I looked down at my dress, hardly what you'd call fancy, with its simple pleats and a hem I'd mended only that morning. I hoped the cobalt blue thread I'd used—the only I had—didn't look glaringly obvious against the light blue of the dress. "Do I look all right?"

Caroline frowned. "Honey, you want to impress him, don't you?"

I nodded.

Caroline began unfastening the buttons on my dress. "Of course you do, which is why you're going to wear my red dress."

"Caroline, I couldn't," I said. "It's so . . ."

"Low cut?"

I nodded.

"Well, yes, my dear, that's rather the point. We're going to get you out of this potato sack."

After Caroline had the final button undone, my dress fell to the floor, where it rested around my ankles. She walked to her closet and returned with the red dress. She held it up proudly. "He'll love you in this." Caroline had spent a month's wages on it after seeing it in the window at a boutique in Pioneer Square. "Here," she said, inching the frock over my head. It clung to my body like a tight bandage, and I tugged at the bodice self-consciously.

"There," she said, taking a step back to gaze at me. "Stunning."

"I don't know, Caroline," I said hesitantly. "Do you think it's really *me*?"

"It's you tonight," she said, holding a beaded necklace against the nape of my neck. "They're not real pearls, but no one will know." I felt a shiver along my spine as she fastened the clasp.

"Perfect," she said, stepping back again to take a final look at me. "Go on; you'll be late." She shooed me toward the door. "You look beautiful."

I turned to face her. "Thank you, Caroline. I know this is your favorite dress. I'll treat it well."

"Spill wine on it if you want," she said. "I'll never wear it again, anyway." She patted her belly. It swelled a little, revealing the early months of her pregnancy. "I had plenty of fun in it."

In an impulsive move, Caroline had married a fisherman named Joe the week after the event at the Olympic. They'd been together, on and off, for a year, but when he'd shown up with his grandmother's engagement ring, she'd said yes. And then, shortly after, he died in an automobile accident and she found out she was expecting his child. Caroline showed up at the apartment with all of her worldly possessions stuffed into a single suitcase. The one-bedroom flat was already cramped with three other women, but we took her in anyway. Her own parents had thrown her out.

"Oh, Caroline," I said, tucking an arm around her waist. "You'll wear it again. You'll see."

"Well," she said with a sigh, "it's your night. Live it up, honey."
I nodded. "I'll try."

Charles waited for me on the sidewalk. He leaned against the car
and watched as I walked outside.

"Hey there, doll," an obviously drunk man called from the
street. "Looking for someone to love?"

"Mind your manners!" Charles shouted to the man. "Where do
you get off speaking to a lady that way?"

The man slunk back into an alley as I gave Charles a grateful
smile. "Welcome to the neighborhood," I said.

"Do you have to put up with this all the time?"

I nodded. "You get used to it after a while. Most of them are
harmless."

He shook his head, surveying the street. A homeless man
kicked a tin can down the sidewalk, grumbling to himself. An old
woman stood up from a bench and approached Charles. A vehicle
that shiny in our part of town was a rare sight, and it attracted a
crowd of onlookers like a juicy plum draws buzzing fruit flies.

"Excuse me, sir," the woman said in almost a whisper. She held
out her hand, displaying dirt-caked fingernails. "Could you spare a
few cents for a hungry old woman?"

"Is that a real Buick?" a teenage boy asked, running his hand
along the hood. Charles looked at me with a helpless expression.

I cleared my throat. "Pardon us," I said with a firm voice. "We
were just leaving."

The woman nodded, taking a step back. The boy shrugged.
The others continued on.

"Sorry about that," I said once we were inside the car. "Rich
people are a novelty around these parts."

He looked conflicted. "Oh," he said, pulling away slowly.

We drove in silence for a few moments, before Charles turned to me. "I wish I had given her something."

"Who?"

"That woman back there," he said. "I could have given her some money. I don't know why I didn't."

I shook my head. "Well, it would take more than a few dollars to solve her problems."

Charles nodded. "Do they hate people like me?"

"Of course they don't," I said, noticing the way the streetlights made his gold cuff link glisten. "You're just from another world, that's all. A world they don't understand."

Charles shook his head, as if trying to make sense of the differences between us. "I'm embarrassed," he finally said, "that I'm so out of touch with what these people are facing."

I touched his arm. "You're different," I said, looking at him in awe. Charles possessed a goodness that others in his position didn't. His heart seemed to feel the pain of the poor—rare, when the trend among the upper class was to simply ignore them.

He stopped the car in front of a restaurant where a woman in a pale crepe dress stood outside smoking a cigarette. She puffed it elegantly through her crimson red lips, then dropped it to the sidewalk and stomped out its last embers with a thick, shiny black heel. "I thought we'd grab a little dinner at the Blue Palms," he said. "That is, if you're hungry." His kind eyes smiled expectantly.

"Yes," I said. "Yes, that would be lovely."

Charles handed his keys to the valet before proceeding to the opposite side to open my door. I felt like an heiress stepping out onto the curb, tucking my arm in his. Two women gawked at us from the sidewalk. They looked at Charles and then at me, studying me from head to toe, then whispering among themselves. I could read their eyes. *Fraud.* They knew I didn't belong. I looked straight ahead, following Charles into the club.

I felt the urge to peek into the mirror on the wall to my left just to make sure I was really the woman staring back. Caroline and I had dreamed of dining at the Blue Palms a thousand times before. We knew a cocktail waitress who worked there on weekends. She'd recounted stories of the socialites and celebrities who poured through its doors. I followed Charles inside the dimly lit foyer, where chic-looking couples handed over their coats to stoic doormen.

Charles whispered something to the concierge at the desk, and he jumped up with a nervous smile. "Yes, so nice to see you again. Your regular table is waiting."

I tried not to think about all the other women Charles had brought here before me. And there must have been a *parade* of them. Instead, I looked straight ahead as we followed the host down a dark corridor, lights streaming up from the floor like in the movie theaters I'd snuck into as a child. Scores of curious eyes looked out from tables all around us, wondering, watching. A band played a ballad onstage, and I kept time with the trombone with each step. One foot in front of the other. *What if I trip? What if I embarrass Charles?*

I felt a gentle hand on my waist, then warm breath near my neck. "I just can't bear to sit down when this song is playing, can you?"

Goose bumps covered my arms. I knew the song, of course. "Stardust." Caroline and I had listened to it at the record store dozens of times, until the shopkeeper had told us we had two choices: buy it or leave. Lacking the funds to purchase the record, we'd sulked our way to the door.

Charles held out his hand to me. "Shall we?"

"I'd love to," I said, following him to the dance floor. I felt eyes piercing my back, but when Charles wrapped his arm around my waist and pulled me close, my insecurities drifted away effortlessly.

"And you said you couldn't dance," he whispered into my ear.

"I can't," I replied. "You just make me look good."

He shook his head. "You know," he said with a serious face, "you're really something, Vera Ray."

Charles whisked me around the dance floor. His firm grasp and confident steps made me feel light on my feet, agile, as he dipped and twirled me. When the song ended, my cheeks flushed as he pulled me close. We stared into one another's eyes for a moment.

"Let's have dinner," he said, just as the band started up another song.

We slipped into a private booth that provided a full view of the stage. The soft, tufted upholstery felt like a cloud to sit on, and with Charles by my side, the effect was otherworldly—at least, a world unfamiliar to me.

He ordered wine and rattled off a few selections from the menu to a waiter who stood before us with a crisp white towel folded across his arm.

"Have you tried oysters?" Charles asked me. "Caviar?"

I shook my head. *Why pretend to have luxurious tastes when he knows I don't?*

"Good, then," he said, turning to the waiter. "We'll have both."

Within moments, the waiter returned with a pewter bowl filled with what looked like shiny blackberries.

"Caviar," Charles said, grinning.

I scrunched my nose.

The waiter next presented a platter topped with a strange array of mollusks resting on a bed of ice. A lemon wedge and an assortment of dipping sauces were artfully arranged on a second plate. I gulped.

"So," Charles began, "you squeeze a little lemon on top, then pick up the shell, just like this. Then you let the oyster slide into your mouth."

"Just like that?"

"Just like that."

It occurred to me that all of this fancy food was quite silly. Why go through the trouble when you could have a fine ham sandwich? But I didn't want to disappoint Charles. "All right," I said skeptically. "If you say so."

I reached for the plate and picked up one of the shells, eyeing the jagged texture and marveling at its sharp edges. My father, a fisherman, had brought an oyster shell home when I was a girl, and I'd cut my finger on its sharp edge. My mother, working the night shift at the factory, hadn't been there to bandage it. So I tore a piece of fabric from a kitchen rag and wrapped it around the wound with enough pressure to stop the bleeding. When Mother returned from her second job, after spending her days tending to a wealthy family's children in a privileged Seattle suburb, I held the injured finger before her. "It's your own fault!" she barked without looking up. "You're five years old; you should know better." Dark shadows of fatigue hovered under her eyes. She didn't mean it. She never meant anything she said after a long day at work. I forgave her, as I always did. And when she fell asleep in the parlor chair, in her work clothes, I pulled a blanket over her.

I held the oyster shell in my hand, feeling the sharpness on my skin, and recoiled, dropping it back onto the plate. I rubbed my index finger and eyed the jagged scar that anchored me to my past.

"Everyone's a little bashful when they try their first oyster," Charles said. "Let me help you."

I let my eyes meet his, so warm, so welcoming. *I'm not that little girl anymore.* He put the shell to my lips, and I opened my mouth as the oyster's cool, silky flesh rolled onto my tongue. I tasted the salt of the sea, its briny pungency, followed by the tartness of the lemon. The bite awakened my senses, opened my eyes.

"That was surprisingly good," I said, reaching for another.

We ate. We drank. And we *danced*. With Charles leading, my feet carried me around the dance floor with an agility I hadn't known I possessed.

Just as a song ended, and after a round of applause for the band, a couple approached us. The woman, with perfectly coiffed hair dyed to a beige blond, waved hello to Charles, her hand displaying a diamond engagement ring the size of a nickel. It sparkled under the stage lights as she held her fingers out to me. The man beside her, presumably her fiancé, looked at me curiously.

"I'm Delores," she crooned, turning to Charles with a wounded look. "Charles, you didn't tell us you had a new girlfriend. I thought you were still dating Yvonne. The two of you were—"

"Yes," he interjected. "This is Vera. Vera Ray."

Delores looked amused. "Of course," she said, scrutinizing me from head to toe. "Miss Ray. It's a pleasure to meet you."

"And you as well," I said, feeling a tightness in my chest.

"How did you two meet?" she continued. "At the country club?" She eyed my dress. Something told me she knew I wasn't a member of the country club.

"No," Charles said, "Vera and I met at—"

"At the Olympic Hotel," I interjected. "My friend and I were there for the opening."

Delores raised one eyebrow. "Oh?" she said, as if trying to make sense of the very idea of me at the Olympic Hotel. "Dear, tell me something." She clasped her hand on my arm. "How ever did *you* get an invitation to that party? I know at least a dozen of the city's most elite who weren't invited."

Charles tucked his hand around my waist and gave me a protective squeeze. "She was *my* guest," he said, the confidence in his voice snuffing out any further talk of my appearance at the hotel.

"Well, then," Delores replied, tugging at her date's sleeve, "we'll leave you now." She giggled. "The way you two have been dancing you'd think you were in that dance-a-thon over on Sixth Avenue."

Charles looked confused. "Dance-a-thon?"

"Oh, you wouldn't have heard about it," she said. "It's not really your crowd." Delores then turned to look at me.

"Perhaps it's *my* kind of crowd," I said in a moment of boldness. My cheeks burned. I knew what she was getting at: I wasn't good enough for Charles. It was written all over my shabby dress, second-hand shoes, and unmanicured hands.

"Goodnight, Delores," Charles said before nodding to her male companion. "Let's get out of here," he whispered to me as we walked back to the table.

I nodded. "Where to?"

"Vera," he said, as if suddenly struck with a thought, "why don't we go to that dance-a-thon?"

I shook my head. "You can't be serious."

"We're an incredible dance team," he said, grinning. "I bet we could win. Besides, I'm tired of this stuffy old place."

"You do know what a dance-a-thon is, right?"

He looked at me with naive eyes. Here was a man who could waltz—but swing? "I think I do."

"Couples dance for hours—sometimes all night," I explained. "The winners are the last ones standing."

"I'd like to be the last man standing by *you*," he said, reaching for my hand.

I could hear band music billowing out from the gymnasium onto Sixth Avenue. Charles and I stood on the sidewalk staring at the double doors, where a crowd of young men puffed cigarettes, wearing shabby suits sized too small or too large.

Charles rubbed his forehead nervously. *What was I thinking bringing him here?* Surely none of his polo-playing friends frequented the makeshift Friday night dance hall. The men eyed Charles suspiciously as we made our way to the entrance.

"Hey, dollface," one of them said to me. "Looking for a dance partner?"

Charles held out his hand. "She has one, thank you," he said, putting an end to the proposition.

"Some broad you got there," I heard the man remark as we walked inside. His voice was swallowed up by the music. But it was the sight before us that captured our attention. Couples everywhere danced with such energy, such passion. I watched as a man lifted his partner into the air and then brought her down again, whipping her from left to right like a ball on a tether.

Charles's mouth fell open. "Wow," he murmured. "I've never seen anything like *this*."

"We can go if you want," I said, looking toward the door.

"No, no," he replied, watching a man dip his partner so low her hair skimmed the floor. "I've just never seen people dance like this. It's . . . amazing. I want to try it. Can you do it?"

"Swing? Yeah," I said. "Well, a little." I took his hand, but before we could make it to the dance floor, an older woman tapped Charles on the shoulder.

"Did you register?" she asked.

"Register?" I replied.

"A nickel apiece," she said. "Covers your admission, the cost of the photo, and a bowl of chili."

Charles looked amused. "And a bowl of chili."

She pointed to a desk just ahead. "You can pay over there."

He pulled a dollar bill from his wallet and handed it to a man behind the desk.

"And your change is—"

"Keep it," Charles said.

"Thank you, sir," the man said, looking at Charles in astonishment. "Did Alice tell you the rules?"

He shook his head.

"We cut off admission in five minutes, so you just made it. Rules are as follows: No sitting. No eating. No drinking. Dancers must not stop dancing or stand in one place longer than three seconds or face elimination. The last couple to remain dancing wins the kitty here." He pointed to a glass canning jar filled with nickels. "Photos are just to your left."

Charles and I walked a few paces and stood side by side against a white curtain.

"Smile now," the photographer called out from behind his camera with an elaborate flash. It was easy to smile with Charles by my side.

"There," the photographer said. "If you come back next Friday, the photo will be waiting for you."

We approached the dance floor timidly. Charles clasped his hands around my waist and began moving his feet clumsily. I smiled, taking his hands in mine and showing him the basic swing step.

"Like this," I said, moving my feet in time with the music. I waved at Lola, a former schoolmate, in the distance. She looked shocked seeing me in Charles's arms. Shocked and jealous, maybe.

"This is harder than it looks," he said, attempting the move again and landing on my right foot. "Sorry."

"You're doing well," I said. It felt good being the one teaching *him* something.

After a while, Charles got the hang of swing, and he twirled me around the floor with the confidence of an old pro.

"I can see why you like this better than the waltz," he said, grinning. "It's a heck of a lot more fun."

I felt a bead of sweat on my brow. "So what do people like you do for fun?"

He flashed a half grin. "You act like I'm from a different planet."

"Well," I said, wiping my brow, "you are, in a sense." I gazed out at the regular folks on the dance floor—sons of factory workers, daughters of dressmakers. And then there was Charles, the son of one of the wealthiest families in the city, and perhaps in the country, by Caroline's estimation.

"Oh, come now," he said. "Don't you think that's being a bit dramatic?"

A diminutive figure entered the gymnasium, and I recognized her instantly: Ginger Clayton, an old friend. Her younger sister had died six months before because her family couldn't afford the medicine to save her. Suddenly I didn't feel like dancing anymore. How could I dine on oysters and caviar while people like little Emma Clayton had lost their lives?

I let go of his hand. "Don't you see?"

He tucked my hand in his again. "Careful," he said. "We'll be disqualified if we stop. What was it again? The three-second rule?"

I looked away.

"Did I say something wrong?"

"No," I said. "Well, yes. I just wish the poor didn't have to suffer so."

The band slowed its tempo, and I was glad for it. It felt strange to be having such a serious conversation when dancing at such a frenetic pace.

"Listen," I continued, seeing concern register in his eyes, "I do believe you care, and I know you're different than most people in your position. I just wish more people with your privileged background cared about the plight of the poor. Times are tough. The widow who lives on the floor below me has to leave her children alone all day while she works because there's no one to care for them. Perfectly respectable people are out on the street, begging for handouts. All this while the rich . . ."

"While the rich do nothing about it?" he said.

"Yes," I replied, nodding.

"Well, you're right," he said with a look of conviction. "We're a despicable lot. I'm the first to admit that. My own parents won't even pay the household help a living wage. Most have to take second jobs just to feed their families. It's not right. I've tried to speak to my father. He won't hear of it. He himself came from poverty. Worked his way up from a farming town in Eastern Washington. He's a self-made man. He believes that hard work and discipline is the ticket out of poverty. In his mind, anyone can make their fortune."

I shook my head. "But that's not always true."

"I know."

"What he doesn't realize is that decent, hardworking people are down on their luck," I continued. "There aren't enough jobs to go around. People who want to work can't."

Charles looked away. "I don't know what to tell you, Vera. I don't like it any more than you do."

"I don't mean to sound like I'm blaming you, or your father," I said, worrying I'd overstepped my bounds. It's just that I was taught that if you have two of something, you share it with someone else. Why can't the privileged do more to help the needy?"

Charles nodded. "That widow you spoke of, what's her name?"

"Laura," I said. "Her name's Laura."

"Where does she work?"

"In a garment factory in the industrial district."

"How many children does she have?"

The band began playing a faster song, so we picked up the pace. "At least five," I said. "The eldest is barely nine years old. It's a terrible situation. I brought a loaf of bread down to her last week. The place was an awful mess. Squalor, really."

Charles looked at me tenderly. "I want to help her."

"How?"

"For one, let's get her out of that wretched factory job so she can care for her family," he said.

"To do that she'll need—"

"Funds, yes. I'll take care of it."

I smiled from a place deep inside. "You will?"

"Yes," he said. "But she must not know of my involvement."

"I can help," I offered.

"Good."

I nestled my head on his lapel. "That's an honorable thing to do."

"No," he said, stroking my hair, "it's the *right* thing to do, and I'm ashamed I haven't done more things like it."

Charles twirled me across the floor before I rebounded like a fire hose back into his arms. The music stopped for a moment as I looked into his eyes. His gaze made me feel tingly everywhere, and when he leaned toward me, I let my lips meet his.

"There you are!" a shrill female voice echoed across the dance floor. I took a step back from Charles and watched as a woman approached. Her tan silk dress and hat trimmed with white feathers looked like a page torn from one of the discarded *Vogue* magazines Georgia sometimes brought home from her housekeeping job. In the ragtag gymnasium, this woman stood out like a swan in a coal mine.

"I've been looking for you everywhere, Charles," she continued with a chastising tone.

He divided his attention between the approaching woman and a man who appeared before us wagging his finger. "I'm afraid you've paused too long," he said. "Please step off the dance floor. You've been disqualified."

"Sorry, Vera," Charles said to me. "It was my fault."

The woman pushed through a crowd of people, and Charles and I followed. "Why is my *sister* here?" he said under his breath.

Away from the dancers, he folded his arms. "Josie?" His tone wasn't exactly welcoming.

"Wow, I didn't think I'd actually find you *here*," she said, annoyed. She tucked a lock of her perfectly coiffed brown hair under her hat before smoothing an imaginary wrinkle from her dress. "I went looking for you over at the Blue Palms and Delores said"—she looked at me with disapproving eyes and took a deep, frustrated breath—"anyway, there isn't much time. It's Mother. She's taken ill."

Charles dropped my hand. "Oh no," he said. "What happened?"

"The doctor's with her now," she replied. "But you need to come quick."

Charles turned to me. "I'm sorry, Vera, I have to go. I'll . . . I'll call on you soon."

"Don't worry about me," I said, trying to hide my disappointment. "Go."

I watched Charles and Josie walk briskly out of the gymnasium. They disappeared in the shadows of the night before I turned back to the other dancers on the floor. Only a few dozen remained. Beads of sweat dripped from their brows. We would have won, Charles and I. We would have danced until dawn.

"My, aren't you a vision, Vera!" Lon exclaimed when he saw me in the lobby. I hardly recognized my own name on his breath. And when I caught a glimpse of myself in the gilded mirror on the wall to my left, a society girl stared back. My waist looked inches thinner, suctioned in by the fancy undergarments beneath the blue silk dress. My breasts brimmed out of the bodice in a way that made me feel like a roast turkey on a platter, buttered and browned and ready to be devoured. I held my hand to my chest self-consciously.

"Your beauty is dizzying," Lon said, slipping a possessive arm around my waist.

I didn't like his hand there, or anywhere. I swallowed hard. *I can do this. For Daniel.* If I played my cards right, Lon might use his resources to help me find my son. I would be his dinner guest. I would smile and look pretty. I would do anything, really, if it brought Daniel home.

Chapter 12

CLAIRE

I ducked my head as I stepped out of the elevator at the office the next day, purposely taking the long, winding route through the sea of gray cubicles. It seemed silly to take such extreme measures to avoid my own husband, but after last night's exchange, I didn't have the heart, or the strength, to face him. Besides, I'd slept in an empty bed again. I knew he probably had stayed at the hospital with Warren, but still, he hadn't even called to let me know. Since when had he become the husband who considered coming home optional?

The sun had returned to Seattle, and the warmer weather had Frank particularly agitated. "How's the story coming?" he asked from the doorway of my cubicle a mere ten seconds after I'd planted my butt in the chair.

I swiveled around to face him. "Good morning to you, too."

"I'm not sure if you've noticed," he said, pointing to the window, "but the snow has *melted*. Before readers forget about the storm entirely, I was kinda hoping to get your story to press. You told me you'd have it to me today, but that's obviously not going to happen, so maybe I can get it, I dunno, before *Thanksgiving*?" He plucked a gnawed pencil from his shirt pocket and inserted it in his mouth. He remained the only boss whom I found adorable when he was mad at me.

"Listen, Frank," I said, folding my arms with deliberation. "You knew this story was going to be a goose chase going into it."

He put the pencil back in his shirt pocket. "You're right," he said. "But I didn't think it would be such an *epic* goose chase."

I glanced at my notebook, wishing I had more to show for the past days' research. "Frank, it's like someone erased this little boy from history."

"So you're saying you don't have a single lead?" he said with a sigh.

"Well," I continued, "I found a child's drawing with the name Eva Morelandsteed written on the back."

"A child's drawing?" By the look on his face, I gathered he wasn't thrilled.

"I think she might be related to the missing boy, somehow. Perhaps a sister, or a friend."

"Well," he said, "I'm taking you off the story."

"What?"

"Claire, you're my best reporter. I can't keep you on a story that's not going to pan out." He set a file on my desk. "We have a lot of stuff to cover this month."

I looked at the green file folder begrudgingly. "What is this?"

He spoke to the tabletop. "A press kit for Seattle Cultural Days. I want you to write the promo pieces."

"You have to be kidding me, Frank," I said. "An *advertorial*?" Frank knew very well that any self-respecting reporter would rather gouge her eyes out than write ad copy.

"Yes," he said blankly. "I just got word from advertising. It's a two-page spread. It needs to run by next week."

I shook my head. "I can't believe this."

He took a step closer. "I'm worried about you, Claire. You haven't been yourself for a long time."

I shook my head. "Why would you say that?"

"Well," he said, choosing his words carefully, "it's just that you've never failed to meet a deadline."

I ran my fingers through my hair. He was right. I'd feared I'd lost my reporter's instinct, my edge, and Frank had confirmed it. *What's happening to me?*

I picked up the green folder and opened it. "Don't worry," I said, turning to face my computer. "I'll get this done. Just give me the weekend and I promise you'll have it on Monday."

"Claire, listen," Frank began, "I didn't mean to hurt you; I was just—"

"It's fine," I said stiffly, clenching my fists under my desk. "I'm sorry I let you down. I thought I could write it. I thought I could find that little boy."

Frank nodded and walked out to the hallway.

A few moments later I heard footsteps approaching. "Knock, knock." I turned to see Abby at the door, with a big box in her hands. "Morning."

"Morning," I said, punctuating the word with an exaggerated sigh.

"Oh, no," she said. "What is it?"

"I think my career may be over, and Ethan didn't come home last night," I replied, unable to take my eyes off the green folder.

"Your career is *not* over," she said. "You're one of, if not *the* best reporter on staff. And as far as your husband goes, fill me in."

I sighed. "Thanks, but I'd rather not talk about it right now. I might lose it. You remember our rule about not crying at work."

Abby smiled, holding out the box to me. "Here."

"What is it?"

She shrugged. "I don't know, but it has your name on it. Jenna brought it to my office by mistake."

I set the box on my desk and reached for the scissors in my drawer to release the tape, which is when I noticed the return address. "Abby, this is from Swedish Hospital." I felt my heartbeat's pace quicken. "What could they possibly be sending me?"

I hated that something as simple as the hospital's logo on the mailing label could create such a visceral response in me. I could hear the beeping of the blood pressure monitor on my arm, see the vivid blue of the curtain in the emergency room, taste the salty tears streaming from my eyes. In an instant, I felt the horror of the accident all over again. I closed my eyes, trying to block the memories, to shut them out, sending them back to the hospital, where I had left them. But when I opened my eyes again, they were there before me, waiting to be confronted.

"Claire," Abby said quietly, "what is it?"

Anger surged through me as I yanked one flap of cardboard open, then another. *What are they sending me?* They'd called repeatedly for follow-up appointments, but I never returned the messages. *Don't they know that every call, every damn bill in the mail, is a reminder of my loss? And now this? Can't they just leave me alone?* An envelope was taped to the inside flap of the box. I tore it open.

> *Dear Ms. Aldridge,*
>
> *We've tried to reach you multiple times about picking up personal items left behind during your hospital stay. The only address we had on record was your*

employer's. It is our policy to return belongings to our patients.

Best wishes,

Katie Morelandsteed

I cautiously peered inside the box and pulled out a ribbed gray sweatshirt. It was a mangled mess, ripped at the side by the ambulance driver—a vague memory that came full focus again—with a bloodstain along the sleeve. I remembered the moment I'd purchased it. Ethan and I had gone shopping for maternity clothes at the Gap. I'd strapped on one of those prosthetic stuffed bellies and paraded out of the fitting room, giving him the shock of his life.

"Your stomach!" he exclaimed. "It looks . . ."

"Huge?" I grinned, lifting up the edge of the sweatshirt to reveal the padding underneath. "Did I fool you?"

"You did," he said, a bit relieved. "For a second there, I thought we might be having twins."

That day, I bought the sweatshirt in three colors, several pairs of pants, all with thick, stretchy elastic waistbands, and a black wraparound dress that *Fit Pregnancy* magazine had claimed to be the most flattering look for moms-to-be. I winced at the memory, setting the sweatshirt aside before pulling out a pair of black leggings with a jagged hole in the knee. Underneath were my underwear and sports bra, neatly folded into a bundle. *Why did they even bother returning this stuff? Why couldn't they just . . . burn it?* At the bottom of the box lay my running shoes. I had others in my closet, but these had been my favorite pair. Mud-stained, perfectly broken in, they'd traveled with me down miles of rainy Seattle streets, across the finish line of several grueling races, but I couldn't look at them then. They'd betrayed me.

I tossed the shoes and ragged clothing back into the box, and looked up at Abby. "Is there a Dumpster outside somewhere?"

Abby knelt down next to me. "Claire," she whispered, "maybe you shouldn't be so quick to throw all of this away."

My eyes burned, and I quickly wiped a stray tear from my cheek, annoyed by its presence.

"Oh, honey," she said. "Come here." She wrapped her arm around my shoulder, and I leaned against her, breathing in her lavender perfume. "You used to love to run," she continued. "Why don't you try again?"

"I can't," I said, shaking my head. "I won't."

She reached into the box and pulled out my old running shoes. "Just the same," she said, "let's keep these. Toss the clothes if you like, but these shoes need to stay." She tucked them under my desk. "When you're ready, put them on."

"I'll never be ready," I said.

"You will," Abby countered. "After my dad died, Mom kept all his clothes in the closet, exactly as he'd left them. They gathered dust for three years before she found the strength to face them again. I was only thirteen, but I remember the day she opened up that old closet and pulled one of the shirts from the hanger. She set it on the bed and lay next to it for a long time, crying, remembering. It took a lot of strength to do that. Strength and *time*. My point is that Mom needed that closure, and if she'd had someone box up his clothes the week after he died like Aunt Pam suggested, she'd never have had the opportunity to face her sadness, to find her own closure. Everyone grieves and heals at her own pace, honey. Give yourself time."

I stared at the shoes under my desk, wishing, as I had every day since the accident, that I'd stayed home instead of going on that damn jog. "I don't know, Abby," I said, looking away from the shoes.

"Trust me," she replied, closing the flaps of the box and setting it outside. "So, did you find the kid?"

"No. Frank took me off the story." I pointed to the file of information for the ad copy I had been assigned. "I'm now writing the special advertising section for next week."

Abby frowned. "No, he didn't." She knew as well as I that getting an ad copy assignment was the equivalent of being grounded.

"Yes, he did."

"Maybe I can talk to him," she offered.

"I wouldn't bother," I said. "He had the *look*."

Abby folded her arms. "Well, I think you should continue your research anyway. Surprise him with a draft. I don't think you should quit this story, Claire."

"But Frank doesn't want it," I said, shrugging. "Even if I did turn something in, it would be too late. The snow's melted. Everyone's moved on. I think I lost this one."

"No," she said. "You didn't lose it. You've only scratched the surface." Her eyes narrowed. "Listen, honey, I've seen you work on hundreds of stories, and never has one gotten under your skin like this little boy's. Write it. Even if it's only for you. Besides, I want to know what happened."

"I do too," I said, before pulling my notebook from my bag and setting it on top of the green folder. "Yes," I said, with more assurance in my voice. "I'll finish this story."

"Good girl," she said.

I glanced at the running shoes under my desk and then back at Abby. "You know what's funny?" I picked up the letter from the hospital. "That name, Morelandsteed. It's the same name on the back of a child's drawing I found."

She grinned. "You think there's some connection?"

I shrugged. "That would be a pretty crazy coincidence," I said, my reporter's curiosity piqued. "But it's an unusual name. Who knows?"

"Follow up on it," she said, nodding and turning to the door. "I'm here till six if you need me."

"Thanks," I replied, looking back to my computer screen, where I keyed in the hospital's URL. Once I found the general number, I picked up the phone.

"Yes, hi," I said to the hospital operator. "I'm trying to reach an employee by the name of Katie Morelandsteed."

"Just a moment," the woman replied.

"This is Katie," chirped a voice a few seconds later.

"Uh, hi, Katie, this is Claire Aldridge, from the *Seattle Herald*. I mean, well, here's the thing. You sent me a package recently. A box of—"

"Yes, *Claire*," she said. "Of course. I hope you don't mind that we mailed the box to your workplace. For some reason we didn't have your home address on file. And, well, anyway, we've been try-ing to reach you for some time. You might think it strange for us to send you all your clothes from the accident, but we've found that acknowledging the remnants of a tragedy can really help our patients heal, and help them—"

"Yes," I said, cutting her off, "it's fine. I'm actually calling about something else. I hope you don't mind my asking, but you don't, by chance, happen to be related to a woman named Eva Moreland-steed? It's a shot in the dark, really; I—"

"Well, actually, yes," she said. "I have a great-aunt named Eva." My jaw dropped. "Really?"

"Yeah, she lives in Seattle, right by Pike Place. She's in her eighties, but you'd never know it. Aunt Eva's as sharp as a whip. Wait, how is it that you know her?"

"It's sort of a long story," I said. "I'm working on an article, and I found something with her name on it from a long time ago. I hoped to contact her."

"Sure," Katie said. "I have her phone number in my cell phone. Let me pull it up for you. She was a librarian for decades, so she's always supportive of research. I'm sure she wouldn't mind."

A few moments later, I scrawled the number down on a scrap of paper. "Thank you, Katie."

"Of course."

I hung up the phone and then punched the numbers in quickly. The phone rang once, twice, three times.

"Hello?"

"Ms. Morelandsteed? Eva Morelandsteed?"

"This is she."

"Hi," I said, clearing my throat. "My name is Claire Aldridge. I'm a reporter with the *Seattle Herald*. I apologize for bothering you, but your niece, Katie, gave me your phone number, and, well, I'm working on a story about the storm that hit Seattle in May of 1933, and I came across some information about a little boy named Daniel Ray." I paused, waiting for Eva's response, but the line was quiet. "Ms. Morelandsteed? Are you still there?"

"Yes," she said. "You'll have to forgive me. I haven't heard that name in a very long time."

I sat up straighter in my chair. "So you know him? Or, rather, you *knew* him?"

"I did," she said. "It was so long ago."

My heart beat faster.

"How did you say you found my name?" she asked suspiciously.

"On a drawing," I said. "A child's drawing over at Café Lavanto."

"Well," she said, a stiff practicality tingeing the edges of her voice, "I'm not sure how I can help you. I was just a small child when he went missing."

"Could we meet in person?" I had learned early on as a reporter that people always divulge more in person than they do on the phone. A senator had once confessed his marital affair to me at a lunch interview at Canlis restaurant during the salad course. I remember crunching into a bite of romaine when he told me about the shade of his mistress's eyes. "Perhaps when we talk, you'll remember something. Even a small detail might help."

"Well," she said, her voice softening a bit, "I suppose that would be all right. Would you like to come by tomorrow morning?"

"I would love that."

"Good," she replied. "I live in the Brighton Towers, a retirement home near the Market."

"I'll see you tomorrow, then."

"You know," she added, her voice trailing off, lost in memories, "my nephew took me up to Nordstrom last week, and we passed the old apartment building."

"You mean Daniel and Vera's?"

"Yes," she said. "It warmed me to see that the old place hadn't been torn down. It's a café now, right?"

"Yes, Café Lavanto."

"Developers treat old buildings like weeds," she said. "They can't wait to tear them down so they can build their fancy high-rise condominiums. They don't know that they're destroying history, and people's memories, with their wrecking balls. Whoever owns that building is a good person, keeping it intact."

I smiled to myself. "I happen to know the owner," I said. "And he's a great guy."

"All right, dear," Eva said. "I'll see you tomorrow."

"Good-bye."

A moment later, an e-mail popped up in my in-box. The subject line read, "Can't wait to see you!" I looked at my desk calendar, where "visit with Emily" was written in blue ink on the slot for the afternoon. I'd promised my old friend Emily Wilson a visit. She'd moved to Bainbridge Island a few years ago, where she lived with her husband, Jack, in an old colonial owned by her ailing great aunt. I opened her e-mail.

If you want to take the 12:00 ferry, I can pick you up at the terminal at 12:45. You won't believe how big the twins are. xoxo

I'd only seen her babies once, when they were just two weeks old. Ethan and I had visited when I was newly pregnant. We shared the news with them then, and I'll never forget holding one of her twins, marveling at how I'd soon be cradling my own baby. She'd felt so delicate, so light. I remember feeling frightened by her little cry, wondering if I was prepared for motherhood. It came so naturally to Emily. She'd lifted the baby out of my arms with such ease, nestling the child to her breast as if she'd done it thousands of times before. I had looked down at my own belly, where a baby was growing inside, wondering if I'd be a good mother, like Emily seemed to be. I closed my eyes tightly, pushing the memory deeper into my mind, forcing it back into its dark corner. I looked at the clock on my desk. Already eleven thirty. I'd have to race to catch a cab to the terminal.

I sank into a booth on the ferry and leaned against the vinyl seat, gazing out at the V-shaped wake the vessel carved through the salty water. Seagulls flapped alongside the aging vessel, yelping and squawking, as if challenging it to a race. Eventually the outspoken birds tired of the game and flapped away.

Ethan loved the island. His parents had a beach cabin there, and we made regular trips. The four-bedroom home overlooking Eagle Harbor, however, was hardly a cabin, in the typical sense. It had a five-piece bathroom, a balcony off the master, and a chef's kitchen, where Ethan would make buttermilk pancakes for me in the mornings. But lately he had been going alone. When my mom stayed on to care for me after the accident, Ethan spent six days at the cabin. My mom never forgave him for that. But as much as I had been hurt by his absence, in some way I'd understood. He had needed to grieve in his own way. He'd come home unshaven, with eyes that seemed vacant, distant.

I reached for my laptop, in its black leather case, and plugged the power cord into an outlet below the bench seat. The Word document I'd saved as "Daniel-Ray-Feature" contained only a title, "Blackberry Winter: The Story of a Lost Boy in the Snowstorm of 1933." I stared at the flashing cursor and wrote a few sentences, then a few more. By the time the ferry's horn sounded, announcing our approach to the island, I had written an introduction I was proud of. *Will I be able to finish the rest? Will I ever figure out what happened to Daniel Ray?*

A short walk down the ramp to the terminal and I spotted Emily, waving her arm out of the driver's side window of her aunt's green 1963 Volkswagen Beetle. "You made it!" she called out, her voice muted by the sound of the engine.

I opened the passenger side door and tucked my bag and laptop case inside before turning to look at the backseat, half-expecting to see the twins tucked into their car seats.

"They're at home with Jack," Emily said, as if reading my mind. She looked happy, with her rosy cheeks and wispy blond hair tucked back into a simple ponytail. The pear-shaped diamond, studded with rubies, on her hand sparkled in the sun that streamed through the window. Emily had recounted the story of the ring to me once. It had belonged to a woman Jack's grandfather had loved a long time ago. I don't remember the details of the tale entirely, but it exuded love from decades past. You could feel it when you looked at it. "Twenty months old yesterday," she said. "Can you believe it?" Her happiness, so apparent, may as well have been written all over her with a permanent marker.

"I can't wait to see them!" I said. It was a true statement, and yet if I was honest with myself, I'd admit that I was apprehensive, too. For every milestone of their lives would be a reminder of my loss.

"Sorry, Claire," she said suddenly. "I know you've been through so much this year. Is it too hard for you to be around . . . ?"

"Babies?"

"Yeah," she replied cautiously. "I don't know how you're holding up so well. I'd be in pieces."

There was no sense lying to an old friend. "I *am* in pieces."

"Oh, Claire," she said, her eyes narrowed, reflecting my pain. "I'm so sorry. I just grieve for you. Listen, if it's hard for you to see the babies, just let me know. I just fed them, so we can go out for lunch instead. We don't have to go back to the house."

I placed my hand on Emily's arm and gave it a firm squeeze. "I *want* to see them. It would break my heart not to."

"You're amazing, you know," she said, navigating the car out of the ferry terminal. "You really *get* friendship."

"What do you mean?"

"My aunt Bee has always said that contrary to what most people think, the definition of a true friend is not someone who swoops in when you're going through a rough patch." She shook her head.

"Anyone can do that. True friendship, she says, is when someone can appreciate your happiness—*celebrate* your happiness, even—when she's not necessarily happy herself." She looked at me with appreciative eyes. "That's you, Claire."

My eyes brightened. "Thanks, Em."

She turned her gaze from the road for a moment. "I really mean that."

"I bet they're huge now, the twins," I said, pausing to look out the window. The island's lush evergreens whooshed by. "What's it like, motherhood?"

Emily sighed, clasping the wheel a little tighter. "It's frightening and wonderful all at the same time. And exhausting. I'll tell you, honestly, for about a month after their birth, I secretly wanted to send them back."

I giggled.

"I'm not lying, Claire," she said. "I'll never forget the moment when Jack came into the bedroom one night and one of the babies was crying in his arms; the other was crying in her crib. It was somewhere around two a.m. I was so tired. Sick tired. I sat up and dangled my legs off the side of the bed, and all I could think was, *I've made the worst mistake of my life.*" She shook her head. "But I got through it. The adjustment period, that is. Now I can't imagine life any other way." She turned down the winding road that led to her aunt's property, and gave me a quick smile.

"I bet Jack is a wonderful father," I said.

"He's amazing with them," she agreed. "He's taking them on a walk along the beach right now. We got one of those double jogger strollers with those enormous turbocharged wheels that can handle the barnacles."

"How's your aunt Bee?" I asked. I wasn't certain of her

age—late eighties, possibly nineties, even—but she didn't fit the mold of an elderly woman. When I'd visited Emily on the island the first time, Bee had offered me a shot of whiskey.

Emily sighed. "She hasn't been well," she said. "The doctor says it's her heart. They have her on all kinds of medications now. She's in bed most of the time. I take care of her during the day, and we have a nurse who tends to her at night." She shook her head. "Bee just hates being cooped up in the house. I caught her trying to sneak down to the beach yesterday afternoon. The poor thing is so frail, she nearly fell off the bulkhead."

"Sorry to hear that," I said. "It must be so hard to see her deteriorate."

"It is," she replied. "And it sounds strange, but the house feels different without her at the helm. Something's changed. I can feel it. Does that even make sense?"

"I know what you're saying. When my grandma got sick years ago, the old house took on a different feeling too," I said. "Like the soul had been sucked from the walls."

"That's exactly it," Emily agreed. "Jack and I moved in with her right after we were married. Bee insisted. At first I worried the arrangement wouldn't work, but we came to love it. It's funny, I think we needed Bee just as much as she needed us. Her health has declined quickly, though, and the changes frighten me. She no longer mills about at six o'clock in the morning, or comments on the sea life outside the window. The newspapers pile up in the entryway because she doesn't read them. *The New Yorkers* too. I actually cried the other day when I pulled the last jar of her homemade jam from the freezer. I stood there realizing that it may be the last jar I'd ever enjoy. She's still here, of course, but I'm starting to miss her already."

I ached for her, because I knew the type of sadness she spoke of. "I'm not sure what's more difficult," I said. "Losing someone quickly or gradually, over time."

Emily wiped away a tear on her cheek with the edge of her hand. "Bee'll be happy to see you. She loves visitors."

She slowed the car as we approached the house. I stared out the window at the rhododendrons in bloom along the roadside, in shades of deep red, light purple, white, and coral. The road wound its way down to the waterfront, where the old white colonial gazed out at the Puget Sound. It looked wise, with its black shutters and stately columns. Wise and a little sad.

"Here we are," Emily said, opening the car door. I stepped out and followed her along the pathway to the front door, where an empty double jogger stroller was parked.

"Mommy's home," Emily cooed into the entryway. I heard a chorus of giggles from somewhere inside, and a moment later Jack appeared holding two cherubs dressed in pink.

"Hi Jack," I said, smiling. "Look at you. You're a natural."

Emily rubbed his back lovingly. "He gets up every morning with the babies so I can write."

"Did she tell you?" Jack said, turning to me.

I shook my head. "What?"

"She wrote a second novel. It's being published this winter."

I smiled. "That's fantastic, Emily!"

"Well," she said, looking out toward the water, "I owe it to this place. It's magic. I've never felt so creative. Anyway, come in! I know you don't have much time, so let's savor every second."

We walked to the living room, and Jack set the twins down on a blanket scattered with toys. "They're beautiful," I said.

"Nora is a firecracker," Emily said, pointing to the larger of the two, who swiped a rattle from her sister's hands. "She already argues with me."

I laughed. "Your Mini-Me?"

Emily nodded. "I'm in for it. But Evelyn—we call her Evie—is our little peacemaker. The girls still share a crib, and when Nora wakes up crying, Evie pats her head. It's the sweetest thing."

"Adorable," I said, handing Evie another toy.

Jack gestured toward the hallway. "Why don't you take her to visit Bee?" he said to Emily. "She's usually up from her nap about now."

"Yes," Emily said, "Bee would love to see you."

I nodded and stood up, following Emily to a closed door at the end of the hallway. She knocked quietly, and moments later, we heard a feeble but friendly, "Come in."

Bee wore a white nightgown. She lay in her bed, propped up by pillows. A stack of books and magazines sat untouched on a table to her right. She stared blankly out the open window, where waves rolled quietly onto the shore.

"Hello, dear," Bee said, sitting up.

Emily saw the breeze rustling the curtains and ran to close the window. "Bee, you must be frozen," she scolded, pulling an extra blanket from a nearby chair and draping it over her aunt.

"I miss the sea air," Bee said. "I'd rather freeze to death than do without it."

"Well," Emily said, fiddling with the thermostat, "fair enough. But let's at least turn the heat up a bit in here."

Bee reached for a pair of glasses on the table. "Oh, you have company."

"Yes," Emily said. "You remember my old friend Claire, don't you, Bee?"

"Of course, Claire," she said, waving me over to her. "How are you, dear?"

"As well as can be," I said to Bee. "And you?"

"Well," she said sarcastically, "as well as one can be cooped up in this damn bed all day."

Her voice may have been feeble, but I was happy to see that her spirit remained strong.

"You're a writer, like Emily, aren't you, dear?"

I nodded. "Yes, I am. Emily and I met in college. She chose the more glamorous life of fiction, while I hit the gritty newsroom."

Bee smiled. "Oh, I remember. You write for the newspaper."

"Yes," I said. "The *Seattle Herald*."

"What are you working on right now, dear? I read the paper cover to cover." I remembered the stack of newspapers I'd seen piled up outside the bedroom door.

"I'm working on a particularly interesting story right now," I said. "About a little boy who disappeared in 1933. The day of the May snowstorm."

Bee looked startled. "I haven't thought about that snowstorm in a long time," she said.

"You remember it?"

She smiled, her eyes lost in memories. "I was just a girl. We were living in West Seattle then. Mother let us play in the snow all morning. It was a dream come true for a schoolgirl hoping to get out of her morning arithmetic lesson. And what a shock to all of us. Snow in May. The cold snap we had this week reminded me of it. So what did you say the little boy's name was again?"

"Daniel," I said. "Daniel Ray. Probably no chance you'd remember him, right?"

"Sorry," she said. "I wish I did." She folded her hands together thoughtfully. "But you might try talking to an old friend of mine. Lillian Sharpe. Well, she was Lillian Winchester when we went to school together in Seattle. Our families were old friends. Her father was one of Seattle's most prominent attorneys in the 1930s. He took on several famous cases. I remember Lill thinking his work was very dull when we were young, but she became quite fascinated by his legacy as an adult. After he passed, she collected all of his files and donated most of them to a museum in Seattle. He took on some high-profile cases back then. Most have long since been forgotten, of course, but let's see. . . ." She paused, as if trying very hard to make the wheels in her mind turn faster. "Yes, he represented the woman who shot her husband. It was the talk of Seattle, that case. You should interview Lillian. It's probably a long shot, but maybe she knows something about your missing boy."

"I'd love to talk to her," I said. "I'll look her up when I'm back in Seattle."

"I just saw her yesterday," Bee said. "At the soda fountain. She didn't like Esther much, but Evelyn . . ."

Emily gave me a knowing look, then rubbed her aunt's arm affectionately. "Bee, you must be remembering something from the past. We didn't go to the soda fountain yesterday."

Bee looked startled, then embarrassed. "Oh yes," she said. "Of course. The days sort of jumble together sometimes."

"I'm lucky if I can remember the year lately," I chimed in.

Bee gave me an appreciative grin, then reached for my hand. "It's nice of you," she said.

"I'm sorry," I said. "What?"

"It's nice of you to care about a story from the past," she continued. "So many young people don't give a hootenanny about anything that doesn't involve the here and now."

"Well," I said, "the story captured me the moment I learned of it. There's just something about a mother and her little boy separated. I couldn't *not* pursue it." I didn't have the heart to tell her that my editor had killed the story. For me, however, it was very much alive.

Bee nodded. "You'll find your little boy," she said assuredly.

"I hope so," I said, standing up.

"Did you take your medicine?" Emily asked, hovering over her like a mother hen.

Bee smirked and turned to me. "She's always nagging me about my medicine, this one."

Emily grinned. "Someone's got to keep that heart ticking."

"It's nice to have someone nagging," she whispered to me. "Frankly, I don't know what I'd do without her."

"All right, you," Emily said, pulling down the shade. "Time for rest. And no more open windows. You'll catch pneumonia."

"Good-bye, Claire," Bee said, shifting positions. "I hope you'll come visit again. I'll be looking for your story."

"I'll send you a copy," I said, walking to the hallway.

I caught the six o'clock ferry home, and Gene greeted me where the cab dropped me off. "You just missed Ethan," he said.

"Oh?" I hadn't heard from him all day; not that I expected to. We held grudges. If there were going to be an undoing of our marriage, that would be it.

"Yeah," Gene continued. "He was all dressed up. In a tux. Left in a cab ten minutes ago."

Where would my husband be going in a tux? Without me? My heart filled with the lonely realization that he was slipping away from me, like sand between my fingers. *I could stop this. I could find him and take him into my arms. Tell him I love him. We could end this nonsense.* The painful memories of the past began to seep into my mind, but I shooed them away. Reconciliation. It's what my therapist had been pushing for all along. One of us needed to make the first step, she'd said. One of us needed to grab the other by the collar and say, 'Look at us! We're dying! We can fix this! We love each other!' I'd been thinking about making that first step for months, but each time I tried to take one forward, we took two steps back, sometimes three. Not this time. I nodded to myself and held my hand out to the driver. "Wait a sec, please!" I yelled, before whipping my head back to Gene. "Did he say where he was going?"

"Yes, some big event at the Olympic Hotel." He looked nervous, as if he worried he'd just divulged a marriage-shattering secret. "I, um, assumed you were joining him."

"Thanks, Gene," I said, ducking back into the cab. I turned to the driver. "Can you take me to the Olympic Hotel?"

I clasped my hands together nervously as the cab approached the old building. I marveled at its ornate facade and intricate columns. Valets buzzed like bees, plucking keys and flying incoming cars off to inconspicuous parking garages. A couple arrived in a shiny black Mercedes-Benz a few feet ahead. The woman's sequined dress sparkled as she took her date's hand, shimmying her svelte body out of the car in five-inch heels. I glanced down at my own shoes, a pair of worn gray ballet flats with a black scuff on the right toe that I hadn't bothered to buff out. I tried in vain to smooth the wrinkles from my shirt. When a tube of lipstick didn't turn up in my purse, I ran a nervous hand through my wind-whipped hair. I regretted sitting on the outside deck of the ferry on the return trip to Seattle; the salty breeze had pulverized my hair into a mangled mess. I gathered my straggly locks into a tight bunch and tucked it into the rubber band I pulled from my wrist. I handed the driver a ten-dollar bill and stepped out of the cab.

I approached a doorman clad in a black trench coat. "Is there an event happening here tonight?" I asked, peering through the gold-trimmed glass doors ahead, trying to make out the scene.

He eyed me suspiciously. "Yes. It's invitation only." He turned toward a young woman, no more than twenty-five, a few feet away. She clutched a clipboard. The PR type. "Talk to Lisa," he said to me. "You have to be on the list."

"Hi," I said to her. "I'm Claire Aldridge."

She scanned the clipboard and then looked back at me with a satisfied smirk. "Sorry," she said. "I can't seem to find your name."

I shook my head. "No, no," I said. "I'm not here for the event. My husband's inside."

She looked doubtful, as if considering the possibility that I was making up a creative story to get access. "If you're not on the list, you're not on the list."

"Listen," I said, "my husband is—" Just then I spotted Ethan. The scene was a bit blurred through the glass doors, but he looked handsome; that much was clear. Tuxedos were made for Ethan. He held a champagne flute to his lips, then nodded and waved at someone across the room. The man knew how to work a crowd. I recalled the way he'd weaved through the tables at our wedding reception with such ease and grace, while I'd plodded along behind him awkwardly, dreading the nonstop stream of well-wishes and mandatory hugging. Social anxiety, my therapist said. Lots of people have it. Not Ethan. Inside, the room sparkled, from the enormous crystal chandelier overhead to the glint of the jewels draped around women's necks.

I pointed to Ethan. I didn't feel like Mrs. Ethan Kensington. Instead I was thirteen again, lanky, wearing cutoff jeans and a Hypercolor T-shirt, nose pressed against the rusty chain-link fence behind my junior high school, alone, watching the popular girls play basketball. This time, I spoke up. "See?" I said. "My husband's right there. Ethan *Kensington*."

She looked at me with scrutinizing eyes, as if it were a good possibility I only wanted to score free champagne and all-you-can-eat stuffed mushrooms and crudités. "Listen," she said, "I can't let you inside if you don't have an invitation."

My heart lightened when I saw Ethan turn toward the entrance. He'd bound through the doors, and I'd run to him. I'd take his cheeks in my hands and tell him I was ready to end this war. Ready to try again. He set an empty champagne flute down on a waiter's tray and selected two more. He smiled as he walked toward the foyer. I waved. But then my heart sank when a woman walked toward him and kissed him on the cheek. He handed her the second glass of champagne. I was so close, I could see the fizzy bubbles in the glass. It took a second before I realized who she was, and then it hit me like an arrow to the heart.

Cassandra.

I shuddered, watching them together. They smiled. They laughed. She placed her hand on his arm flirtatiously. Part of me wanted to charge through the doors and tear her hand off of my husband's sleeve. Instead, I reached into my bag and fished out my cell phone. I dialed Ethan's number, and held the phone to my ear. A moment later, I watched through the doors as he pulled his phone out of his pocket. He glanced at the screen, said something to Cassandra, and walked a few steps toward the door. I slunk back, worried he would see me through the glass.

"Claire?" His voice sounded distant, foreign over the phone line, even though he stood mere feet from me. "Is everything all right?"

I felt too numb to answer. I thought about all the things I wanted to say to the man I loved, all the things I had rehearsed on the cab ride over. But when presented with the opportunity, I could only stare at my scuffed shoes.

"Claire, are you still there?"

"I'm here," I said, my voice cracking. I bit my lip.

"You don't sound well, honey," he said. "Listen, why don't I come home? I'm just at a work function. I can cut out early."

I peered through the window and watched Cassandra pop an hors d'oeuvre into his mouth. She grinned at him, and helped herself to another on a nearby tray.

"Sorry," he said. "I'm eating on the fly tonight."

"Right," I said, pulling myself together. "Never mind. I didn't mean to interrupt. I have to go."

I watched as Ethan walked back to Cassandra's side. She spoke, her face animated, and he laughed, before they meandered deeper into the crowd.

"Excuse me," the woman with the clipboard said in a voice that was both syrupy sweet and exceedingly annoyed. "We really have to keep this entrance free to invited guests."

"Yes," I said, with no attempt to try to mask the defeat in my voice. "I was just leaving."

Chapter 13

VERA

Sitting at the table with Lon was painful. Not because of the pressure of the corset binding my waist or the heat of his gaze, like fire, on my chest. No, it was seeing the faces of the people I'd worked with, the faces of disappointment. Lou, the old jolly doorman, once a father figure to me, looked away as I walked in on Lon's arm. Two maids whom I'd counted as friends, Jenny and Vivien, gave me sour looks in the lobby before turning back to the sconces they were dusting. I didn't blame them for feeling betrayed. Primped and pressed in clothes that didn't belong to me, I stood for everything we all detested about the upper class and their penchant for taking what they wanted. But I couldn't worry about that now. I felt a lump in my throat and closed my eyes, long enough to see Daniel's face, his soft cheeks, those blond silky curls hanging over his blue eyes. He always waited there in the dark quiet of my mind.

"What's the sad look for, dollface?" Lon asked before prying open a crab leg with his teeth. A drip of butter rolled off his chin. "Why don't you eat?" he said, pointing to the decadence laid out on the table.

The tears were coming. I couldn't stop them now. "I'm sorry, Mr.—I mean, Lon," I said. "It's my son. I miss him terribly."

"Now, now," he said. "I'm sure he's just fine."

Just fine? I dug my fingernails into the upholstery of the chair. *How can everyone be so dismissive about a lost boy? A child of three is missing, and no one cares.* I buried my face in my hands, feeling Lon's warm, moist hand on my shoulder a moment later.

"I'll make some calls in the morning," he said, trying to console me.

"In the morning?" I cried, looking up at him. "I beg your pardon, but couldn't you call tonight?"

Lon shook his head. "All the offices are closed, darling," he said. "Tomorrow."

I nodded.

"Now," he said, "let's get you upstairs. You can relax there."

I stood up hesitantly, dabbing a crisp cloth napkin against my cheek to blot a fresh tear. Lon held out his hand to me, and I took it reluctantly. He gave it a suffocating squeeze as he led me through the restaurant out to the lobby. I saw the elevator ahead. Servants weren't allowed to use the guests' elevator, with its ornate trim and shiny brass knobs. But I'd stepped inside it before, the first time I'd been a guest of the hotel. With Charles. I'd ended up in a bed of soft down. The bed where Daniel was conceived.

Four Years Prior

Charles picked me up at seven. A week had passed since he had exited the dance floor in such a hurry, ushered away by his prickly sister. I'd thought of him every day after that, particularly in the evenings, after my shifts at the restaurant, when the apartment was quiet. That night, I slid into the front seat of his Buick. It smelled of finery—leather; good, sweet-smelling tobacco; and cologne. "Hi," he said, grinning. I felt my heart race faster the moment our eyes met.

"I've missed you," he said, tucking a stray lock of hair behind my ear. His fingers sent a chill down my neck. A *good* chill.

"I've missed you, too," I said. "How's your mother?"

"Much better," he replied. "Pneumonia. The doctor was able to catch it just in time." He tilted his head to the right, peering deeper into my eyes. "I've been feeling terribly, leaving you at the dance hall like I did."

"Don't think of it," I said. "Your family needed you."

He shrugged. "Well, it wouldn't have killed my sister to be a little kinder. Don't be offended by her, though. That's just Josie. She disapproves of every girl I've ever taken out."

"Oh," I said, looking at my lap.

Charles inched closer to me. "That came out wrong," he said. "I don't mean to imply that she disapproves of *you*, Claire. She's just, well . . ."

"A snob?"

He smiled playfully. "Why, yes."

"It's all right," I said.

He stepped on the gas pedal and turned the car into the street. Nobody I knew had a car. I relished the sound of the engine and the jazz playing on the radio. "Why don't we head over to the Cabaña Club? We could grab some dinner, and maybe try our luck with dancing again."

"I'd love that," I said, pressing my cheek against his shoulder.

Seattle looked glorious from inside the Buick, its windshield like a pair of rose-colored glasses blurring the world outside into a lovelier place. From my comfortable seat, I did not see the shadowy apartment buildings where dozens of poor families I knew dined on stale bread, nor did I notice the trash-strewn alleys where young children played jacks, unattended, while their mothers, as mine had, worked late into the night in the homes of the city's elite. Instead, I let myself dream about what it might be like to live in Charles's world, a place where life was handed to you, pressed and polished, on a platter.

Charles pulled over to the side of the road, leaning across the seat to peer out my window. I didn't mind him hovering so close.

A Closed sign hung over the door of the club. "Rats," he said. "Well, how about we just head over to the hotel instead? It's a beautiful night. We can have dinner on the balcony of my parents' suite."

"Your parents' *suite*?"

"Yes," he said. "They do a lot of entertaining there. Father uses it a few nights a week when he works late and needs quiet. Or when he's had it out with Mother, which happens more often these days."

"Well, I guess," I said shyly.

Charles drove to the entrance of the hotel, just a few blocks down the street, pulling the car into the circular drive, smooth as silk. He handed the keys to a valet and nodded to the doorman. We walked straight into the elevator, where Charles hit the button for number seventeen.

I gulped.

"First time in an elevator?"

"Yes," I admitted, feeling a tugging sensation in my stomach as we jerked upward.

"Don't be afraid," he said, pulling me toward him with both hands on my waist.

I looked up into his eyes. "What happens if it . . . falls?"

"It won't," he said, squeezing me tighter. "I promise."

When the elevator jolted to a stop, the doors opened, and a man in a white suit stood waiting. "Good evening, sir," he said to Charles, before tipping his cap at me. "The suite is ready for you. Will you be dining inside or out tonight?"

Charles turned to me. "Does the balcony sound all right?"

I nodded, so caught up in the grandeur of the moment, I forgot my voice.

The steward slid a key into the lock and held the door open for us. I followed Charles inside, and gasped at the sight. Tufted silk sofas, oriental rugs, drapes made of velvet the color of rubies—the place looked like a palace, or at least how I'd always imagined one to look.

Charles slipped off his jacket and tossed it nonchalantly onto a sofa to our right. He walked to the bar by the far window and flipped on the radio, letting the soothing sounds of big band seep through the air, before selecting two martini glasses from the cabinet. I watched as he unlocked another cabinet and pulled out two ornate glass decanters, pouring liquid from each into a shiny silver shaker. Next he scooped ice inside, then closed the top before shaking the vessel with an expert hand.

When he handed me a glass, I marveled at the thin layer of ice at the top. I was careful to keep my hand steady or risk sloshing the drink all over my dress. I stole a look at myself in the reflection of the window as I held the drink to my lips. Fashionable. Like I belonged. I swallowed the ice-cold liquid, so strong a fit of coughing ensued.

"Sorry," I said, setting the glass down on a side table. "I guess I wasn't expecting it to be so strong." I scolded myself for the naive comment.

"The first sip is always the hardest to take," Charles said, popping a green olive into his mouth. "After that, it goes down like butter."

I picked up the glass again, and after a second sip, and a third, the drink had lost its bite, just as he had promised. My cheeks felt warm and my head light. When I finished the glass, he refilled it. I stood at the window staring out at Seattle, sparkling, effervescent. The spring cherry trees on the street below had just burst into bloom, and from the seventeenth floor, they looked like cheerful clouds of pink lining the streets. The city was full of promise, which is exactly how I felt. I felt the stubble of Charles's chin on my neck as he perched his head over my shoulder to share the view with me.

"It's beautiful out there, isn't it?" he whispered into my ear.

"Yes," I said.

A crescent moon hovered low in the sky, like a painting hung just for us.

"Where would you want to go," he said, "right now, if you could be anywhere in the world?"

I thought for a moment. Caroline and I had talked an awful lot about Paris. And New York. But in that moment, I didn't want to be anywhere other than where I stood.

"Right here," I whispered, turning to face Charles.

"Me too," he said, taking my face tenderly in his hands.

As he leaned closer, the steward cleared his throat. "I'm sorry to interrupt, but dinner is here, sir. Will you still be taking it on the balcony?"

"Yes," Charles said, weaving his fingers into mine. He showed me to the balcony, where a table, two chairs, and a half dozen carefully tended stone urns filled with flowering plants waited. Like a magician, the steward produced two plates from a cart somewhere behind us. I sank my fork into a tender piece of fish, its buttery flesh yielding to the tines. A bite of steaming hot roll was washed down with a sip of red wine. I squinted, unable to make out the French words on the label, just the date, 1916. I'd been a scrawny little girl then, chasing my younger brother and sister around the dusty streets outside the ramshackle building we called home. To think this wine was being bottled at that very moment.

"I haven't forgotten about the woman in your apartment building," he said.

My heart swelled. "You haven't?"

"No," he replied, pulling an envelope from his pocket. "I talked to my father. He owns a new housing development in West Seattle. They all have yards, new appliances. I think it would be a perfect place for her, and her children."

"Oh, Charles!" I cried. "Your father agreed?"

He shook his head. "No, he refused. He doesn't believe in handouts."

"Oh," I said, confused.

"I'm taking care of it myself," he continued. "I don't need my father's permission to do a good deed. I have my own funds. She can move into her new home next week if she'd like."

I shook my head in disbelief. "That's so very generous."

He handed me the envelope. I lifted the flap and peeked inside to see a stack of bills. "Charles!" I couldn't wait to give her the money. I'd passed her on the stairs the other night, and she looked so tired, so gaunt, I worried she might pass out right there.

"After you told me about that poor woman, I couldn't get her— or your—words out of my head. I've been thinking, Vera—together, we could do a lot of good for people."

I beamed and couldn't help but sway as the radio played a slow melodic song.

"Dance with me," Charles said, standing up and reaching for my hands.

He helped me to my feet. I pressed my cheek to his chest, and we moved in time to the music. "I'd like to spend every day like this, with you," he said. "Forever." My lips met his and a force rivaling electricity surged through my body. He lifted me into his arms and carried me to the bedroom, laying me atop a down comforter as soft and enveloping as whipped cream. I sank into it willingly, and didn't protest as he nestled his body next to mine. He kissed me again and again. I closed my eyes, trying to memorize the feeling of being loved. Truly loved.

Upstairs in Lon's suite, I walked to the window, looking down to the street below. There might as well have been bars attached to the glass. I felt caged, jailed. He hovered behind me, his breath rapid and warm on my neck. "I miss my son so much," I cried.

"Now, now," Lon said, turning me around to face him. "To-morrow we'll find your son. Tonight, we'll find"—he paused, unfastening a button on my dress—"each other."

His touch repulsed me, but I didn't push his hand away. With his wealth, we could plaster the city in posters, litter the streets with leaflets, hire a search team. "Promise me you'll help find Daniel?" I searched his eyes. "You're my only hope."

"You have my word," he said, confidently running a finger along the sash of my dress.

Lon turned out the light, and I held my breath as he pulled me toward the bed.

Chapter 14

※

CLAIRE

I sat in the cab for a while, staring at the hotel, memorializing the moment that Ethan had slipped away from me.

The cab driver didn't share my emotional sentiments. "Where to, miss?" he barked, tapping his fingers on the dash impatiently. "I don't have all night."

I didn't feel like going home, not after tonight. "Café Lavanto," I said instead.

The café looked dark when I arrived, but I was glad to find the door still open. A college girl with a short blond bobbed haircut shook her head from behind the counter. "Sorry," she said. "We're closed. I must have forgotten to lock the door."

"Oh, I—"

"It's fine, Brittany," Dominic said, emerging from the back room with a stack of papers in hand. He turned to me. "It's good to see you, Claire. Want something to drink?"

Brittany, cleaning the steamer wand of the espresso machine with a damp towel, seemed visibly annoyed by my presence. I shook my head. "No," I said. "I just . . ." I stared down at my feet. "Do you have a minute to talk?"

He nodded, setting down the papers on a nearby table. "I'm all ears."

We sat in a pair of upholstered chairs by the windows, gazing out at the street. A couple walking a pug passed by, holding hands over the dog's leash. Brittany stopped at the door before letting herself out. "See you tomorrow," she said.

Dominic waved and then turned back to me. "What's wrong?"

I sighed. "You went through a bad breakup, right?"

"A doozy," he said.

"How did you know when it was . . ." I paused. "Over?"

"Things were shaky for a long time," he said. "We stopped laughing. She'd work late and not call me. I started spending more time with my friends. It snowballed. And then there was the added fact that she was—how do I put this nicely?—crazy."

I returned his grin, but the smile faded quickly. There was nothing funny about what I was about to say. "I'm afraid my marriage might be over."

"Claire, I'm so sorry."

I clasped my hands together and stared ahead. My heart ached, and I couldn't think of a single way to quell the pain. "It's the betrayal I can't get over."

"I know," he said. "I've been there. It hurts. I wish I could say something to make you feel better."

"Well, just being here helps," I said. "This place is a comfort to me."

Dominic rubbed his forehead as if recalling an uncomfortable memory. He looked at his watch. "Hey, you know what you need?"

I shrugged. "What?"

"A beer," he said. "I'm taking you down to Kells. My buddy's in a band that's playing there tonight. They cover U2 songs. You'll love it. You can drink yourself silly, sing your heart out, and then I'll drive you home and make sure you're safe."

"I don't know," I said apprehensively.

"Come on," he said. "There's nothing that a Guinness can't fix."

"Well," I said, grinning, "I do like U2."

Dominic smiled with satisfaction. "Good. I'll just go get the extra helmet."

I waited at the bar, glancing at the paperwork Dominic had left on a table to my right. The disarray reminded me of Ethan's home office. I was forever tidying his mess. Manila file folders were his Achilles' heel. I felt a sudden pain in my heart as I gathered the papers, tapping them into a neat pile.

"Oh," Dominic said nervously, setting down the extra motorcycle helmet and swooping in to collect the pages in my hands. "I'll take those. Sorry, I left a bit of a mess out here."

An awkward pause hovered between us as Dominic shuffled the papers into a drawer below the bar. He smiled, erasing any lingering tension, and handed me the helmet. "Ready?"

"Yes," I said, following him out to the street to his parked motorcycle.

Dominic blazed a trail through the crowd of sweaty, beer-fueled college students at Kells. I instantly regretted going, but then the unmistakable sound of U2 came from the stage. I expected to see Bono himself clutching the microphone, but I didn't care that a guy with a pot belly and balding head was standing in. Dominic handed me a beer, something light brown and frothy, and I took a sip, and then another. We leaned against a patch of free space at the bar together. When a spot on the dance floor cleared, Dominic took my hand in his. "Want to dance?"

I had already finished a second beer, so I said yes without thinking. And when the band began playing "With or Without You," I pressed my weary head against Dominic's chest. I missed my husband terribly, but I liked the way Dominic held me, so safe, so secure. When the song ended and the band began playing the opening rifts of "One," I didn't object when his hands slipped lower on my waist.

"Claire?"

I heard my name, yes. A familiar female voice. But whose? I looked over Dominic's shoulder, then felt a tap on my back. I turned around, and my mouth flew open. My God. Ethan's sister, Leslie. We had skirmished pretty much since the day we met, but I could now see the conflict escalating to World War III proportions.

She gave Dominic a long look, then eyed me suspiciously. "What are you doing here, Claire?"

"Oh hi, Leslie," I said, feigning composure. "This is my friend Dominic."

"Friend?"

"Leslie," I said, "I don't know what you're implying, but I can tell you right now I don't owe you any explanation."

"Tell that to Ethan," she said, pulling out her cell phone.

"Yes, do," I said. "He won't bother answering. He's at the Olympic Hotel with Cassandra."

Her mouth gaped.

"Good night, Leslie," I said, dragging Dominic by the arm.

"Sorry," he said. "I didn't mean to cause trouble."

I sighed. "If he can drink champagne with his ex, I can drink beer with you." I waved at the bartender. "Another round, please."

I don't remember the ride to Abby's place, or climbing the stairs to her apartment. Later, I discovered that Dominic had found her number in my phone and called for directions. I do, however, remember waking up and feeling like I'd been hit with an ax to the head. "Where am I?" I groaned.

Abby handed me a cup of coffee. Swirls of steam drifted from the green mug. I watched them disappear into the air. "I don't drink coffee," I said ungratefully.

"You do this morning," she said. "Drink up."

I took a sip. "What happened last night?"

"Someone had a little *too* much fun," she said.

"Oh gosh," I said. "Do I want to know?"

Suddenly, I remembered Kells, Dominic's warm embrace, Leslie. I covered my face. "This isn't good, Abs."

"No, it isn't," she agreed.

"Did I kiss him?"

"I don't think so," she said. "He's a decent guy. I don't think he would have let you kiss him, even if he wanted to kiss you."

I nodded.

"He carried you up six flights of stairs," she said. "You were singing the whole way."

"No."

"Yes," she said. "And you woke up the crazy lady in the apartment on the fourth floor."

I buried my face deeper in my hands, then looked at my watch, suddenly panic-stricken.

"Don't worry," she said. "It's Saturday."

"I'm not worried about work," I said. "It's Eva."

"Eva?"

I fumbled for my bag, and was happy to find it next to me, beside the couch. "She used to know Daniel Ray. I'm meeting her today." I pulled out my planner and flipped to the current week. "Good. I have an hour."

"Go shower," Abby said. "Towels are in the cabinet. Use anything you need."

I took another big gulp of coffee. Ethan would be proud, but I wasn't drinking it for him. "Thanks, Abs," I said. "You're the world's greatest friend."

"I know," she said, folding up the blanket she'd strewn over me the night before. "But I'd like to point out that you drooled on my Pottery Barn pillows."

"I'll buy you new ones."

"Nonsense," she said. "What's a friendship without a little drool?"

I gave her a grateful smile that had nothing to do with the pillows. "I love you."

She shooed me to the bathroom. "Go brush your teeth."

The flower stands at the Pike Place Market brimmed with new blossoms. A bucket of fresh-cut hydrangeas, indigo blue, caught my eye, but even their cheerful petals couldn't elicit a smile. All I could think about was Ethan and Cassandra, and how we were entwined in a colossal mess. I pulled a bottle of Advil from my bag and popped two pills, washing them down with a swig from the water bottle Abby had provided. I tucked the bottle back inside and felt my cell phone buzzing, notifying me of a missed call. I clicked a button and saw that it was Ethan. So he'd talked to Leslie. That or he wanted to apologize for last night. Either way, I didn't want to speak to him. I had nothing to say.

I checked the address in my planner, walking along the sidewalk until I came to the entrance of Eva's building. Inside the lobby an arrangement of sun-faded silk flowers sat atop a round table, their petals thick with dust. The wallpaper bubbled and peeled at the edges, and the scent of boiled vegetables wafted in the air. I took the elevator to the eleventh floor, stopping at unit 1105 and knocking quietly.

Moments later the doorknob turned and an elderly woman appeared. Her white hair was tucked into a bun, revealing a thin face and kind brown eyes. She smiled. "You must be Claire."

"Yes," I said, extending my hand. Funny, I knew she was an old woman, and yet I'd only imagined a little girl, with pigtails and a calico jumper. "Thank you so much for inviting me."

"Come in," she said, gesturing inside the apartment. I sat down in a blue recliner near the window, tucking aside a small cross-stitched pillow to make room for my purse. Plain, but tidy, the space smelled of lemons and baby powder. It reminded me a little of my grandmother's small condo in San Diego. I missed her.

"Can I make you a cup of tea, dear?"

"No thank you," I said. "I'm fine."

She sat down in a chair beside me, crossing her hands in her lap. "Now," she said, "what can I tell you?"

"Yes," I replied, pulling my notebook and a pen out of my purse. "As I mentioned on the phone, I'm writing a feature about a little boy who disappeared the day of the snowstorm in May of 1933. I believe you two were acquainted?"

"Yes," Eva said, her eyes clouded with memories. "Yes, we were." She closed her eyes briefly and opened them again. "Daniel was the son of my mother's best friend, Vera Ray. We were like sister and brother."

"So you lived together?"

"Well, for a short time when we were babies. Our mothers were both unmarried. My father died before I was born, and Daniel's, well, he wasn't in the picture. Vera and Daniel moved into their own apartment, though, just after she got a job at the Olympic."

I thought of the scene from last night and cringed. "The hotel?"

"Yes," she said. "Vera was a maid there."

"And your mother was too?"

"No," she said. "Mother worked in a factory in the industrial district."

I turned a page in my notebook. "So what do you remember about his disappearance?"

She took a deep breath and fixed her gaze out the window, where the red-lettered sign of Pike Place Market presided and a ferry streamed slowly through the bay. For low-income senior housing, the view was extraordinary. "My memories have faded some," she said, rubbing her right hand. "But I remember Aunt Vera. I called her that, Auntie. I remember when she came to stay with us, right after Daniel disappeared. Vera had always been generous with smiles, but not anymore. I remember watching from the hallway as she sobbed. Her body trembled from her sorrow. I didn't understand it then, of course. But I do now." She pointed to a framed photo on the wall of three children. The lighting and dress dated the shot to the 1960s. "The boy," she said. "My eldest. He died in a car accident twenty years ago. A head-on collision. A drunk driver was going the wrong way on an on-ramp. I'd thought of Vera many times as a young mother, of course. The thought of losing a baby was horrific. But when the highway patrol called me to tell me about Eddie's death, I felt a kinship with Vera. I finally knew what she went through."

"I'm so sorry," I said.

She nodded. "I've had many years to come to terms with it. But I still grieve."

"Do you believe that Daniel was . . . ?" I couldn't will myself to vocalize the thought.

"Killed?"

I nodded.

Eva threw up her hands. "I don't know, dear. I've thought about it an awful lot over the years. Mother and I always wanted to believe that he only wandered off. That some nice family took him in. But the chances of that are slim. Mother knew that. Not Vera. She refused to believe the worst. She held out hope, until the very end."

"The end?"

Eva frowned. "Mother shielded me from the details, of course," she said. "I was only a little girl, too young to understand. But eventually I heard the whole story."

"What happened?"

"Her body was found floating in Lake Washington," she said.

I gasped.

Eva shook her head regretfully. "By the time they found her, her skin was so puffy, so waterlogged, that the medical examiner couldn't make a ruling."

I covered my mouth. "My God."

"The police ruled it a suicide," she continued, "but anyone who knew her didn't believe that. She'd never leave this earth willingly without the knowledge that her son was safe." She paused, eyeing my wedding ring.

"When you're a mother, dear, you'll understand."

But I do understand. I swallowed hard and stared at my notebook, willing my emotion away. "So you think someone murdered her, then?"

"I have my suspicions," she replied. "But no one really knows. In those days, we didn't have justice in the same way we do now. If the daughter of a prominent family were found bobbing in the lake, you better bet an investigation would be launched. But for Vera Ray, daughter of a fisherman? The sad fact is that no one really cared. It's why the police hardly batted an eye when Daniel went missing. Why waste police resources on the poor? It was the prominent thinking of the time."

"So sad," I said, shaking my head. "So there wasn't even an investigation?"

"They did interview a man in connection with the crime," she said. "A mason, I believe. Picked him up after getting a tip from someone. But the suspect died in jail. Heart attack. The case fizzled after that. It broke Mother's heart that nothing more became of it. She always believed she'd find justice for her friend."

I thought of my visit to the police archives, which had turned up nothing. "Do you know if they have the transcripts?"

"I wondered the same thing myself," she said. "I set out to find them in the 1950s, but was told that all records from that year were destroyed in a fire."

The whistle on the teakettle sounded. "Sure you don't want a cup of tea?"

"Actually," I said, "that sounds nice."

Eva returned with two cups. She handed me one, and I held it close, letting the steam warm my face. I took a sip and set the cup down on the nearby coffee table. "Do you know much about Daniel's father?"

Eva sighed. "Just that he was very rich," she said. "Vera was proud. It didn't make for a good match."

"They never married?"

"No. But she always wore a bracelet he gave her. That made me think she still loved him."

I thought of my bracelet tucked under my sleeve. From Ethan. *Would I take it off? Would I take my wedding ring off?*

"It was a dark time for Mother," Eva continued. "Losing her best friend in such a tragic way, it affected her."

"How terrible," I said. I pulled an envelope from my bag and handed it to Eva. "Some things I found."

She lifted the flap of the envelope and reached inside, placing the contents on her lap. She held the photo up to the light. "That's Vera, all right," she said. "She was so beautiful."

I nodded. "And the man? Daniel's father?"

"Yes," she said. "At least, I think so. I never met him, of course. But look." She pointed to a spot on the photo. "He has Daniel's chin."

I produced the *Seattle Post-Intelligencer*'s photo of the boy, and held it up to the picture of his parents. "You're right," I said. "I can see a resemblance." Daniel had a heart-shaped face, and his chin revealed a tiny dimple, nearly identical to the man in the photograph.

"Ah, yes," Eva said with a sigh. "Daniel would have been a handsome one, just like his father."

"Do you know Charles's last name?" I asked, flipping the photo over and rereading the inscription: "Vera and Charles."

Eva shook her head. "Mother didn't speak of him. I never knew."

"Thank you," I said, closing my notebook. "I've taken up enough of your time."

"Wait," Eva said, holding up the drawing she'd made as a girl, marveling at the brittle yellow page. "There is *something*."

"What?"

She held out the drawing for me to see and pointed to the woman drawn behind the children. "There was a woman," she said.

"Where?"

"The image is a bit of blur," she said. "It might be nothing."

"Keep trying. The memory might be significant."

"Well," she said, holding a hand to her wrinkled cheek as if trying very hard to recall a memory. "Daniel and I used to play in a park near Sixth Avenue. We'd wait there for our mothers to get off work. Sometimes a strange woman would come and watch us. She seemed out of place there, in her fine dresses and hats, smack dab in the working-class part of town. She was friendly enough, talked to Daniel mostly, but I didn't like her. Mama taught me not to talk to strangers, and there was something about her that frightened me."

"What do you think it was?"

"I'm not certain," Eva said. "And really, the woman might have just been taking pity on us. I don't know. But I have never forgotten the memory, even after all these years, or her hat."

"Her hat?

Eva nodded and pointed to the stick figure's head. "They're feathers, I think," she said. "I must have been drawing the feathers on her hat."

I finished writing out her quote, then drew a big question mark on the page. *How will I follow up on that?*

Eva's eyes looked strained, so I stood and gathered my things. "Thank you ever so much for sharing your memories with me."

"Anytime, dear," she said. "I hope you solve this mystery. For mothers everywhere." She paused and tilted her head to the right. "I just assumed you hadn't any children of your own. Are you a mother too, honey?"

It was the first time I'd heard the question since the accident. I bit my lip. Without thinking, I spoke from my heart. "Yes," I said. "I am."

I rarely worked on weekends, but I made my way into the office on Saturday, looking forward to some uninterrupted writing time. A sign on Ethan's door read, ON ASSIGNMENT. I checked my cell phone and saw that he'd tried to call again. I tossed the phone back into my purse and turned on my laptop, pulling up the document I'd begun on the ferry the day before. It felt easier to lose myself in Daniel and Vera's story than to sort out my own.

I leaned back in my chair. *Who was the woman at the park that Eva spoke of? And the mason?* I recalled the name I'd written in my notebook at Café Lavanto the previous week and thumbed through the pages until I found it: Ivanoff. I pulled up the online newspaper archives and searched for the name, and two entries came back, both from the *Seattle Herald*. I clicked on the first headline, which appeared as part of a police blotter: MAN JAILED IN DOMESTIC VIO-LENCE CHARGE.

> Sven Ivanoff, a mason, has been arrested and taken to jail on charges of injur-ing his wife, Arianna Ivanoff, who sus-tained injuries to the head and neck.

So he had a violent streak, this mason. I clicked on the next head-line. FOUL PLAY SUSPECTED IN IVANOFF CASE. I shivered. "Police have charged Sven Ivanoff with the murder of a woman whose body was found floating in Lake Washington last week. Ivanoff, a mason, was the last person to be seen with the woman, who is believed to be a prostitute."

A prostitute? I shuddered. If this was indeed Vera, her life had taken an unfortunate turn. I shook my head in disbelief. *There has to be more to the story.* I remembered Emily's aunt Bee's suggestion to speak to her friend Lillian. Perhaps she had crucial information. I searched for her name, and when a number came up, I dialed. A man with a deep, gravelly voice picked up immediately. "Hello?"

"Oh, I must have the wrong number," I said. "I'm trying to reach someone by the name of Lillian Sharpe."

"Yes," he said. "My wife. She's right here. Who may I say is calling?"

"My name is Claire Aldridge, from the *Seattle Herald.*"

"Hello, this is Lillian."

"Ms. Sharpe," I said.

"Yes," she replied.

"I hate to disturb you, but I'm working on a story about a little boy who went missing in 1933. During the storm."

"Yes," she said.

"You remember?"

"Well, no, not the boy you speak of, but the storm. Everybody remembers that. It nearly shut down the city. And right before summer. Just like the storm we had this week. Such a strange coincidence."

"I know," I replied.

"How can I help you, Ms. Aldridge?"

"I was just chatting with an old friend of yours, Bee Larson," I said.

"Bee! How is she?"

"Not well, I'm afraid. She's confined to bed now. Heart problems."

"Bless her heart," she said. "I'll have to pay her a visit. Is she still on the island?"

"Yes," I replied. "I was visiting her niece yesterday. Bee told me your father was a prominent attorney in the 1930s."

"Indeed he was," she said. "He took on some of the most famous cases of the time."

"Could one of those cases be the murder of Vera Ray?"

She sighed. "I wish I could recall. The name doesn't sound familiar, but it's possible."

"Bee mentioned something about his case files and archives," I said. "Do you happen to have them?"

"I do. My granddaughter, Lisa, spent a good portion of last summer reorganizing them for me. She's a journalist, like you."

"Is it possible that I could take a look?" I asked. "I mean, if you don't mind."

"Of course not, dear," she said. "My father would have gladly shared them with you. He was a truth seeker, just as you seem to be. They're at the old house, in Windermere."

I knew the neighborhood, of course. One of the finest areas of historic Seattle. Ethan had a cousin who lived in an enormous home along the lake.

"I grew up there, but it's empty now. My husband and I are in a retirement facility," Lillian continued. "I just can't bear to sell the old place. I hoped one of my boys would move in, but they had other plans. I can't say I blame them. The house is in disrepair." She sighed. "Listen to me rambling. I could meet you there if you like. As long as you don't mind a little dust and cobwebs. We haven't had the place cleaned in some time."

"I would be so grateful," I said.

"I've had to part with some of it, but I do have an assortment of boxes in the spare bedroom, all things that Lisa thought to keep. Hopefully you'll find what you're looking for there."

"Thank you so much," I said. "Could I come by tomorrow morning, say, nine thirty?"

"You choose the hour," she said. "My husband and I are early birds, up at sunrise. The address is 5985 Windermere Boulevard. It's an old white colonial with a big blue spruce in front."

"Great," I said, writing the address in my notebook. "See you then."

My phone buzzed in my bag. *Not again.* I pulled it out and opened a text message. From Dominic. "Meet me at the Market at one for lunch?" I smiled, and typed a quick response. "I'll be in front of the first flower stand. Bring Advil."

Dominic waited at the corner of the market, a bouquet of hydrangeas wrapped in brown butcher paper in his hands. "For you," he said, tucking the enormous bunch into the crook of my arm.

"They're beautiful," I said, feeling awkward about accepting them, especially after last night.

"How's your head?"

"Pounding," I replied.

He pulled a pill bottle from his pocket. "Here," he said, handing me two white pills.

I washed them down with a sip from the water bottle in my purse. "I'm starving. What did you have in mind?"

He pointed to a creperie across the street. Ethan and I had eaten there when I was pregnant and craving crepes. "How about La Bouche?"

I shrugged. "OK."

We crossed the cobblestone street. My heels sank into the large grooves. I loved the exposed brick in this part of Seattle. It's how the city must have looked when Vera and Daniel walked through the Market so many years ago.

Dominic and I sat down on two stools facing the street. The waitress took our crepe orders. He ordered mushroom, and I goat cheese and roasted red pepper, the same thing I'd sent Ethan down for on multiple occasions when a pregnancy craving struck.

"Listen," I said, "I'm really sorry for my behavior last night."

"No need to apologize. You have nothing to be ashamed of."

"I think I do," I said. "I'm married, and I was acting like a—"

"You were acting like a woman who was hurt," he said. "And for the record, you did not kiss me."

I arched my eyebrows. "I didn't?"

"You tried to," he said, grinning. "And I thought about letting you, but I didn't."

I exhaled deeply.

"What's with your sister-in-law, though?"

The memory was fuzzy, but I recalled Leslie's accusatory stare. "She's never liked me."

"Sounds like a real peach."

I took a sip of water. "You're telling me. By now, she's probably recounted the story to Ethan and her parents in great detail. But in her version, I'm sure I had my tongue down your throat."

"Naturally," he said, smiling.

Moments later, the waitress reappeared with our crepes. I took a bite of mine. The mélange of roasted red peppers and warm goat cheese tasted just as luscious as I remembered.

Dominic dabbed his mouth with a napkin. "All joking aside, how are you doing?"

I shrugged. "It's weird. I feel like a storm's coming—a big one that I'm not prepared for. I have this sense that it's going to pummel my house, my life, everything I've been holding on to so tightly, for so many years. I'm bracing for it. I know it's going to hurt." I sighed. "And after what I went through this year, I'm not sure I have the strength to handle it."

He gave me a confused look.

I hadn't told him about the accident, not yet. I clasped my hands together and took a deep breath. "We lost a baby," I said. "A year ago." The words whizzed out of my mouth before I could think them over.

"Oh, Claire," Dominic said, his eyes filled with sorrow. "I don't know what to say."

Outside the window, a woman jogged by. Her ponytail swayed as her strong legs carried her through the market, dodging pockets of tourists. I followed her with my eyes until she disappeared around the corner. I wanted to stand up, run after her, and shout, "Be careful! In a mere blink of the eye, everything you love can be taken from you!"

Dominic opened his mouth to speak, but his cell phone struck first, ringing loudly inside his jacket. He looked at the screen, then smiled apologetically. "I have to take this. I'll be right back."

"No worries," I said, turning my attention back to the neglected crepe.

Dominic stepped to the sidewalk, and I watched him hold the phone up to his ear as he paced nervously. *Who is he talking to?* The crowd in the café was loud, but because the window had been propped open, bits and pieces of the one-sided conversation seeped in.

"I don't know what to say. . . . Well, I'm a little speechless right now, I guess. . . . I understand, but I wasn't planning to . . . All right, I'll give it some thought. . . . I'll call you . . . yes."

I nervously stuffed a bite into my mouth when he returned to the counter.

"Sorry," he said.

My curiosity swelled. "Something important?"

"Just my . . . sister. She needed some business advice."

"Oh," I replied. It didn't add up, but I decided not to press him. If he had a secret, he'd reveal it in time.

After lunch, we walked through the Market, stopping at the park overlooking the bay. I could smell salmon grilling on alder planks at a nearby restaurant. Seagulls patrolled the salty air above, swooping down to accept scraps of food and bread that tourists offered. Dominic leaned against the guardrail. "Can we talk about something?"

"Sure," I said, leaning back beside him. Our arms touched.

"What you said, back there," he said. "About the baby."

My eyes met his.

"It seems"—he ran a hand through his hair, trying to find the proper word—"wrong that your husband isn't there for you right now after what you went through."

Dominic was right, at least in a sense. On paper, Ethan's behavior appeared despicable. Wife loses baby, followed by midlife crisis, followed by reconciliation with ex-girlfriend. In my heart, however, I knew that I was just as much to blame. I'd pulled away from him, too. In my grief, I'd frozen, shut him out. And just as my heart was starting to thaw, it was too late.

"I'm just saying," he continued, "he should have been there for you." He paused, turning to me. "*I* would have been there for you."

He draped his arm around me. I didn't pull away.

Chapter 15

※

VERA

The morning light streamed inside the window as I opened my eyes. I hated the feel of the silky sheets on my naked skin, hated the feel of Lon's rough leg on mine even more. I peeled my body away from his hot, moist skin and sat up, wrapping a sheet over my body. He snored so loudly, the pillowcase quivered with each rise and fall of his chest.

My dress and undergarments lay on the floor beside the bed. I'd died a little inside each time Lon removed a piece of clothing. I cringed, remembering the heaviness of his hands, fumbling to unfasten a button, only to resort to ripping it in eager frustration. I had numbed the pain with champagne. Too much champagne. And now my head spun. I closed the bathroom door and vomited into the toilet, purging the contents of my stomach and the memory of last night. I felt a sudden urge to bathe, to wash every breath, every fingerprint of Lon's from my body. I turned on the faucet and watched as the water fell like raindrops from the steel showerhead, ricocheting off the marble tiles. I'd polished hundreds of showers, maybe even this one, in suites at the hotel, scrubbing the grout with precision. Estella was a stickler about grout.

I lathered my body with soap, but even with every inch of my skin covered in a thick film of bubbles, I still felt filthy. Tainted. I scrubbed harder, until my hand cramped and I dropped the bar of soap. My lip quivered as the tears came. I couldn't stop them. I prayed that Lon wouldn't hear my cries. The water rushed over me, and after a while, I couldn't differentiate between the shower's stream and my tears.

I closed my eyes and Daniel's face appeared again, calling to me, comforting me. I remembered why I was there. I turned off the shower with new strength, patting myself dry with a fluffy cotton towel that waited on the rack. I selected a dress from the closet and put it on. As I waited for Lon to wake up, I sat by the window, thinking about Daniel, and his father.

Four Years Prior

Charles kissed my neck, and I smiled, rolling over to face him. "Good morning, beautiful," he said, tracing my face with his index finger.

I looked away shyly. *Was last night a dream?* We both looked up when we heard a knock at the bedroom door.

"Breakfast is ready, sir." The muffled male voice sounded like the steward from last night.

"Thank you," Charles said, sitting up. He walked to the bathroom and returned with a fluffy white robe. "Will you be comfortable in this?"

I nodded. "As long as we don't have any breakfast guests."

"Just us," he said.

I grinned, slipping into the robe, and followed Charles out to the front room.

"Will you take breakfast on the terrace, sir?"

I looked down at my feet, not wanting to make eye contact with the steward. *What does he think of me?*

"No," Charles said. "There's a breeze this morning. The table will be fine."

"As you wish," the man said, distributing the contents of two silver platters onto the table. I eyed the glasses of orange juice. We could get oranges in Seattle, but grapefruit were harder to come by. Last year I'd saved my tip money for a whole week and bought a single grapefruit. It had cost a fortune, but I'd felt very fancy slicing into its thick skin, until I discovered that the flesh inside was rotten.

The steward bowed and let himself out, and I relaxed a little when he did.

"I want to do this every day," Charles said, smiling at me from across the table.

"Me too," I said.

I took a sip of orange juice, taking in its tangy sweetness. I wished I could share some with Caroline and the others. I thought about tucking a croissant in my pocket for Georgia. She'd always wanted to try one.

"I was wondering," Charles said between bites of omelet. "What are you doing tonight?"

"I'm afraid I have to work," I said.

"Work?"

"Yes. It's a little thing one does to earn a living," I said sarcastically.

"Very funny," he said playfully. He looked at me for a long moment. "What if you didn't have to work again?"

"What do you mean?"

He placed his hand on mine. "What if—"

The hinge of the door squeaked. Someone was coming into

the suite. I felt like sinking my head deeper into the robe and hiding under the table, especially when I saw who it was: Charles's sister, Josie. A maid followed behind her, carrying a dozen shopping bags.

"Charles?" she said with arched eyebrows. "What are you doing here?"

"What are *you* doing here?" he countered. "I thought you were in Vancouver on a shopping trip with Mother."

"We came home yesterday," she said, walking toward us. "I was just picking up some things in town, and I thought I'd stop . . ." She paused the moment she recognized me. I could see the look of astonishment in her eyes.

"Josie, you remember Vera," Charles said, as if there was nothing awkward about reacquainting his sister with me, while I was clad in a *bathrobe*. "Vera Ray."

"Of course," she sneered, staring at me for a moment longer than was comfortable. In the morning light, I noticed a familiar quality I had missed at the dance marathon. Where had I seen her before? "Yes, Vera, from the dance hall."

"Hello," I managed. I wished I'd decided to dress before breakfast. The robe was a terrible mistake.

"*Well*," Josie huffed. "Clearly I'm interrupting an *intimate* moment, so I'll go." She eyed the envelope of cash on the side table, the one Charles had given me the night before for the widow in my building. *What must she think of that?* I prayed that Charles would explain, but he ignored his sister's shocked expression and continued eating.

"See you," he simply said. The maid followed with Josie's parcels. The door slammed behind them.

I spent eight more glorious weeks with Charles before the fairy tale came hurtling to an abrupt end. There were gifts—one night at dinner, he slid a sapphire bracelet around my wrist—flowers, trips, phone calls. It was enough to make my roommates green with envy.

Even so, I waited to tell him about the baby. I'd known about the pregnancy for almost two weeks, and I wanted to give it more time to be certain. I knew he'd be overjoyed. We were having a child together. A child conceived in love. And yet, I worried. Everything was perfect, and I feared the news could change that.

And then, one night in the hotel suite, he knelt down and asked me to marry him. I said yes, of course. He might as well have been a boy from the factories; I'd have married him anyway. I had fallen in love with his goodness, his heart, not his money. And when he gazed into my eyes, I almost told him about the baby right then and there, but the nausea had subsided, and I worried I'd miscarried. I couldn't bear to think of telling him I had lost his child. So I waited.

"It's about time you meet my family," he said. "Why don't you come for dinner at the house tonight?"

"I don't know," I said, feeling apprehensive about the previous interactions with Josie.

"They'll love you."

I scrunched my nose. "I'm not so sure."

"You're worried about Josie, aren't you?"

I nodded.

"Well, don't," he said. "You're the woman I love, and that's that."

I nestled my head into the fold of his shirt, breathing in the comforting scent of pipe tobacco and cologne.

"You make me so happy, Vera."

I couldn't help but smile. "I do?"

"You do. I love your strength." He traced my nose with his fingertip. "You're a force. You can look at me with those eyes and make me question everything I ever believed about the world." He placed his hand over my heart. "But, here, inside, you have so much love. It beams from you."

I grinned playfully. "You're sure your parents wouldn't rather you marry a society girl?"

"I can assure you, my love," he said, inching his face closer to mine, "I would rather banish myself to the farthest corner of Alaska than marry a society girl."

"All right," I conceded. "I'll meet your parents. But only if you really believe it's a good idea." I tucked my hand in his. He kissed my palm. "Have you told them yet? About our engagement?"

"Not yet," he said. "I think I'll surprise them tonight."

I fussed over what to wear for hours before Charles picked me up that night. Caroline's red dress seemed too tawdry for a dinner at the home of my future in-laws; besides, it fit too tightly. I wasn't far along, but Caroline and the other girls had made suspicious comments about the few pounds I'd gained. I eyed my old blue dress critically. *Much too drab.* I didn't want to pretend to be anyone I wasn't, and yet I needed them to accept me. It was a delicate dance. Eventually, I settled on the yellow frock Charles had purchased for me weeks ago. I'd worn it on many of our dates. I hoped he hadn't tired of it.

I retied the sash a dozen times in the car on the drive to his parents' home. No matter how hard I tried, I couldn't get the ribbon to hang properly.

"You look fine," Charles said, sensing my anxiety.

"I just want tonight to go well," I said, turning to him.

"It *will*," he assured me, wrapping a lock of my hair around his finger.

I pulled back. "Careful," I said. "You'll ruin my hair."

He disobediently sank his hands deeper into my scalp.

"You're incorrigible," I said.

I'd been so distracted by my dress, and my hair, and my worries that I hadn't paid attention to where we were, but we'd been driving for several miles, so we must have traveled a ways from downtown. Charles turned the car between two stone pillars—the entrance, according to a placard, to Windermere.

I'd heard of the privileged community, of course. Before her death, my mother had cared for the children of the wealthy inside this very neighborhood. And Georgia looked after the children of a wealthy family who lived within. She caught a ride on the milk truck every morning at five, which deposited her at the home just before the children woke. Her employer, a stern woman who slept until noon each day, complained that the truck soured Georgia's clothes. The woman made her change into a uniform in the servants' quarters before entering the main residence.

"So you grew up in this neighborhood?" I said, admiring the well-appointed homes, a mansion with a gabled roof to our right, a Victorian estate to our left. I wished Charles would slow the car so I could study each with greater attention. I'd never seen such elaborate dwellings.

"Born and raised, I'm afraid," he said, as though the revelation marred his record. I admired the carefully tended gardens on either side of the road, not a weed in sight. A row of azaleas, their blooms a symphony of crimson, begged to be noticed, but Charles kept his eyes on the road, oblivious to their beauty. "When I turned eighteen, I couldn't wait to fly the coop," he continued.

"Why?" I asked wistfully, intoxicated by the neighborhood's beauty.

"I guess I just came to despise it all," he said. "The way everyone pretends to be so perfect." He looked at me for a moment before turning back to the road. "I can assure you, what goes on inside those homes is far from perfect."

He didn't have to tell me that; I already knew. Mother had recounted a story of a disturbed little girl she cared for in this very neighborhood years ago. The child had taken a candlestick to her mother's dressing room curtains and burned them so badly, she almost set the whole house ablaze.

He turned onto a side street, where the houses appeared even more extravagant, then veered the car down a long driveway. At the very end was a gate, where a man in a black suit stood. "Good evening, Mr. Charles," he said, tipping his cap and swinging the gate open. Charles proceeded around the gravel-lined circular drive, parked the car, and got out to open my door.

"I want to introduce you to Old Joe," he said to me. "Joseph!" he shouted to the man at the gate. "Did you miss me?"

The older man with graying hair smiled heartily. "Welcome home, Mr. Charles," he said, reaching for a rake to resettle the disturbed gravel. I marveled at Charles's world—a foreign place where servants appeared around every corner, making sure every pebble in your wake was returned to its rightful place.

I looked up at the house—so beautiful, so perfect, it frightened me. "It looks like a . . . *palace*," I said under my breath, entranced by its grandeur.

"Mother saw a château in France she liked and Father had his architect reproduce it," he said, sounding a little embarrassed by the obvious opulence of his family's whims.

Twin cypress trees framed the entryway, nearly brushing up against the slate roof, where a massive chimney presided. I surveyed the handsome stonework that made up the residence's thick, commanding walls, crowned by intricate cornices. A pair of urns bracketed the front door. Each held emerald green boxwoods clipped and trimmed into perfect spirals.

"Charles!" A woman with outstretched arms approached from the front door. Her ivory dress swished as she walked. I immediately noticed her tiny waist, accentuated by a wide blue sash. Her upswept hair struck a regal note.

"Mother," Charles said, leaning in as she took both of his hands in hers before kissing each of his cheeks. I waited for her gaze to turn to me, and it did.

"Why, Charles," she said, "who is this?"

"This is Vera," he said, beaming with pride. "Vera Ray."

I held out my hand and prayed she wouldn't notice my chapped, red fingers, raw from the washbasin at the restaurant and nicked by one too many paring knives. "It's a pleasure to meet you, ma'am."

Her skin felt like cool white velvet against mine. I wished I'd taken the time to soak my hands in bacon drippings, the way Caroline had advised. Now I'd pay for it.

"You may call me Opal," she said, casting a glance at my shoes. The dress may have been couture, thanks to Charles, but the shoes were undeniably shabby. My forehead began to perspire. *Is the hole in my right shoe or my left?* I took a guess and wedged my right toe behind the heel of my left. I didn't dare look down at my feet, which would only draw more attention to the offending heels. To think I had saved almost three months' wages to put a pair of black leather pumps on layaway at Frederick and Nelson. Charles would buy them for me in an instant, of course. But I didn't ask him for things. It didn't feel right.

"I've been so looking forward to introducing Vera to the family," Charles said, kissing my hand lightly.

"How . . . charming," Opal said, her voice a few octaves higher on the word *charming*. Her smile quickly disappeared and her eyes narrowed. I felt clumsy in her gaze. "I believe you've already met Josephine."

I recalled the strained circumstances under which I had encountered Josie, Charles's sister. Twice. "Yes," I said, certain my cheeks had flushed to a cherry red.

"Well," Opal continued, "I'm glad you dropped in, son. Will you stay for dinner?"

"Yes, of course," Charles said. "Is Father here?"

"He's in his study," she said. "I'll have Greta ring him."

Ring him. I marveled at the way they regarded one another with such formality. *Can't she just dash down the hall to the study and call him up?*

We followed Opal inside. The instant Charles held out his outerwear, a housekeeper stepped forward to retrieve the garment as it fell from his fingertips.

"Greta will take your wrap, Ms. Ray," Opal said. She spoke to me slowly, as if to a child.

I nodded, letting the green shawl slip from my shoulders. I'd made it myself from scrap linen Caroline had brought home from the factory. At the time, I'd thought it rivaled any of the fine wraps I'd seen in shop windows. But inside Charles's family home, it seemed more suitable as a dust rag. I nervously handed it to the housekeeper, who looked at me curiously. "Thank you," I said, awed by the home's interior. We passed through a long hallway lined with oil paintings. Their subjects depicted a comfortable life, in which pampered terriers lounged on sofas, country houses nestled among rolling hills, and women socialized beneath parasols. The hallway wended toward a large room with a grand piano and windows overlooking an enormous lawn outstretched to a lake.

I sat down on a green velvet sofa next to Charles, unable to take my eyes off the breathtaking body of water, soft like the gray velvet wingback chairs in the lobby of the Olympic Hotel.

"You look as if you've never seen water before, Miss Ray."

"Well, it's the first time I've seen Lake Washington, ma'am," I said, before considering the implication.

Opal held a hand to her mouth. Laughter escaped. "Why, that's like saying you've never seen the moon."

"Mother," Charles said protectively, "Vera lives in the city."

"Why, of course, dear," Opal said quickly. She offered me a cup of tea, and when I lifted my arm to take it, my limbs felt leaden. *Why am I so stiff, so awkward in this place?*

Opal set her cup on the saucer and held up her index finger. "I know," she said. "You could take her out for a boat ride, Charles."

He looked skeptical. "I don't know, Mother. It's awfully windy today. It might not be the best time for—"

"Nonsense," Opal countered. "The young lady says she's never seen the lake. You *must* show it to her."

"But isn't it almost time for supper?"

"I'll tell the cook to hold off for a half hour," she said. "That should give you enough time to take her around."

Charles turned to me. "What do you think?"

The gray clouds overhead loomed, and the wind shook the tree branches outside the window with such force, I could only imagine what it would do to my hair. But not wanting to disappoint Opal, I obliged. "It sounds grand," I said, hiding my apprehension.

"It's settled, then," Charles said, standing up.

I followed him out to the back deck, and together we descended the stairs that led to the lawn. I had been too captivated by the lake to notice the spectacular sight below the house, a veritable zoo of animals clipped out of hedges. Rabbits. Dogs. A turtle. A mare and her foal. I stopped to admire a hedge carved into the unmistakable shape of an elephant.

"These are remarkable," I said, running my hand along the elephant's scratchy trunk. "The precision, it's uncanny."

"Joseph has a gift with boxwood," he said. "Father would rather have them all cut down. But Mother loves them. She spends a great deal of time out here. They bring her comfort."

I imagined Opal petting the boxwood giraffe to my right in her extravagant way. "I don't think your mother fancies me much," I said. A cool breeze rolled off the lake, and I wished I hadn't relinquished my shawl.

"Of course she *fancies* you," Charles said, pulling me toward him. "How could she not? You're lovely in every way. Just be yourself, and they'll see the woman I love so." He kissed my cheek lightly. "And she's going to love you even more when I announce our news tonight."

I stiffened. "Do you really think we should tell them tonight?"

Charles nodded. "I can't bear to keep it a secret any longer."

"But," I said, fumbling, "I worry they'll think it's so sudden. I mean, won't it be jarring to hear we're getting married moments after meeting me?"

Charles shrugged. "Vera, don't you see?" He pointed up toward the house. "That's my past, and you"—he tucked a lock of hair behind my ear—"are my future. Telling them is inconsequential. There's nothing to fear."

I exhaled. "All right," I conceded.

I followed him onto the dock, where two boats lay overturned. "Now," he said, examining both, "which one has the hole?"

My eyes widened. "Hole?"

"The last time I was here, Joseph mentioned that one needed repair." He ran his hand along the hull of one. "Aha, here it is. Found the hole."

"Good thing," I said. "I don't swim."

"I can swim for both of us," he said with a smile, kneeling down on the splintered, sun-bleached planks of the dock to untie the rope that secured the second small boat to a rusted cleat. When Opal had mentioned a boat ride, I had pictured something a little more substantial. The small craft hardly passed as a dinghy, not unlike the ones my father had taken me out in as a child on the Puget Sound. We'd capsized in one, and I'd almost drowned. I hadn't been in a boat since.

"There," he said, reaching for my hand.

"I don't know," I said, suddenly feeling unsure.

"Come on, don't be scared. You'll love being out on the lake. There's nothing more peaceful."

"All right," I said, taking his hand. He steadied me as I stepped inside and sat down with a thud on the wooden bench, narrowly missing a bird dropping. Charles sat down in front of me, tucking each oar into the appropriate slot.

"Now, don't you worry," he said, securing the oars into position. "I was a lifeguard at the club every summer during college."

He rowed out a few hundred feet. I watched in awe as the boat carved its way through the lake, slicing through the water like a knife through soft butter. A heron, startled by our presence, squawked in disapproval. It dragged its feet along the water, disrupting a colony of pale green lily pads before becoming airborne.

"It's beautiful out here," I said. "How lucky you were to grow up with *this* in your backyard."

"I'm not any happier for it," he said.

I shook my head. "What do you mean?"

"People think that wealth buys happiness," he replied, pointing back up toward the lawn. "Spend a night in that house, and you'll see otherwise."

I gave him a confused look.

"Mother is always in a mood," he explained. "Father locks himself in his study, and when he's not there he's at the hotel. And Josie is, well, Josie. She's always been troubled. When she was five, she nearly burned the house down."

My heart began to beat faster. *Could she have been the child my own mother took care of?* I sat up straighter. "What do you mean, she almost burned the house down?"

"I was in school then," he said, shaking his head as though the memory came with disturbing baggage. "Josie was cared for by a governess. One day when Mother was in town Josie managed to light the curtains on fire with a candlestick. She almost burned the house to ashes. Mother dismissed the woman on the spot, of course. But it wasn't her fault. Josie's always been devious like that."

"Oh," I said, reeling. *So my own mother took care of Josephine!* I shook my head, remembering the way Mother had complained about the little girl in Windermere. I'd grown to resent the girl who occupied my mother's time and attention, and when she'd lost her job with the family, I was glad, even though it meant we might not eat.

"What is it, Vera?" Charles asked, sensing my distant stare.

"Oh, it's nothing," I said, trying to purge the memories. *Does Josephine know who I am?*

"Anyway," he continued, "you can see why I wanted to spend as much time out here as possible. As a boy, I was always out on the lake, or following Joseph around. Father was much too busy with his business endeavors."

Charles pulled up the oars and we glided for a few moments. I held out my hand, letting it skim the water. A white lily tickled my palm and, on a whim, I lifted it a few inches from its watery home.

"Look," I said, indicating the stunning blossom.

"Careful," he said, gently tugging my hand back. "They're fragile, these lilies."

I smiled at him curiously. "You're the only man I've ever met who cares for flowers."

Charles shrugged. "I suppose it was Joseph's influence." He turned his eyes back to the lake. "Lilies are special. They haven't always been around these parts, you know. I found the first one right over there when I was a boy. Just one. Joseph showed me. Each year there were more. And now . . ." He waved his hand toward a point in the distance, where scores of white flowers the size of my hand bobbed on the water. "Well, just look at them."

"They're breathtaking," I said, grinning at the sight before us.

"They're picky about where they'll grow," he said. "Too much or too little sun and *pft*, they perish. They're shy, lilies. Shy and prideful."

I smiled.

"Delicate, too," he said. "They won't hold up if you pick them. Josie used to come out here with her friends and gather them by the armful, just for the heck of it. An hour later they'd shrivel on the dock." He paused, clearly disturbed by the memory. "I hated to see them die that way. For nothing."

I glanced back at the lake. The ripples on the water jostled the lilies up and down, like schoolchildren playing in the surf.

"They're happy out there," he said. "When you take them out of their home, they suffocate."

The wind had picked up, and it was whipping my hair into a matted mess. I replaced a fallen clip just as a raindrop hit my cheek. "Oh, no," I said, feeling another on my arm.

Charles reached for the oars. "We'd better get back."

By the time we reached the dock, the sky opened up and unleashed its fury, rendering any attempt I made to preserve my hair futile. Still, I tried, in vain, to reshape my limp curls. My waterlogged dress clung to my body. I tugged at the fabric self-consciously, hoping it didn't accentuate the increasing roundness of my stomach, even if I was the only one who could tell.

"Look at us," Charles said after tying the boat down. "A couple of drowned lake rats."

He took my hand and we ran together across the lawn toward the house. I hated to think of how I looked. A glance into the gold-rimmed mirror ahead confirmed my horror. Rouge streamed down my cheeks like pale pink watercolor. My hair hung, flattened, in soggy tufts.

"Oh, dear," Opal said. "Greta!" she barked. "Find Miss Ray some dry clothing in the guest quarters."

"Come with me, Miss Ray," the housekeeper said. I followed her down the hallway, conscious of every drip falling from my dress onto the hardwood floors, buffed to shining. We turned a corner and Greta opened a door on the west wing of the house. "There should be an extra dress in here," she said. "The family has frequent weekend visitors. They keep the wardrobe well stocked."

It seemed odd to think of people coming to stay without packing bags, but perhaps this wasn't a concern for the well-to-do. Wherever they landed, things were simply provided.

Greta held out a cream-colored dress with a low neckline. "This looks to be your size," she said, holding it up to me. "I hope it fits."

I would have wished for a more elegant garment. The dress looked lumpy and large at the waist. I worried how I'd appear when I met Charles's father. Greta peeled my wet clothes from my body. I avoided her eyes when she unfastened my corset, torn under the left arm and dingy from being washed so many times in salvaged wash water. Laundry soap was a luxury my roommates and I could not do without, but we pooled our resources and stretched every ounce. *She dresses the ladies of the house in their French silk lingerie, so what will she think of me, wearing such rags?*

Whatever her thoughts, however, she kept them private, dutifully handing me a fluffy white towel. I wrapped it around my body. Its thick, soft fibers blunted the chill in the air, halting my shivers. Greta produced a set of spare undergarments from the nearby dresser. "I'll hang these"—she ducked to pick up the pile of soggy rags—"out to dry. That is, if you do want to keep them?"

I nodded meekly, embarrassed by the exchange. She stepped out to the balcony, and I sat down on the bed. *What a strange world Charles comes from.* I felt like the lilies on the lake—out of my element, frightened, gasping for breath in these new surroundings.

Greta returned and helped me slip into the corset, a size too small; it squeezed my breasts together uncomfortably. I worried I looked like one of the call girls who frequented the saloons on Fifth.

"Are you sure there isn't another corset in the drawer?"

Greta shook her head. "It's the only one."

I stepped into the dress, and after she fastened the buttons, I took a long look at myself in the full-length mirror near the bed. My breasts bulged out of the low-cut bodice. The fabric didn't taper down like the yellow dress I'd arrived in. Instead it hung from me like a paper sack. *How can I go out there looking like this?*

Greta didn't seem to sense my concern, and if she did, she didn't let on. "Here," she said, handing me a hairbrush and a washcloth in her practiced way.

"Thank you," I said, running the brush through my tangled locks, setting the clip in place as best as I could. I took another look at myself and sighed.

Greta's eyes met mine, and for the first time, I detected a glimmer of compassion. "Don't be ashamed of where you come from, Miss Ray," she said softly.

I nodded. I knew exactly what she meant, and her words warmed me.

"Now," she said, "shall I take you back?"

I wanted to scream, *No, don't make me go back in there! I can't face them looking like this!* But I nodded, held my head up high, and followed her out the door. In the hallway, when I thought no one was looking, I tried in vain to pull the dress higher on my chest.

"There you are!" Charles called from behind the piano. "Come sing along with us." Josie sat beside him, mouth gaping as I approached. Whatever she knew or didn't know about me, I decided not to care. Instead, I remembered what Greta had said and held my composure.

"Hello, Josie," I said as sweetly as I could muster. She wore a mauve dress with a fashionable drop waist. Diamond earrings dangled from her lobes.

"Hello," she said icily. "Charles and I were just singing the song of our alma mater. Would you like to join us? On second thought, perhaps we should sing yours. Where did you go to high school?"

I looked at my feet as they stared at me expectantly. "I, I . . ."

I felt Charles's comforting hand on the small of my back.

"I didn't attend," I said meekly. Greta's words rang in my ears. *Don't be ashamed of where you come from.* "I had to drop out to go to work. My father died, and Mother passed shortly after."

Josie feigned concern. "Oh, you lost *both* your parents?"

"Enough music for now," Charles said, salvaging the moment. "I'm starved."

"Your father will be here in a few minutes, darlings," Opal crooned, looking at me with an amused expression. She took a final swig from her goblet, stopping at the bar to fill it again. I watched as an amber-colored liquid flowed from a crystal decanter. "Let's make our way to the dining room."

The table, clad in white linen, gleamed with polished silver and crystal. I sat down in a chair next to Charles. He squeezed my leg under the table. "I'm glad you're here," he whispered.

I patted my hair, still damp from the boat trip, as Charles's father walked into the room. "Opal!" he barked. "I don't know why you insist on taking dinner at seven thirty every night when the rest of the world dines at six." I stared straight ahead, trying to remain inconspicuous, as someone hovered behind me, ladling soup in a shade of mint green into my bowl.

"William, this is Charles's friend Miss Ray," Opal said, gesturing to me.

Charles's father sat in a chair at the head of the table and tucked a napkin into his collar. "You didn't say you were bringing a dinner guest, son," he said. But when he turned to face me, he smiled. "And such a pretty one."

"You're too kind," I said, feeling the urge to cover my chest with the napkin on my lap.

"I've been wanting you to meet her for a while now," Charles said, reaching for my hand. "I—"

"Mother," Josie said, interrupting, "do you think the cook put a bit too much salt in the soup?"

Opal nodded. "I ought to fire her. Everything that comes out of that kitchen tastes like brine."

"Oh, Mother," Charles said. "It's not that bad. I rather like it. And besides, isn't Mrs. Meriwether the breadwinner for her family? I believe Joseph said she's a widow."

William cleared his throat. "You've taken a liking to widows these days, my boy," he said, turning to Opal. "Just last week he suggested that I offer free room and board to a woman from the city and her five children."

I remembered Laura from my building and gave Charles a knowing look.

"Next, you'll be asking me for tuition money for her children to attend Yale."

Josie laughed.

"Your brother has a heart of gold," he continued. "If he had his way, he'd give a handout to every commoner in this city."

William turned his gaze to me again. "Miss Ray," he said, "I don't recognize your name. Who are your parents?"

Josie glared at me, but I refused to make eye contact with her.

"They're both deceased, sir," I said.

"I'm sorry to hear that," William replied.

Opal snapped her fingers and a young woman in a white dress

and black apron scurried from the kitchen. She held her head low as Charles's mother instructed her to clear the plates. "Yes, ma'am," she said quickly.

She piled the soup bowls onto her tray, and stopped suddenly when our eyes met across the table. "Vera?"

It took a moment before I recognized her in the maid's uniform, but the familiar face of a childhood friend shone through.

"Sylvie," I said self-consciously, immediately wondering what Charles's family would think of the exchange.

"What are you doing here?" she said.

"I'm . . ." I felt all eyes in the room burrowing into me. My cheeks burned.

"She's here with me," Charles said, filling the awkward silence.

"Well, would you look at that," Josie sneered. "Two friends reunited. Vera, tell us, is she a friend from the dance hall?"

Charles's parents stared at me disapprovingly as I set my napkin on my plate and stood up. *How could I ever think I'd fit into this world?*

Tears blurred my vision. No, I would not let them see me cry. I lifted the hem of my skirt and ran, down the hallway and out to the foyer, where I let myself out the front door. I sat down on a stone bench on the porch, contemplating my next move. Moments later, I heard the creak of the hinge behind me. Expecting to see Charles, I turned, and was disheartened to find Josie standing beside me with a satisfied smile.

"He's in there explaining to my parents that he's proposed to you," she said, shaking her head at what she obviously believed was a laughable idea. "You should see Mother. She's devastated." She looked back to the house and smirked. "I know who you are, Vera Ray," she continued. "I knew your mother, too. I assume you're a thief like her. Like mother, like daughter, right?"

I shook my head. "I don't know what you mean."

"So your mother didn't tell you about all the things she stole from our family? The jewelry? The coins from father's study?"

"Josie," I stammered, "you—you must be mistaken. My mother would never—"

"I watched her take a diamond bracelet from Mother's jewelry box," she said.

"I don't believe it!" I cried. "How dare you speak of my mother that way? She was a good woman. She did her best to take care of you, Josie. But you tormented her."

Her icy stare frightened me. "I know your angle," she said. "Just like your mother, you see my family as your meal ticket."

I shook my head, wiping a tear from my cheek. "You have it all wrong."

"Well," she said, "if you expect me to stand back while my brother is duped by a common whore, then, my dear, you're mistaken."

The words stung. "A common . . . ?"

I couldn't let the vulgar word cross my lips. "What makes you think that I . . . ?" Then I remembered the envelope in the suite. The money Charles had set aside for the poor widow. Josie had seen it. She'd thought it was for *me*.

"No, no," I continued. "You have it all wrong. That money was for—"

Josie shook her head. "And now you're having his child."

I placed my hand on my belly.

"How long did you think you were going to keep *that* a secret?"

I gasped. *How does she know?* I hadn't told anyone. Not even Charles.

"You didn't have to tell me," she said. "It's obvious."

"But I—"

"How much?" she said.

I searched her face. "I don't understand."

"How much do I have to pay you to get out of our lives, to get out of Charles's life?"

I shook my head. "Why would you do this?"

"Because he can't be permitted to end up with a woman like you," she said. "It would destroy Mother. And Father would write him out of"—she gestured to the house and gardens—"all of this. Do you think he would love you then? Well, Miss Ray, I know my brother better than you, and I can tell you the answer is no."

I loved him with every inch of my heart, but would my love be enough to make him happy, without . . . the privileged life he was accustomed to?

I knew it then. I couldn't fit into Charles's world any more than he could fit into mine.

"So how much do I need to give you?" she asked again. "How much to get you out of here?"

I held up my hand. "Nothing," I said, rising to my feet. "I understand."

I walked up the gravel path and to the road. Charles's voice rang out in the distance, calling to me like a lighthouse to a lost ship, and yet I kept walking. The charade had to end. Josie may have been cruel, but she was right. It would never work, Charles and me.

"Vera!" he shouted, catching up to me. I felt his hand on my shoulder. "Please wait. I'm so sorry about the way they treated you in there. Let's go. Let's leave together."

I blinked back tears. "I can't, Charles," I said. "This is what I have feared all along, but today, it just confirmed everything for me. I love you. So much. But I can't marry you."

I hated to see my words wound him so deeply.

"Why not?"

"Don't you see?" I ran my hand along his face. "We could never make it work. We're from two different worlds."

"But that doesn't matter," he pleaded. "It doesn't have to."

"But it does," I said. "I'm sorry, Charles. I'm not the woman for you." He would have given up everything for me, but I loved him enough that I wouldn't let him do it.

He stood dumfounded as I ran past the clipped boxwood hedge, pushing open the iron gate. I walked along the road, unsure of how I'd get home, miles away from the city. When I heard the sound of Charles's car approaching and his voice calling my name out the window, I ducked behind a tree. "Vera!" he screamed. "Vera!" His desperate tone broke my heart. I wanted to shout, *Here I am, Charles! Let's run away together. Let's start a new life on our own terms.* But in my heart, I knew that Josie was right. I crouched lower until the Buick was out of sight.

On the main road, cars barreled past, splashing mud onto my dress. *What does it matter?* I held out my hand, trying unsuccessfully to flag down a car, and then another. Finally, a truck pulled over. White, with a rusted hood and piles of tile stacked in the back. A man waved to me from the front seat. "Where to, miss?" He spoke in a thick foreign accent that reminded me of the Russian families who lived in my building.

"I'm trying to get back to the city," I said, wiping away a tear. "Can you take me?"

"That's where I'm headed," he said.

I climbed inside the truck and closed the heavy door with all my might. It smelled of must and gasoline. As he revved the engine and turned in to traffic, I cast a backward glance on the entrance to Windermere.

"The name's Ivanoff," the man said, casting a sideways glance at me. "Sven Ivanoff."

Chapter 16

CLAIRE

I stuffed a piece of pizza in my mouth, then washed it down with a sip of red wine. "He called," I said to Abby. We both sat on the floor in front of the TV in my apartment, pizza box open on the coffee table, wine bottle at the ready.

"Wait," she said. "Which one?"

"Ethan."

"And?"

"He left two voice mails. The first: 'Claire, I stayed at my parents' suite at the hotel last night after the party. Had too many drinks. You understand.'"

"Oh, honey," she said. "That doesn't sound good."

I frowned. "It gets worse. The second, which I just got an hour ago, went like this: 'Claire, I'm heading to Portland tonight for a conference. Will be back on Sunday.'"

Abby shook her head. "What conference?"

"That's the thing," I said. "I did some searching, and take a wild guess."

"No," Abby said. "Don't tell me he went with—"

"Cassandra? You guessed it. Well, I'm not one hundred percent certain, but the only conference that I could find in Portland is a food writers' convention. So, you do the math."

"That doesn't bode well," Abby said, taking a sip of wine. "*If* it's true."

I shrugged. "After seeing them together last night, I have no doubt it is."

I set my foot on the lower ledge of the coffee table and a stack of photo albums toppled over onto the rug. One flipped open, spreading its pages out as if to taunt me. I picked it up and leaned over the page. There we were, Ethan and I on our wedding day, I in my strapless white gown. Ethan's mother had made a fuss about strapless being inappropriate in a Catholic church, but Ethan had put a stop to it. He'd been on my team. I longed for those days. I longed for him. I ran my hand along the photo, letting my finger rest on his cheek. I'd tucked a photo of my grandparents on their wedding day next to ours when I put the album together. The black-and-white print had faded over the years. I'd looked at it hundreds of times as a girl, memorizing the look of love on both of their faces. True love. But not until that moment did I notice a piece of paper in my grandmother's hands. I squinted, trying to make out the words.

"Abby, look at this," I said, pointing to the photo. "Can you tell what that says?"

She reached for her glasses on the table and took the album in her hands. "Well," she said, "I think it says, 'Sonnet 43.'"

"What does that mean?"

"A little rusty on our English lit, are we?" she said in a mocking voice.

I rolled my eyes. "Well, while you were reciting poetry, I was hunched over the copy desk, line-editing the newspaper. There wasn't time for *fluff*." Abby had been an English literature major, while I had taken the journalism track. It was a long-running feud.

"All right, all right," she said. "But do you want to know what this is or not?"

"Fill me in, Shakespeare."

Abby smirked. "It's Elizabeth Barrett Browning, silly. You know, the famous poem, 'How Do I Love Thee? Let Me Count the Ways.'"

"Oh," I said, remembering it in an instant. "I do know that one."

"Of course you do," she continued. "It's only the most important love poem in the history of love poems." She pulled up the verse on her phone and read out the lines.

I leaned back against the couch, keeping my wineglass close at hand. "How romantic," I said, glancing at the photo again. "I bet she read it to him at their reception."

Abby nodded. "You can see the words echoing in his ears. Look at his face. He cherishes her."

"He did," I said. "It's all Mom talked about growing up, which is why she's had two failed marriages, I think. She could never find her prince charming the way Grandma did." I sighed, closing the album.

Abby leaned her head against my shoulder. "What are you thinking about?"

"I'm afraid of failing, Abs. I'm afraid that our marriage was put to the test, and it wilted under pressure."

Abby opened up the album again, pointing to the black-and-white photo. "I don't care how perfect you say their marriage was; I'm sure they had their own problems."

I gave her a doubtful look.

"Listen, I know you, Claire, and I know you love Ethan deeply. So why not fight for him? Cassandra has her hooks in him, but only because you stepped aside."

I took a bite of pizza crust and then tossed it back into the box, thinking of the fine food she and Ethan were probably enjoying at the conference. "So what do you think I should do? Drive down there?"

"No, but for starters, you could return his call," she said. "He's called you, what, twice now and left messages?"

"Yeah."

Abby grinned. "Call him."

I picked up my cell phone and scrolled to his number. The connection went through, and my heart beat the way it would when calling someone after a first date. After the third ring, however, I let out a disappointed sigh.

"Voice mail," I mouthed to Abby.

"Leave him a message," she whispered.

I shook my head.

"Do it!"

"Uh, Ethan, this is Claire. I got your messages. Listen, when you get back from the, um, conference, can we talk? I miss you." I paused, and Abby poked me in the thigh. "And *I love you*."

"There," I said. "I sounded like a total idiot. Are you happy?"

"Good girl," she said, refilling my wineglass.

A moment later my cell phone buzzed. The vibration startled me and I spilled wine on the coffee table as I reached for the phone. Abby sopped up the mess with a stack of napkins by the pizza box. I looked at the screen. "Abby, it's him."

The phone buzzed again. "Well, aren't you going to answer it?"

I took a deep breath and picked up, holding the phone to my ear. "Hi Ethan." I couldn't wait to hear his voice, to hear him tell me how much he missed me, that the message I'd left had touched him. After all, I couldn't remember the last time I'd uttered the words *I love you.*

But instead of his voice on the line, I heard only commotion, a distant jostling sound. I detected the jingle of car keys, then a door slamming. "Ethan?" I said. "Can you hear me?" I turned to Abby dejectedly. "I think it's a pocket call." I continued to listen until I thought I heard the muffled sound of a female voice.

I hung up.

"What happened? What did he say?"

I wiped a tear from my cheek, before pushing the photo album away with my foot. "I think he's with *her.*"

"How do you know?" Abby said.

I folded my arms, staring ahead, crestfallen. "There was a woman in the background."

"Claire, it could have been anyone. Maybe it was a waitress at a restaurant."

I shook my head. "No. It was her. I know it was."

Abby held out her hand. "Not yet," she said. "Don't mourn the marriage yet. Don't write the obituary. Wait until he's back from Portland. Talk to him. Then make your decision."

I shrugged.

"For now, we'll have pizza and wine." She reached for the remote control. "And Lifetime Original Movies."

I sighed, never more grateful for my friend than at that moment.

Before my trip to see Lillian Sharpe in Windermere on Sunday morning, I stopped at the assisted living facility where Ethan's grandfather was recovering. After the terse exchange with Glenda at the hospital, boundary lines had been drawn, and it was clear I was to leave Warren well enough alone. But he'd called me over the weekend. He missed me. For Warren, I decided to break the rules.

"How are you?" he said as I entered. He motioned me toward the bed. The room resembled a hospital with a few extra furnishings—a sofa, a mini-refrigerator, and a dresser and closet.

"I've been better," I said. "I'm researching a story that's turning out to be quite a goose chase."

"Oh?"

Before I could give him the details, my phone rang. I pulled it from my bag. "Ethan," I said to Warren, dismissing the call and tossing the phone back into my purse.

"I've been worried about you two," he said. "Marriage trouble?"

I sighed. "Yes, I'm afraid so."

"Let me tell you about my wife," he said, smiling up at a spot on the wall, as if he could see his beloved there gazing back at him. "Annie was a lot like you. Spirited. Driven. A bit of a temper."

I grinned. "I would have liked her."

"You would have *loved* her, Claire. She was passionate about life, just as she was passionate about me."

The phone rang beside his bed. "Now, who would that be?" he said, giving the phone a puzzled look. He picked up. "Hello?" He paused for a long moment, his eyes showing signs of disappointment. "I can't believe you didn't find it. . . . You thought this was it. . . . All right. . . . No, now is not the time for . . . I'll call you later."

I occupied myself with a magazine on the side table, wondering what Warren was talking about.

He turned back to me. "I'm sorry about that. Now, where were we?"

"Your wife," I said.

"Ah, yes, my wife."

I patted his arm. "I bet you miss her so much."

"I do," he said. "Losing your true love is like losing your right hand. It feels just like that. Everything takes more effort. Everything feels different when she's gone."

"I've never thought about it that way."

He nodded. "I want to tell you something." He clasped his hands together. "A few years after she and I were married, we separated."

I shook my head in disbelief. "What happened?"

"She left me," he said. "I didn't have an affair, mind you, but I did have an inappropriate friendship with a woman. A secretary at the office."

I raised my eyebrows. "Inappropriate?"

"I was dumb as a doornail. Thirty-year-old men are, you know."

I nodded in agreement.

"It started out innocently enough," he continued. "I'd stay late at work. We'd flirt. Then we started having drinks together after hours. I was playing with fire. Well, Annie found out, and you can believe she was livid. She packed her bags and moved back home with her mother.

"So you think I should move out?"

"No," he said. "I'm just saying that when I lost Annie for that short period of time, I realized how precious she was to me. I never forgot that lesson. We both loved each other more for that early blip in our marriage. Annie came to appreciate it, actually."

"I wish I could imagine that happy ending," I said. "Ethan seems to have a different outcome in mind."

A nurse came in and gestured to the clock. "Sorry to interrupt, Mr. Kensington, but it's time for your physical therapy."

He nodded and held up his finger. "Just a minute." Then to me he said, "Call him back. Give him one more chance to prove himself. Think of me and Annie."

I hugged him. "You're right. Thanks, Warren."

The nurse helped him out of his bed. "You know, they're wasting their time on me," he said playfully. "I'm an old geezer."

"An old geezer who needs his physical therapy," the nurse sparred back.

Warren winked at me. "We didn't get a chance to talk about your article," he said.

"Glenda will be glad," I replied. "She forbade me from bothering you with any of my—what did she call it?—oh yes, 'drama.'"

"To hell with Glenda," he said without mincing words. He loved his daughter-in-law, I knew that, but not her meddling ways. "Come back and tell me about your story as soon as you can."

I nodded. "I will."

"Now, call that husband of yours," he said as the nurse led him out the door. "Promise?"

"Promise."

The cab dropped me off in front of Lillian Sharpe's home in Windermere, the kind of neighborhood my parents might have driven through on Sundays when I was a kid, daydreaming about a better life. I looked up at the enormous home. Lillian had been right; it had the look of a place that hadn't seen visitors in a very long time. The paint peeled. The moss-covered shingles on the roof looked weary. And while the grass had been mowed and the beds weeded, the garden didn't appear to be loved the way the neighboring yards did. I stared at the empty driveway and looked at my watch. Five minutes early. I sat on the stoop, waiting for Lillian to arrive. My heart fluttered thinking about how I might be one step closer to understanding why Daniel Ray had disappeared.

Moments later, a gray Volvo sedan barreled into the driveway; a woman with bobbed white hair sat behind the wheel. She stepped out of the car and greeted me with a warm smile. "You must be Claire."

"Yes," I said, walking toward her with an outstretched hand. "Thank you so much for meeting me here. I hope it wasn't an inconvenience."

"Not at all, dear," she said, staring up at the old house, then exhaling deeply. "My, I have missed this place."

"You raised your family here?"

"I did," she said. "Two sons."

"When did you and your husband move out?"

She paused for a moment. "My first husband died," she said. "Some time ago. I remarried last year." She sighed, looking up at the house. "I haven't been able to bring him here. Of course, I want to share it with him, as I want to share everything with him, but I worry that I may need to keep this place to myself." She shook her head. "Too many memories."

"I can understand that," I said.

"Well," Lillian said, "listen to me blabbering. You've come to look for information, and I'd like to help you find it. My father had the most interesting career. He was a partner in the largest law firm in Seattle—Sharpe, Sanford, and O'Keefe—but he always had time for the little guy. He took on cases even when he knew he wouldn't get paid for them. He was a good man." She walked to the front door of the house, inserting a key into the lock. "Here we are, home sweet home." Her voice echoed against the lonely walls.

I followed her inside, brushing a cobweb from the doorway. The hardwood floors creaked beneath my feet. Everywhere furniture was covered in white fabric. "It must have been a wonderful home to raise a family in," I said, imagining the sound of little boys' laughter in the air.

"Yes," Lillian said, reminiscing. "We had so much happiness here." She pointed to a hallway ahead. "My father's records are down this way. He was fastidious about his files. Kept copies of every document relating to each case he ever took on. Few attorneys bothered with such documentation back then, but my father cared about details. Besides, there had been too many strange incidents with the police department. Corruption, Father believed." She nodded. "He always kept records in case anyone tried to falsify a document."

She stopped in front of a room at the east end of the house. I watched as she began to turn the door handle, pushing against it with her frail arm, but it stuck. "That's strange," she said. "It's almost as if something's blocking the opening."

"Let me try." I reached for the handle and gave the door a solid shove. Whatever lay behind it was heavy, but I pushed hard until the offending object budged, opening up enough space for Lillian and me to squeeze through.

Lillian gasped. "My God. What's happened in here?"

Glass lay on the floor in jagged shards. "Be careful," I said, pointing to a sharp piece right in front of her feet. A window had been broken; it didn't have the look of an accident. On the floor lay dozens of overturned boxes, spilling out reams of paperwork and files.

Lillian raised her hand to her mouth. "Who would do this?"

I held out my arm to steady her. "Someone who wanted information your father had."

She shook her head in disbelief. "All these years, the house has never been tampered with, not once, and now this?"

I knelt down, pushing some of the papers, ankle deep, aside. I picked up a page, holding it up to Lillian. "The State vs. Edward Ainsburg." I sighed. "Talk about looking for a needle in a haystack."

I attempted to sort through the paperwork before rising to my feet again. "Whoever was here was looking for something. Maybe they didn't find it." I turned to Lillian. "Any chance that he kept his files elsewhere in the house?"

"No," she said, visibly startled by the disarray, the intrusion.

I knelt back down. "All right, it's at least worth a try. Maybe I'll get lucky."

Lillian paused. "Wait. . . . Yes, there is one place we might look. How could I forget? Come with me."

We walked up a set of stairs to a room filled with books. I marveled at the old leather-bound volumes that clung to the high shelves. If I lived in the home, I'd spend most of my time there, I decided.

"It's Father's old library," she said, smiling. "After he passed, when Bill, my first husband, and I moved here, we kept this room exactly as it was. I wouldn't let him remove a single book." She closed her eyes. "I didn't want to lose a single piece of him." She ran her hand along the bookcase, reading every groove, every notch with her fingertips.

I took a step closer. "What are you looking for?"

Lost in thought, she didn't answer. But a moment later, one of the shelves shifted. "Found it!" she cried.

I watched with anticipation as the shelf pushed inward, revealing a space behind the wall.

"It's where he kept the family's valuables," she said. "Funny, I'd almost forgotten about this place. Come in and have a look with me."

I crouched down and followed her inside the space, about the size of a typical bedroom closet. A sweet, musty scent lingered. Lillian pointed to a square shadow high on the shelf. "His cigars," she said, taking the box down and holding it to her nose.

I turned back to the doorway, feeling the urge to wedge it open. I didn't want to take the chance of being locked behind a wall. And if someone had broken into the home, what if they returned? What if they—

"It must feel a little spooky in here," Lillian said.

"Well," I replied, "a little."

"I spent hours in this little room as a girl," she said. "Father let my friend Martha and me play dolls in here while he worked. He'd light a little kerosene lantern for us. We had the most fun."

My heart beat faster as I scanned the dim space, wishing for more light than the tiny stream from the room behind us provided. It didn't take long for defeat to set in. The space had obviously been cleaned out at some point. What remained—a framed photo of a woman, a pair of faded opera tickets, a child's wooden train—was merely memorabilia from long ago.

"I'm sorry," Lillian said. "I had hoped you might find something of importance in here." She turned to the doorway, just as something caught my eye.

"Wait," I said. Shrouded in shadows, the outlines of a dark, rectangular shape came into focus. I knelt down and reached my arm out until my fingers touched what felt like leather. I detected a clasp and a handle. "Could this be an old briefcase?"

Lillian squinted to make out the shape. "Why, yes," she said. "Father took it to work every day."

I followed her back out to the library, opening the case with eager hands. Inside, a bundle of twine-bound papers waited, as neatly stacked as the day they'd been tucked inside. I tugged on the knot, but it didn't loosen, so I attempted to pry it off from the sides, leaving a fresh paper cut on my index finger. "Ouch," I said, shaking my hand.

I tried again, this time more carefully, and succeeded. Lillian leaned over me as I fanned the stack of pages, at least two inches thick. I shook my head in astonishment when I read the words on the first page: "Deposition of Sven W. Ivanoff."

"My God," I said, gasping. "We've found it."

Lillian sat down on an upholstered bench near the door. It was a lot of excitement for someone of her age, and I worried about her.

"They're the files you were looking for?"

"Yes," I said. I skimmed the first page, nodding. "It seems your father may have represented the suspect in the murder case of Vera Ray, the mother of the little boy who went missing in 1933."

Lillian's face looked ashen. "I can't believe this," she said. "I'm trying to make sense of why he decided to hide them away here."

I shook my head. "I think there's more to this story than everyone believed, and perhaps your father knew that. Maybe he wanted to prove it." I looked at her. "Do you remember your father talking about any case more than another?

"No," she said. "He suffered from dementia. It came early, in his sixties. We lost many good years with him, sadly. There might have been cases he intended to work on, but never got to. I'm not certain. But he wouldn't have put something in the space behind the wall unless it held great importance to him."

My grandfather had also had dementia. Grandma had started to notice when he kept putting cereal boxes in the refrigerator. Maybe Lillian's father had simply tucked the files away for no apparent reason, or maybe he had known his mind was ailing and was attempting to preserve them before someone else destroyed the truth. The air in the room felt thick, eerily so. I tucked the loose pages back inside the briefcase and stood up. "Do you mind if I take these with me and go through them at the office? I'll return them to you, of course. And I promise to keep them safe."

"Yes, dear," she said. "If you feel you can bring the truth to light, keep them. My father would be glad to know they're in good hands."

We walked out to the stairway, and I looked over my shoulder, feeling the urge to run, to leave the home as quickly as my feet could carry me, but I kept my pace slow and steady.

When we made our way back outside, where the birds chirped and the sun shone down on my face, I breathed a sigh of relief.

"Can I drive you back, honey?" Lillian asked, walking to the car.

"That would be wonderful, thank you," I said, opening the passenger door of the Volvo. I turned to look at the house a final time, eyeing the upper bedrooms cautiously. *Are we being watched?* Silly, I told myself. As Lillian pulled the car out of the driveway, I clasped the briefcase tighter in my arms, knowing I was in possession of something very important. It was up to me to find out why.

Just as I sat down at my desk back at the office, my phone rang. I picked it up, annoyed. I didn't want to do anything but immerse myself in the contents of the briefcase.

"Claire?" Ethan's voice sounded far away. A world away. "Honey." My heart softened, but I remained silent.

"I tried you at home. I didn't think I'd find you in the office on a Sunday. I miss you."

He got my voice message. "I'm working on a story. I miss you too," I said, caving, willing away the jealousy, the anger that had taken up residence in my heart. I wanted to ask him what he was doing in Portland, and whether Cassandra was part of the equation, but I bit my tongue.

"I spent all day yesterday interviewing candidates for the Journalists' Guild Scholarship," he said. "It was grueling."

"Oh," I said, feeling relieved. "I thought you were—"

"I'm coming home on the train tonight. I'd love it if we could have dinner."

My eyes brightened. "You would?"

"Yes," he continued. "That is, if you want to."

"I do."

"Seven o'clock, the Pink Door?"

"Yes," I said. "I'll be waiting."

I hung up the phone and redirected my attention to the briefcase. Lillian's father had carried it with him every day of his working life, no doubt. It felt a little like looking inside an old doctor's bag. You couldn't pull out the stethoscope without thinking of the physician who had held it up to hearts hundreds of times over. Yes, I could feel Lillian's father's presence. Secrets waited inside this case, and I think he wanted me to find them.

Chapter 17

VERA

Lon slept till noon. I watched the clock tick above his head, praying he'd wake soon so he could make the calls he'd promised to make on Daniel's behalf. People listened to Lon. He was a powerful man.

I sat up straight in my chair as he opened his eyes. He held his hand out to me, gesturing for me to come toward him. The hand that had ravaged me last night. I felt my stomach turn.

"Come here, dollface," he said, rubbing his eyes. "Come lay down beside me."

"Lon," I said as sweetly as I could, "you promised that you'd help me find my son. I've been very patient."

"Sure, beautiful," he said, yawning. "But I don't get out of bed without breakfast, and"—he winked at me—"a woman."

I shook my head. "No," I said firmly, "you promised."

Lon sat up. His eyes switched from playful to angry. "Who do you think you are, giving me orders like that?"

My hands began to shake. "I, I—"

"Do you think for a moment that I care about your damn son?"

he said, laughing sinisterly. "For God's sake, how can you even think he's still alive? It's been days." He reached for the half-empty bottle of champagne on the bedside table and took a swig.

I felt as if I had stepped out of my body and was watching the scene unfold in the suite as an outsider. Lon's lips moved, laughing, mocking me. I sat there, frozen, frightened, for the first time feeling complete and utter hopelessness.

Lon stepped out of bed. I averted my eyes from his naked body. "Now, if you know what's best for you, dollface," he said, taking a step toward me, "you'll give up on this nonsense about finding your son and come to bed with me." *My God. I have to get out of here.*

I eyed the door. If I was quick, I could run. I could get there before he got to me. He wouldn't chase me down the hallway without clothes on. I could escape.

"Dollface," he said again, fingering the trim of my dress.

I pulled away from him, and the force tore the fabric. A flap hung down at my side, revealing my corset underneath. "Don't you call me dollface!" I screamed, running toward the door.

I felt his anger behind me, burning hot like a dry oak log in the fireplace, stoked and crackling. *I have to get out of here.* I tripped on the rug and lost my shoe. With no time to retrieve it, I reached for the doorknob and flung the door open, running into the hallway with such speed, I surprised myself.

"Don't walk out on me, you whore!" he shouted. "Come back here right now!"

His voice echoed in the hallway. *Is he chasing me?* I didn't turn around to look. *Keep running.* I knew the hotel well, every crevice, every mouse hole. Just ahead was a maid's closet. *He'll never look for me there.* I opened the little door near the Rainier Suite and stuffed myself inside. Lon's voice had quieted. There was just silence and the sound of my heart pounding in my chest. A bead of sweat fell from my forehead and trickled down my cheek. Then I heard footsteps outside. I held my breath. A moment later, the doorknob turned. I clutched a mop. If he came near me, I'd strike him.

The door opened with a squeak. There, peering inside, stood Gwen. "My God," she said with a gasp. "You nearly gave me a heart attack, Vera."

Never in my life had I been so grateful to see the face of a friend. Once I started to cry, I couldn't stop.

"Oh, honey, let's get you out of here," she whispered.

Gwen unlocked the Rainier Suite just ahead, and we hurried inside. "Vera," she said, surveying my torn dress, much fancier than the ones I used to wear, and tear-stained cheeks, "what happened to you?"

"I made a terrible mistake coming here," I said, "with him."

"You mean Lon?"

I bit my lip. "You know?"

She nodded, handing me a freshly pressed white handkerchief from a silver tray by the bed. "You know how the maids talk."

I blew my nose. "I can't imagine what you must think of me, Gwen."

"I think you're a good mother, that's what," she said before pursing her lips. "And I think the hotel ought to throw that monster out for treating women the way he does."

I took a deep breath. "He promised to help me find Daniel. And I believed him."

"The man's a rat," she said. "After what he did to Susie, sending her away like that when she was to have his child. Just despicable."

I nodded. "I knew better. My mind was clouded by the hope of finding Daniel."

"Oh, honey, do not blame yourself. Not for a single minute. You did what you had to."

I sighed in defeat. "But I failed."

Gwen shook her head. "I won't let you talk that way. You did what you had to do," she repeated emphatically.

I sat down on the big, fluffy bed, laying my head against the headboard. "Look at me," I said, "dirtying this room, creating more work for you."

"You certainly are not," she countered. "Besides, the room's vacant tonight. And Estella's off today. So stay as long as you want. I'll have Bruce bring you a tray of food. You're skin and bones."

I looked down at my arms, pale, bony, with a fresh bruise developing on my right wrist. "Only if it's not too much trouble," I said. "I don't want to burden anyone."

"You don't worry about a thing," she said. "Now, rest. You're safe. He can't find you here. Pretend you're a hotel guest for a moment. Maybe take a nap. I would if I were you, honey."

I eyed the bed, so luxurious and warm. I hadn't slept a wink last night, not with that monster slumbering beside me. "Thank you, Gwen," I said, setting my heavy head down on the pillow. I let my eyelids close. *Just a few minutes. Then I'll go. Then I'll leave this place and find my son.* When I closed my eyes I saw, as I always did, my Daniel.

It was half-past eight when I opened my eyes. How had I slept so long? I sat up quickly, smoothing my dress. In my haste to leave Lon's room, I hadn't brought a sweater. I walked to the mirror on the wall and took a long look at myself, ashamed by the image of the scantily dressed woman before me. I didn't have time to fret. I surveyed the sky outside the windows. Dark clouds had rolled in. *I have to get out of here.*

I stepped outside into the hallway, cautiously, quietly, aware of every creak the floor made as I stepped. I kept my eyes out for Lon at every turn. *Is he still looking for me?* When I reached the elevator, I pressed the button and prayed it would come quickly. I heard heavy footsteps down the hall and my heart began to race, but moments later, an older couple walked past. The man tipped his hat at me, and I gave him a relieved nod. Still, when the elevator doors opened, I leapt inside, holding my breath until the doors closed again. *Safe, for the moment.* The elevator deposited me in the lobby. I kept my head down to remain as inconspicuous as possible, but I looked up when I saw a man I recognized. Our eyes met for a brief moment. I couldn't place him at first, so out of context. Then I realized who he was. Mr. Ivanoff, the mason. He held an iron crowbar and appeared to be working on a fireplace in the lobby. He nodded at me, but I didn't stop, especially after I'd heard what he'd done to his wife. As kind as he'd been to my Daniel, a man who could lay hands on his wife wasn't a man I wanted to associate with. I looked straight ahead.

Just as I pushed through the double doors that led to the street, I heard a man calling from a distance. "Wait!"

I glanced back inside the lobby to see Lon's assistant running toward the door, waving his hands. "Come back here, Miss Ray!" he shouted. "You can't just run off like this. Mr. Edwards spent a fortune on your wardrobe."

I ignored him and continued outside. My heart pounded as I ran down the street. I kept running, finally ducking into an alley four blocks away. I slid behind a stack of lumber, gasping for breath. A rat with a crooked tail scurried by in the shadows. *My God, where can I go next? Back to Caroline's? No, I couldn't do that to her. Then where?* It was getting dark; I couldn't stay on the streets, where I'd be prey for the men in the saloons. I buried my head in my hands. *Charles.* At first I brushed off the thought. Too many years had passed. I was probably just a distant memory to him now. *He doesn't know about Daniel, so how would he feel knowing that I'd kept him from him all this time?*

I shook my head. *Charles loved me once. He wouldn't turn me away now. But would he recognize me, this woman I've become?* I looked down at my hands, chapped and red from hours spent elbow-deep in wash buckets at the hotel, a stark contrast from the bright-eyed young woman he'd known four years ago. But perhaps he would see beyond that.

I sighed and stood up, walking out toward the street. I waved at a grocery truck passing by, and the driver slowed the vehicle to a stop. "Any chance you're passing through the Windermere neighborhood tonight?"

The driver, an older, kindly man, smiled as if he took pity on me. "No," he said. "But I can make a detour. I'm making a delivery up north. I can drop you off on the way."

I looked at the front seat, crammed with boxes and crates. "You'll have to ride in the back," he said.

I nodded, walking around to the rear. I climbed up onto the truck bed, pushing a crate aside to make room. As the truck sped forward, I took comfort in thinking of Charles.

"Here you are," the driver said, slamming the brakes in front of Windermere. He tipped his cap at me. "Hope you find what you're looking for, miss."

"Me too," I said. "And thank you."

The streetlights were sparse, and my eyes were weary. Finally, the Kensington home appeared in the distance. I picked up my pace, walking through the gate and past the fountain. I gazed up at the home, remembering the day Charles had first brought me. He'd been proud of me. He had loved me. *How would things have turned out had I stayed and ignored Josephine's warnings? Daniel might be . . .*

I startled at a rustling sound overhead. A bird flapped its wings, flying toward the lake. I dismissed my fears and continued walking toward the house, passing the urns at the entryway. They brimmed with recently planted violets. I knocked timidly and waited. I knocked again, louder. And then, I heard footsteps approach. The door creaked open, revealing Charles, just as I remembered him. That warm smile. Those kind eyes.

"Vera?" he exclaimed, with shock in his eyes. "I—I—Josephine said you'd . . ."

"Hello, Charles," I said quietly. I reached my hand out to him, brushing his cheek. "I've missed you so."

I wished I'd taken a moment to brush my hair. I might have borrowed Gwen's lipstick, too. But how I looked was of no importance. All that mattered was Daniel.

"Charles," I continued, "forgive me for coming here like this, for—"

"No," he said, smiling warmly. "Please don't apologize. Can I help you?" He looked at my left foot, shoeless, toes poking through the stockings. "Are you in some kind of trouble?"

"Yes," I said, hating the desperate tone in my voice, but I couldn't hide it. "I know this is going to sound terrible. I should have told you long ago—"

Women's voices echoed behind Charles, and moments later

Josephine and a blond woman I didn't recognize appeared at the door next to him. The blond woman tucked her arm inside his. A diamond ring sparkled on her left hand. "Charlie, honey, who is this?"

I stepped back.

"So you're back, are you?" Josephine said. "I knew it." She turned to Charles. "Asking for a handout, is she?"

"Josephine, stop!" Charles shouted. "She's here because she needs help." He turned back to me, his eyes as big as saucers. "What is it, Vera?"

"She'll tell you anything to get what she really wants," Josephine continued. "Your money."

I shook my head. "No, please. I'm here because something terrible has happened. My little boy has vanished."

Charles's mouth fell open.

Josephine held out her hand. "Don't listen to another word," she said. "She was never worthy of you. Mother saw her on the arm of Lon Edwards at the hotel the other night."

Lon's reputation wasn't good, and I couldn't deny my association with him. I looked down at my feet. "Yes," I said, "but—"

"That will be all, Miss Ray," Josephine said, attempting to close the door, but Charles interceded.

"Josephine," he said, "that's enough!" He turned to the other woman and smiled sympathetically. "Elaine, will you excuse me for a moment? I'd like to speak to Miss Ray alone."

The woman shrank back, as if injured. "Well, if you must," she said. "But don't be long, dear. You'll miss dinner."

Charles walked outside and pointed to the stone bench to our left. "Won't you sit down?"

I nodded, and he sat down beside me. His hands fidgeted

nervously in his lap as his eyes met mine. "My God, Vera," he said. "I didn't think I'd ever see you again."

I looked away. I couldn't bear to stare into the eyes I'd loved, still loved.

"You broke my heart, you know," he said, glancing back at the house, then at me again. "I wanted to spend the rest of my life with you."

My heart ached to hear his words. "Oh, Charles," I said, turning to face him. "I was so wrong to leave the way I did. But would you believe me if I told you that I left because I loved you?"

His eyes narrowed. "I don't understand."

"Josephine," I continued. "She said your parents would disown you from the family fortune."

Charles shook his head. "And so what if they did?" He sighed, burying his face in his hand. "Could you actually think so little of me to believe that I would choose money over love?"

"No—no," I stammered. "I didn't want to be the reason for you losing . . ." I paused to look around the expansive property, and my eyes stopped at the elaborate fountain ahead. "All of this."

He stared straight ahead. "I only wish you would have left that decision to me."

I reached out and placed my hand on his forearm, but he stiffened and pulled it back. "I'm married now, Vera," he said. "Her name is Elaine. She's a good woman. We're expecting our first child. We only just found out."

The words echoed in the night air, taunting me. "Yes," I said. "Yes, of course." I stood up. "I was foolish for coming here."

Charles stood up. "Vera, wait. Are you in some sort of danger? If you need a place to stay, Greta can make you up a room."

I shook my head. "No." *What would Elaine think? He's about to start a family, a real family, with a proper wife. How can I tell him about Daniel now?* "My being here will only cause trouble for you," I said. "I'll be fine."

Charles took a step closer to me. "You're sure?"

I could see the emotion, the longing, in his eyes. His presence felt magnetic. I wanted nothing more than to feel the comfort of his arms, to tell him about our son and to have him help me find him.

I opened my mouth to speak just as the door cracked open. Elaine walked out to the porch with crossed arms and an impatient expression. "Charles, darling, dinner has been plated. Your soup is getting cold."

"Good-bye Charles," I said, walking down the steps to the gravel drive.

"Vera, wait, I—"

"Good-bye," I said again, disappearing into the darkness. I turned back once more, with an aching heart, and watched as Elaine territorially threaded her arm through his. He kissed her cheek like a gentleman and escorted her back to the house.

I blotted a stray tear with the edge of my sleeve. The moon hovered overhead, a silent witness, shining brighter now. *Where will I go next? What will I do?* I stumbled along the side walkway, looking down toward the lake. Crickets chirped as soft waves pushed up onto the marshy shore. I remembered what Charles had said about the lilies, how they were special, not of this world. I longed to look at them again, to watch them bob in the moonlight. Daniel would have liked to see them. He would have been gentle, just like Charles as a boy, dipping his hand in the water and touching their petals ever so lightly. He would appreciate their beauty, like his father did.

With a heavy heart, I walked toward the lake.

Chapter 18

Claire

I lifted the papers from the case. They carried the scent of the space behind Lillian's wall: cigar smoke, must, a tinge of old leather. The first page confirmed that Lillian's father, Edward Sharpe, had indeed represented Sven W. Ivanoff in the murder trial of Vera Ray. The next few pages were filled with legal jargon and various motions I did not understand. But deeper in the stack lay the material I'd been waiting for, the transcribed sworn testimony of Mr. Ivanoff. I shivered, thinking of what might lie in those yellowed typewritten pages. An admission of guilt? The horrific details of Vera's death? I began reading:

```
E. R. Sharpe: Mr. Ivanoff, please state for
    the record your name and address.
S. W. Ivanoff: Sven W. Ivanoff of 4395 Fifth
    Avenue.
Sharpe: You have pled not guilty to the mur-
    der of Miss Vera Ray. Is this correct?
Ivanoff: Yes, sir.
```

Sharpe: Please state how you were acquainted
with Miss Ray.

Ivanoff: I knew her for about four years.

Sharpe: When did you first meet?

Ivanoff: We lived in the same building. She
lived on the floor below. But that wasn't
how we first met. I was over in Windermere
doing some work on a house. Saw her walking the roadside. She had the look of a
lady who needed help.

Sharpe: So what did you do?

Ivanoff: I stopped the truck. Pulled over.
I asked her if she needed a lift. She
asked me if I could take her back to her
apartment in Seattle. That's when I realized we lived in the same building.

Sharpe: Now, Mr. Ivanoff, the prosecution
seems to paint a picture of Miss Ray as a
woman of questionable morals—a prostitute, even. Did you have any reason to
believe that this was true of Miss Ray?

Ivanoff: No, sir. She was a decent woman. A
good woman. Just trying to make ends meet
like the rest of us.

Sharpe: And when you drove her back to her
apartment building in the city, was there
anything inappropriate, or shall I say,
intimate, about the encounter?

Ivanoff: No, sir. I'm a married man, sir.

Sharpe: What did you talk about on the drive
back to Seattle?

Ivanoff: She said she had to make a very
hard decision. Sounded like relationship

trouble, if you ask me. I didn't ask her
many questions. She didn't seem to want to
talk much. But she did say something
about one of the ladies at the house she
had been at, that she hadn't been kind to
her. We both agreed that rich folks
can sometimes be as mean as the devil
himself.

Sharpe: So you got the impression that someone had been unkind to Miss Ray in the
Windermere neighborhood where she had
been visiting?

Ivanoff: Yes, sir. She was shaken up. You
could tell she'd been crying. I felt sorry
for her.

Sharpe: All right. So you dropped her off
at the apartment building, and that was it?

Ivanoff: Yes, sir. I only saw her off and on
after that. I'd tip my cap at her. Once I
fixed a loose brick in her fireplace.

Sharpe: Why did you help her with it?

Ivanoff: The landlord was a real tyrant.
Made the tenants pay for repairs themselves. I helped as many people as I could.
After the storm, a branch from the cherry
tree outside hit one of the old lady's
windows. She couldn't pay for the repair
bill, so she had to live without a window.
I had some scrap wood in the truck, so I
boarded it shut for her. Cold as an icebox, that apartment.

Sharpe: It sounds as if you were the unof-
ficial handyman of the building.

Ivanoff: You could say so. Somebody had to help those poor folks. I tried to lend a hand whenever I could.

Sharpe: And when you fixed Miss Ray's fireplace, did you get any indication that she was trying to proposition you?

Ivanoff: Heavens, no. Like I said, she was a decent woman. Besides, by the time I visited her apartment to fix the fireplace, she had a newborn baby. I was surprised at first. I didn't even know she was expecting. She was such a little thing. Seemed hard to believe she could have carried a child. Besides, I'd never seen a man around her place. Not once. But it was her business. I didn't ask questions. She loved that little baby. Cooed at him the whole time I was workin'.

Sharpe: Did she tell you the child's name?

Ivanoff: Why, yes, sir. She called him Daniel.

Sharpe: And was there any monetary exchange for your services?

Ivanoff: No, sir. She tried to give me the last few coins from her pocketbook, but I wouldn't accept them. She offered me a slice of bread instead. That was nice. The missus had been sick, and hadn't baked bread in weeks.

Sharpe: Can we clear something up about your record now? You were arrested previously for allegedly striking your wife during a bout of drunkenness. Can you explain what happened?

Ivanoff: It's true that I drink more than I should. But I would never lay a hand on my wife, or any woman, for that matter.

Sharpe: Then what happened the night your wife was harmed?

Ivanoff: I was at the saloon down below the apartment. It had been a long day. I had drunk more than my share of ale. My wife came down to find me, to bring me home. One of the men at the bar didn't like seeing a woman in the place. He called her a terrible name, he did.

Sharpe: What did he call her?

Ivanoff: An ugly Russian. Pointed to her fingers, and called them fat, fat as pierogies, he said. Made her cry. I couldn't let him speak to my wife that way. So I stood up to tell him what I thought of him, and he popped his fist at me, straight at my jaw. Lost a tooth that night.

Sharpe: Can you please stand and show the court which tooth?

Ivanoff: Sure thing. It's this one right here. Fell right out. I never did find it.

Sharpe: Mr. Ivanoff, can you tell me what happened to your wife that night? Why was she taken to the hospital?

Ivanoff: She tried to break up the fight, and that bastard hit her. She got hurt real bad.

Sharpe: So, you did not strike your wife?

Ivanoff: No, sir. The police came by the saloon, and somebody told them it was me. Guess they thought it was better to arrest an immigrant. They took me into the station. It was a terrible mistake.

Sharpe: And I understand your wife came to plead with the police the following day for your release. Why didn't they listen to her?

Ivanoff: Corrupt, I tell you. They jailed an innocent man and wouldn't listen to reason, even with the facts. They ruined my reputation. I don't understand this country. In Russia, men are honest.

Sharpe: Let the record show that I have, here, a signed statement from Mrs. Arianna Ivanoff stating that her husband, Sven Ivanoff, did not harm her on the night of May 7, 1933. Now, Mr. Ivanoff, let's talk about what happened the night of Miss Ray's death.

Ivanoff: Well, I knew she was in a rough spot, having trouble paying her rent and all. I'd heard that her son was missing. Broke my heart. He was a good little boy. Reminded me of my own son.

Sharpe: Mr. Ivanoff, did you have anything to do with the disappearance of Daniel Ray?

Ivanoff: No, sir.

Sharpe: Please describe for me your encounters with Miss Ray in the week leading up to her death.

Ivanoff: Well, sir, I remember being in the
saloon, the day of the snowstorm. I saw
her come home from work, like usual, and
shortly after she came running down the
stairs, screaming for her little boy. I
knew something terrible had happened.

Sharpe: Did you try to help her?

Ivanoff: Yes sir. I walked out to the street,
but she'd already run off.

Sharpe: When did you next see her?

Ivanoff: About a week later. The snow had
melted, I remember that. I was working on
a job at the Olympic Hotel. Saw her there
all gussied up, on the arm of a rich man.
I didn't recognize her at first. She saw
me. Looked away. I think she was ashamed.

Sharpe: Why do you think she was ashamed?
What did you think she was doing there?

Ivanoff: We all do things for the ones we
love. I didn't fault her for trying to get
help from an influential person if it helped
to find her son.

Sharpe: The prosecution has characterized
Miss Ray as a common prostitute, a woman
of questionable morals who neglected her
son so she could make extra cash as a call
girl. They have also suggested that you
paid Miss Ray for such services and that
you are responsible for her death. How do
you respond to these allegations?

Ivanoff: They're made up. Completely false.
Miss Ray was neither a bad mother nor a
prostitute. She loved her boy just as my

Arianna loved our son. Miss Ray's dedication to that child was unquestionable. And I can tell you this, sir, she was no call girl.

Sharpe: How do you know?

Ivanoff: Just by the look in her eye when she was with that man at the hotel. She didn't want to be there with him. Anyone could see that. She looked so sad, so lost. I only wish I could have helped her.

Sharpe: So let's go through the time line of the night she was murdered.

Ivanoff: I was getting off work at the hotel, piling my tools in my truck, when I saw her run out of the hotel. She didn't look well. Her dress was torn. Her hair wasn't up like it usually was. She was crying. It looked as if she was running from someone. I tried to get her attention, but she was running so fast. I secured the last load onto my truck, and started out on Fourth Avenue. That's when I noticed her get on the back of a grocery truck. She sat right there between the crates of produce and bread. I followed the truck. I wanted to be sure she was OK. Truck dropped her off right in front of a fancy street in Windermere, near where I'd first seen her years ago. I pulled the truck to the side of the road, not wanting to intrude. I waited there for a while.

Sharpe: How long would you say?

Ivanoff: Oh, at least twenty minutes. I
thought she might be coming back, and if
she did, I wanted to offer her a ride
home. See if I could help her. The missus
could make her a warm meal, make her a
place to sleep on the sofa.

Sharpe: So you were worried about her safety?

Ivanoff: Yes, sir. And, as I say, when she
didn't come back up that driveway twenty
minutes later, I decided to go after her.
It was an instinct, I guess. I felt that
she was in danger.

Sharpe: You left your truck on the street
and walked down the road that led to the
Kensington residence?

I took my eyes off the page and gasped. *My God. Kensington?*

Ivanoff: That's right, sir. I walked down
the gravel path, past the fountain and
hedges, and looked through the window of
the house. I didn't see anything so I
walked around the side yard, down to the
lawn behind the house. It was the fanciest
home I'd seen in my life. I couldn't understand what Vera was doing there.

Sharpe: What did you see when you reached
the lawn?

Ivanoff: Nothing, at first. Just a big lawn
that connected to Lake Washington. The sun
had set, so there was little light. I was
going to turn back, when I heard something.

Sharpe: What?

Ivanoff: At first I thought it was the sound of an animal. It was so high pitched, so shrill. But then I heard it again, and I knew. It was the sound of a woman crying out for help. She sounded awful scared, or hurt, maybe.

Sharpe: What did you do next?

Ivanoff: I tried to figure where the cry was coming from. Then, I saw movement near the dock. Just a shadow at first. I ducked back behind a tree, and then I saw her.

Sharpe: Vera?

Ivanoff: No, another woman. She was running away from the lake back up to the house.

Sharpe: Did you get a good look at her?

Ivanoff: It was hard to make out her face, but she had dark hair. I suppose you could say she was tall.

Sharpe: And did she let herself inside the residence?

Ivanoff: Yes, sir. It didn't make sense. Someone clearly needed help down there. I started to run down the lawn, but then the screaming stopped. I, I . . .

Sharpe: Mr. Ivanoff, are you all right? May we continue?

Ivanoff: I'll do my best, sir.

Sharpe: What did you see when you reached the lake?

Ivanoff: Dear Lord, it was terrible. I ran to the dock, and I saw her there, floating

in the water. She'd lost one of her
shoes. . . .

Sharpe: You saw Miss Ray in the water?

Ivanoff: Yes, sir. She was floating next to a
small rowboat that was sinking. It must
have had a leak. I tried to reach her from
the dock. But she was too far out. I'd have
gone after her but I can't swim, and
besides, I think I was too late. Her face
was underwater. Eyes open,. It was the most
horrible thing I've seen in all of my days.

Sharpe: What did you do next?

Ivanoff: I couldn't bear to think of leaving
her there all alone, in the cold. But I
knew after my record with the police,
they'd point the finger at me. They'd never
believe a Russian immigrant. They'd pin
me with the crime, the way they'd done the
last time. I couldn't take that chance.

Sharpe: So you left?

Ivanoff: Yes. She looked so peaceful lying
there next to the water lilies. Besides,
her soul had gone to a better place; that
much is certain.

Sharpe: And what did you do next?

Ivanoff: I began walking back up the lawn.
I didn't want anyone to see me. Rich folks
would take one look at me and think I was
up to trouble. But then I heard some sounds
coming from the house.

Sharpe: What did you hear?

Ivanoff: A woman was crying hysterically,
and a man was shouting at her.

Sharpe: Could you make out what they were
saying?

Ivanoff: No. But I crouched down behind a
hedge and watched the man run down to the
lake.

Sharpe: Mr. Ivanoff, do you know the name of
the man you saw?

Ivanoff: No, sir. But if you ask me, he loved
Miss Ray. He knelt down and cried there on
the dock. He took his shirt off and looked
like he might have gone in after her, but
that woman ran down and pulled him back.

Sharpe: So you began walking back to your
truck?

Ivanoff: Yes, sir. I passed by the house on
the way. It was a warm night. The windows
were open in the upstairs rooms. I heard
a child in the house. A boy. He was crying.

Sharpe: Did you think he might be Miss
Ray's son?

Ivanoff: I did. And when I got back to the
city, I phoned the police. I told them
that a crime had occurred at the residence
in Windermere, and that I thought Vera's
boy could be there.

Sharpe: Mr. Ivanoff, what did the officer at
the station tell you?

Ivanoff: He said they wouldn't be looking
into my tip.

Sharpe: Why not?

Ivanoff: He said that the Kensingtons were some of the city's most upstanding citizens.

Sharpe: Let the record state that we have a document from the Police Department proving that Mr. Ivanoff did make a call to the police station to report the crime. Mr. Ivanoff, what do you think really happened to Miss Ray that night?

Ivanoff: I think she traveled to that home to get help and they turned on her. That woman, whoever she was, put her in that boat knowing of the hole. When she could have saved Miss Ray, she didn't. I hope she pays for what she did.

Sharpe: Thank you, Mr. Ivanoff. There will be no further questions.

I lifted my eyes from the last page with a heavy heart. The story had come into focus. My own husband's family had been accomplice to one of the most tragic crimes in Seattle's history, had covered it up, even. No wonder Edward Sharpe had kept the files hidden so long. Mr. Ivanoff had spelled things out in excruciating detail.

I fanned the remaining pages, and my eyes stopped when I read the medical examiner's notes about Vera's personal effects:

Found on Ms. Ray: A hair clip, a hotel key, and bracelet. All remitted to Mr. Charles Kensington on June 13, 1933.

Daniel's father was a . . . Kensington.

I was supposed to meet Ethan for dinner in thirty minutes. *Could I tell him?* I remembered the break-in at Lillian's home and quickly tucked the pages into the briefcase, slipping it under my desk. It would be safe there.

At the restaurant, Ethan ordered a bottle of 2001 merlot from a winery we both loved. "What's the occasion?" I asked, noting the year of our wedding.

"Just being together these days is an occasion," he said, smiling.

"I know," I replied, taking a sip of wine.

"Hey." He held up his glass. "You forgot to clink glasses. That's bad luck."

I tapped my glass against his. "There. The five-second rule applies."

He smiled. "How have you been?"

At face value, it was a strange question for a husband to ask his wife, and yet we'd become so distant, it made sense.

"Well, I've been better," I said, looking at the menu instead of into his eyes. The menu was safer.

I wanted to ask him about Cassandra, but I didn't have the guts. "What's good here?"

"The lamb is fantastic," he said. "With the orzo. It has a light crust of—"

I slammed my menu down. "Since when are you a foodie? You were never a foodie. You used to pride yourself in being *anti*-foodie."

Ethan looked startled.

"Don't pretend that you don't know what I'm talking about. You've been spending an awful lot of time with *her*. She's rubbing off on you."

"Claire, Cassandra's just a friend. And since when do you take offense with me enjoying my food?"

I sighed. "I'm sorry," I said, looking away. The restaurant was filled with couples. Happy couples. *Why can't* we *be happy?* "I didn't mean to attack you like that."

"Can we start over?" he asked, setting his menu aside.

"Yes," I replied. "Reset button."

"Now, what can we talk about that's safe? Work?"

I nodded apprehensively.

He took a sip of wine and then leaned back in his chair with a sigh. "How's work? Got any good stories brewing?"

"Well," I said, taking a long sip of wine and questioning whether to reveal the secret or not. "I'm working on a story that's pretty fascinating."

"Oh?"

"Yes, about a little boy who vanished in 1933, the day the snow-storm hit, just like the one we had this week."

Ethan picked up a piece of bread and dipped it in the plate of olive oil between us. "Did you find out what happened to him?"

"Sort of," I said. "It might actually shock you, if I tell you."

"Try me," he said, amused.

"Well," I said slowly, "turns out, he's a Kensington."

Ethan stopped chewing the bread in his mouth, then swal-lowed the bite quickly. "What do you mean?"

"It's a long story, but the short of it is that one of your great-greats had a fling with a poor woman. She got pregnant, and three years later, I think his sister abducted the boy. At least, I suspect that's how it went."

"My God," he said. "Do you have names?"

I nodded. "The boy's father was a man named Charles Ken-sington."

Ethan shook his head. "You can't be serious."

"Yes," I said. "Why? Who is he?"

"My God, Claire, that's my great-grandfather."

"It's a heartbreaking story," I continued. "I think I finally have the information I need to write a draft."

Ethan frowned. "You know you can't write about this."

"What do you mean?"

"It would ruin the family name, the newspaper. It would destroy Grandpa."

"I think you have it all wrong, Ethan," I said. "I know Warren. He'd want to air the truth."

He set his napkin on his plate. "No. We can't take the risk of hurting him when he's so ill."

"Well," I said, "fortunately, you're not my boss, Ethan."

"You're right," he said. "I'm your boss's boss."

I gasped. "You'd really kill this story because it involves skeletons in your family's closet?"

"Yes," he said. "I would."

The server appeared, but I waved him away. "I'm not the only one looking for answers. You should have seen the scene at Lillian Sharpe's home in Windermere. Her father was involved in the murder trial of the boy's mother. Someone had ransacked the place looking for his files. The truth is bound to come out eventually."

"But my paper won't be the one breaking the news," he said, laying a fifty-dollar bill on the table and reaching for his coat.

I hadn't anticipated going to Café Lavanto. I'd instructed the cab to drop me off at home, but I shook my head when the driver pulled the car in front of the building. "No," I said. "Change of plans. Take me up to Fifth, please."

I knocked and Dominic unlocked the door to the café. "Mind if I come in?" I asked.

"Please," he said warmly. A fire crackled a few feet away. Soft music played from the speakers overhead. He smiled at me in a way that made me swallow hard. "Come, sit down."

Something seemed off about the café. A few cardboard boxes sat near the door. *What else has changed? New paint? Curtains?* I felt too disoriented to focus on the details. Dominic reached for a bottle of wine on the bar and pulled a corkscrew from his pocket. "Wine?"

I shrugged. "Sure, why not?"

I watched as he poured two glasses, handing me one. "To new beginnings," he said.

I nodded, clinking my glass against his. But I set it down before I had taken a sip. "Wait, you said 'beginnings,' plural. What did you mean by that?"

"Well," he said, looking around the café, "there is something I should probably tell you." He paused. "I should have told you about this earlier, Claire."

"What is it?"

"I've made a big decision, about my business. About this place."

"What, you're going to convert the space upstairs into the loft you always wanted? Add a lunch menu?"

He shook his head. "No. Claire, I've decided to sell it."

My mouth flew open. "But—but you said you'd never do that. You said you loved this place. That you couldn't see it get into the hands of another set of condo developers. Am I missing something here?"

"I did say all of that," he continued. "And I meant it. But yesterday, a developer made me an offer I couldn't refuse. He'd been trying to convince me to sell for a while and I was determined not to, but his latest offer was so generous that when I considered my circumstances, I realized I'd be a fool not to accept it. Listen, it's a life-changing amount of money, Claire. I could see that my mother is properly cared for, then buy a place, and"—he leaned closer to me—"settle down."

"No," I said, standing up. "I can't believe you're saying this." I felt torn. I knew he was facing financial pressure to support his mother, and yet I couldn't stand the thought of the beloved building being torn down. "There's too much history in these walls," I countered. "You just can't put a dollar amount on something so special."

"I'm sorry, Claire," he said. "Believe me, it was an agonizing decision. I wish there was another way."

I pushed the glass away.

"Claire," Dominic said, trying to get me to smile, "please say this won't change anything between . . . us."

He lifted his hand and stroked my cheek gently. I closed my eyes as he pulled me toward him. His embrace was warm, comforting, but I pulled back.

"I'm sorry, Dominic. "I have to go."

Chapter 19

"Warren, this is Claire," I said over the phone the next morning.

"Hi honey," he said in almost a whisper.

"Why the hushed voice?"

"The nurse thinks I'm sleeping."

"And why would she care if you're sleeping or not sleeping?"

"She said she has to give me a shot when I wake up."

"A shot."

"Yes."

I stifled a laugh, but not the sarcasm. "Six years old, are we?"

"Apparently, yes," he said.

"Listen," I continued, "needle anxiety aside, how *are* you feeling?"

"Very well, dear," he said. "I don't know why they're keeping me here. Doc said I might be able to go home later today. I sure hope so. Anyway, how are you?"

"I've had a lot on my mind," I replied. "Which is why I'm calling, actually." I paused, thinking of Glenda's warning not to bother him with my "drama." A moth flew onto my computer screen, right above the first line of my story. I waved it away and it flew toward me, taunting me. I batted it down again. Glenda or no Glenda, I wouldn't say anything about the article, about the Kensington connection. Not yet. I could, however, ask a question. "Warren, I was just curious," I began, thinking of how to phrase the query. *Be delicate.* "Curious about the Kensington family tree. It occurred to me that I've never asked Ethan much about his ancestors. You know, great-aunts, uncles. I'd like to learn more about Ethan's family—er, my family."

"Well," Warren said, sighing, "the Kensingtons were one of the original Seattle families. A very important clan, we are."

"And not the least bit conceited, either," I added playfully.

"Claire, you're a Kensington, through and through."

I grinned. "So your parents, will you remind me of their names? I don't recall Ethan telling me."

"Ah, yes," he said, obviously relishing the chance to travel back in time. "Mother's name was Elaine. Father was Charles."

My heart beat faster.

"He was a good man. A good father."

"Did you have any . . . brothers?"

"A younger sister, yes, but no brothers," he said. "But I did for a time. Well, the closest thing to a brother, anyway. He was Aunt Josephine's little boy. He and Aunt Josephine came to stay with us for a while before he died."

"Died?"

"Yes," he said, sighing. "Fell down a ladder. Bumped his head. Died right there on the gravel driveway. I was there when it happened. Josephine blamed me. I was a little older. She said I dared him to climb the ladder. I didn't. I was too afraid to step foot on it, but he didn't have an ounce of fear in him, that one. He had it in his mind that he wanted to see a robin's eggs, so by golly, he climbed that ladder."

"What was his name, Warren?" My heart beat faster.

"Thomas," he said. "But that wasn't his given name. I can't remember what it was. But we called him Thomas. The old house wasn't ever the same after he died. Aunt Josephine never fully recovered. Children shouldn't die before their mothers."

"No, they shouldn't," I said, opening up my notebook.

"What was Josephine's husband's name?"

"You know," he said, pausing, "I don't quite remember. He died, I was told."

"Died?"

"In any case, he was never around. For as long as I can remember, it was just Thomas and Josephine."

So, in her grief, she took Daniel and claimed him as her own? But why?

"Warren, do you know where Thomas is buried?"

"Why do you ask?"

"Oh, just curious. I've always had a thing for cemeteries."

"Bryant Park," he said. "Where all the Kensingtons are buried. It's the cemetery on the hill by the university."

I felt a deep pain emanating from my chest, my heart. "I know the cemetery," I said. "It's where the baby was . . . "

"Oh, honey. How insensitive of me. Of course I remember. I—"

"It's fine," I said. But it wasn't. I hadn't been back to that cemetery since Ethan and I had watched our firstborn, tucked inside a tiny mahogany box—eerily tiny—lowered into a hole in the earth. Our baby was the youngest, and newest, addition to the Kensington grave site, where dozens of deceased family members rested. Glenda had already seen to it that ten feet of earth next to the baby's grave was reserved for Ethan and me. There was much I didn't like about my mother-in-law, but I will always appreciate that she arranged for us to one day be reunited in death.

"The only thing I remember about Thomas's funeral is the big mound of dirt and that little coffin," Warren said, reminiscing. "It was trimmed in gold, all the way around. I couldn't understand why they'd put such a pretty thing in the ground. Father had to hold Josephine back. She almost threw herself into the hole after they lowered the coffin down. It was all very strange for a six-year-old boy to watch."

I sighed. "So if you were six, how old was the little boy? Thomas?"

"He was a little younger than me," he said, pausing.

I heard commotion on the other end of the line, and a nurse's voice. "I'll let you go," I said. "I promise to come visit soon."

"Sure, honey. Anytime you like."

The keys to Ethan's BMW lay on the kitchen counter. I'd only driven it a time or two, preferring cabs to a vehicle with a manual transmission. Shifting gears on Seattle's notoriously hilly streets frightened me, especially after the time I'd rolled back so far between first and second gear. I'd vowed never to drive the car again. It was Ethan's domain, not mine—an unspoken agreement since the accident. Like much of our lives, since last year, a line had divided my world from his. But the keys glistened in the morning light. It would be easier to drive to the cemetery than to hassle with a long cab ride or navigate the bus lines. I hated buses. I nodded, scooping up the keys and dropping them into my bag.

I took the elevator down to the parking garage and stepped into the car, setting my bag on the passenger seat. I took a deep breath. Ethan. The car smelled of his cologne, his skin, and—I picked up a petrified french fry near a cup holder—his secret love of fast food. I smiled to myself, tucking the fry into a plastic trash bag in the backseat.

The tires screeched as I navigated out of the garage, taking a right onto the street. It felt good to be behind the wheel of a car again. I felt in control. I flipped on the radio and the U2 song "With or Without You" drifted from the speakers. I hardly noticed the big hills before turning onto the freeway. I turned the volume up, letting the music soothe me as I drove, taking the exit that led to the cemetery. They'd given me a Valium the morning of the baby's funeral. It had made me feel drowsy and secure, like being cloaked in a big fluffy comforter, warm and protected. I wished I hadn't taken the pill, though. I should have felt the emotions in all of their rawness. I should have let myself grieve. I'd needed to grieve. And now, as I drove the car through the gates of the cemetery, I did so fully conscious, feeling every tug at my heart, every dark memory, every regret.

I stepped out of the car, cautiously, locking the doors with a swift click of the button on the keychain. I looked out ahead over the grassy hill. As children, my little brother and I had often played in a cemetery near our home. Dad had cautioned us not to step too close to the headstones. "It's disrespectful to step on the dead," he had said. After that, I'd made sure to tread more carefully. But once, my brother had hidden behind a headstone and jumped out, screaming, "Boo!" In a frightened state, I'd leapt back, landing on my feet right in the space beside the headstone of a little girl who'd died in the 1940s. I'd felt terrible about that. Dad had said it wasn't a big deal, that I hadn't disturbed the little girl's grave, but I cried the whole way home, too sad to ride my bike, so Dad pushed it for me.

The sun shone down on my head. I was grateful for its warmth after last week's snowstorm. I thought about what the cemetery must have looked like with the headstones covered in snow, like cakes piped with white icing.

I stared ahead, recognizing the willow tree in the distance. The baby was buried just beneath it. A breeze blew a blossom from the nearby magnolia against my cheek, and I swiped it away. I shivered, turning back to the car. *I don't have to do this. I could turn back right now.* Then I remembered Vera. I was here for her. I could be strong for her. I took a step, and then another, winding my way through the grave sites until I reached the willow tree that presided over the Kensington family plot.

With magnetic pull, the baby's headstone drew my eyes to it. Ethan had picked it out, with his parents' help. We'd kept it simple. No name. Few details. It's how I'd wanted it. Ethan couldn't understand why I didn't want to know the child's gender. He had accused me of being emotionally cold, frozen. Perhaps I was. But it was the only way I knew how not to succumb to my sadness. If I didn't *know*, I didn't have to *feel*. The hospital grief counselor had advised that while a funeral wasn't necessary, it could give us closure. A couple who had lost twins recently, he'd explained, had buried the ashes of their children under two plum trees they'd planted in their backyard. Another couple had buried their stillborn daughter under a rose tree in their garden. Ethan had insisted that our child needed a funeral, but to me, it only seemed to add to the pain. I had been distraught, and a nurse had to come in to give me a sedative.

I knelt down beside the grave, running my hand along the edge of the headstone, wiping a bit of moss off the edge with my hand. I pulled a package of tissue from my bag, and used one to rub dust from the shiny granite. BABY KENSINGTON, the first line read. BORN MAY 3; IN THE ARMS OF JESUS 13 MINUTES AFTER BIRTH.

I didn't bother to wipe away the tear on my cheek. No one was watching. I could let myself grieve. "Mommy misses you," I whispered, as the wind whistled through the willow tree. I longed to hold my baby, to feel the softness of a cheek against my breast. I remembered the way they'd been engorged with milk, pulsing with pain, the day I came home from the hospital. How cruel, I'd thought, to have milk for a child I could never feed. I stared at the headstone. Every part of me ached for what I had lost. And when the stream of tears came, I did not try to stifle them.

Startled by a rustling noise, I looked behind me, where an older man in overalls with dirt stains at the knees stood with a rake on the hill above. *How long has he been watching me?*

He set the rake against a tree and walked toward me. I wanted to tell him to go away, to leave me alone, but something about his face—friendly, kind—told me not to. "This your child, miss?" he asked, pointing to the headstone.

I nodded.

"The name's Murphy," he said, pulling a wrinkled hand out of his work glove. "James Murphy. I'm the caretaker here."

He gave my hand a squeeze, and I tucked it back in my pocket. "I'm Claire Aldridge," I said, eyes fixed on the headstone.

"Must be a special one, this child," he said, kneeling beside me.

I didn't answer. *He probably says this to everyone.*

"I've been tending these grounds for more than forty years," he said. "Never seen a blackberry vine grow here, least not in my time. The soil's too dense. But look." He paused, pointing to a sprig of light green peeking out from behind the headstone. The crinkly leaves covered a thorny vine with a single white flower, its petals so delicate they might as well have been lace.

I reached down to touch its stem, but pulled my hand back quickly, feeling a sharp prick. Blood dripped from my finger. "Ouch!" I cried.

"Careful," he said. "Those thorns are sharp."

I put my finger in my mouth to stop the bleeding.

"We grave minders have long believed in the legend of the blackberry," he continued. "Do you know it?"

I shook my head.

"They choose souls to protect. The special ones."

I noticed the way the blackberry leaves lay against the headstone, almost embracing it.

"I'm surprised the storm didn't kill this little shoot," he said, touching the tiny flower delicately with his index finger. "Special," he said again, rising to his feet, brushing dirt from his knees. "Well, I'll leave you now. Just thought you'd like to know."

"Thank you," I said, looking up at him with more gratitude than the words could express.

I sat there for a long time, thinking about the child I'd never know, milestones I'd never see. First steps. First words. Kindergarten. Sixth-grade science fairs. Swing sets and sidewalk chalk. Summer camping trips. Spelling bees. I stood up and steadied myself against the trunk of the willow tree. I'd come here to find Daniel, not to sink deeper into my grief. *I came for Vera.* I took a deep breath and wound my way through the rows of Kensington headstones, most made of marble punctuated with elaborate finials and urns. Headstones for wealthy people. Ruby Kensington. Elias Kensington. Merilee Kensington. Where was Daniel? Eleanor Walsh

Kensington. Louis Kensington III. My eyes squinted at a smaller headstone. A child's rocking horse was etched into the top. My heart beat faster as I read the words. THOMAS KENSINGTON, SON OF JOSEPHINE KENSINGTON. BORN APRIL 21, 1930, DIED JUNE 9, 1936. I wrote the words in my notebook.

The dates figured perfectly. Josephine must have taken him when he was three, and he'd died just a few years later. There he was, little Daniel—well, as Warren had said, they called him Thomas then—resting in the earth beneath my feet. I shook my head. *No, he is not resting. Not without his mother.*

I drove straight to the office, parking the car in the lot next to the *Herald* building. I walked quickly to my desk, passing the girls from sales on a cigarette break without stopping to say hi. At my desk, I pulled up the draft of the story on my computer, and I wrote, referring to my notebook for bits and pieces of my research from the previous week. Eva. Café Lavanto. The Kensington family. Press clippings from decades ago. The testimony from Mr. Ivanoff. And now the gravesite that tied it all together. I wrote through lunch, barely noticing my hunger, when I usually felt famished by noon. At two, I sat back in my chair and gazed at the completed story on my screen. I wrote the last sentence, then scrolled to the very top, where the cursor flashed next to the headline. "Blackberry Winter: Late-Season Snowstorm Holds Key to Missing Boy from 1933." Below the headline, I typed my name with sure fingers. "By Claire Aldridge." I couldn't remember the last time I'd felt so proud of my byline.

I printed the article, five pages in total. Even though he took me off the story, Frank would want to see it. But I walked to Abby's office first. She turned away from her computer and I dropped the pages on her desk, then sat in her guest chair while she read in silence. She looked up at me periodically with a shocked face, then turned back to the draft, continuing to read.

"Wow," she said, handing the pages back to me.

"So what do you think?"

"Just, wow," she said again. "You realize that you're incriminating your husband's entire family with this feature."

I shrugged. "It's the truth."

Abby looked doubtful. "Truth or not, you know the Kensingtons are never going to let you print it."

"They have to," I said. "It needs to be told."

"It does," she agreed, looking thoughtful. "But wait, what about Vera? Did you ever find her grave?"

I sighed. "No," I said, glancing back at the pages in my hand. "And the story doesn't quite feel complete without that information, at least for me."

Abby frowned. "What do you think the Kensingtons will think of all of this?"

"I don't care what they think anymore," I said. I looked to the window that looked out on the street, where a young mother walked by on the sidewalk holding the hand of her little boy. He wore a yellow raincoat with matching boots. I turned back to Abby. "It's time the world learned what happened to Daniel Ray."

She looked at me a long while. "I'm proud of you, honey. You've come a long way."

"Thanks," I said, turning toward the door.

Frank was on the phone, so I set the pages in front of him at his desk and whispered, "I know you killed the story, but for what it's worth, here it is. I had to finish it."

His grin told me he'd forgiven me.

Back at my desk, the red light on my phone blinked, alerting me to a voice message. I dialed the password and listened. "Claire, this is Eva. Sorry, I was out walking when you called. It feels odd leaving this information over a message recorder, but I'll go ahead anyway so as not to delay your research. You asked where Vera was laid to rest, and you can find her at a little cemetery on First Hill, just north of the city. Ninth plot on the left, right next to the chain-link fence. I used to visit her more, but in my old age, well, I haven't gotten up there in a long time. I'm glad you're able to visit her, dear."

My heart raced. I reached for my bag and jacket, but nearly ran into Frank in the doorway. "This," he said, motioning me back to my chair, "is a work of art."

I smiled cautiously. "You really think so?"

"Yes. Your finest research. And the writing"—he shook his head as though marveling at a fine painting—"it's beautiful. Made me cry." He looked at me, astonished. "You're back, Claire."

"Thank you," I said. "But all the stuff about the Kensingtons, I—"

He held up his hand. "This is history. It must be printed. Don't you worry. I'll smooth it all out with the editorial board."

"All right," I said, standing up again.

Frank raised his eyebrows. "Where are you off to?"

"Just following up on another lead," I said. "I'll e-mail you the story tonight."

"I'll look forward to it," he said, following me out.

I parked in front of the cemetery later that afternoon. A far cry from the beautifully tended Bryant Park, the First Hill Cemetery, encircled by a rusty chain-link fence, looked all but forgotten. Brown grass and weeds grew up against headstones, many of which had been marked with graffiti. I was careful to lock the BMW before I walked through the gates, where large cedar trees loomed, casting dark shadows on the ground.

Where did Eva say Vera's grave was? Ninth plot on the left. I walked farther inside the cemetery, counting the headstones as I went. No finials or marble; just simple, unadorned stone. A poorman's graveyard. I came to the ninth headstone and crouched down, attempting to read the inscription, but moss obscured the words. I used the edge of the BMW key to scrape off a clump that covered the letters. VERA RAY, it read simply, 1910–1933.

I shook my head. No reference to her being a loving a mother. A dear friend. A sister. A daughter. Just a name and a few unspecific dates. What was wrong with this world? A world where a name like Kensington made you special and a name like Ray rendered you dispensable, forgettable? I stared at her grave intently. *I won't let them forget about you, Vera.*

I felt a fluttery feeling inside when I noticed a thorny vine growing along the edge of the small headstone. White flowers burst from its velvety green leaves. I remembered what the man at the graveyard had said, about blackberries being special, choosing souls, protecting them. *Of course they'd choose Vera.* I felt a shiver come over me as a car sped by on the street beyond the ramshackle fence.

I thought of Ethan on the drive back to the office. Sure, he'd been apprehensive about the story, but once he read it, he'd understand how important it was. My heart told me that. I couldn't wait to take a draft to him. Of course, Glenda wouldn't be thrilled, but that didn't matter to me. Warren's opinion, however, did. His heart was weak. Could he handle learning about these dark family secrets? Would they cause him too much pain? After all, he hadn't known that his cousin had not only been *kidnapped* but was also his *half brother*.

Frank was waiting for me in my office when I returned. A pencil dangled from his lips.

I dropped my bag to the floor. "What is it?"

"The story's been killed."

"What? By whom?"

He shook his head, disappointed. "It's out of my hands. You'll have to take it up with your husband."

My cheeks burned as I charged through the cubicles to Ethan's office. He'd warned me that he wasn't comfortable with the story, but I didn't believe he'd actually kill the piece.

Ethan's back was turned to the door when I walked into his office. I closed the door behind me. "How could you?" I screamed.

He turned around, holding my article in his hands. "It's a good story, Claire," he said. "Really. Bravo."

"You can't kill it," I said. "You just can't."

"I can." His eyes looked distant, vacant. I didn't know what I hated more at that moment, the death of this story, or the death of our marriage.

I sat down in a chair in front of his desk and let out a huge sigh.

"Listen," Ethan said, sitting down, "I didn't make the decision."

I looked up. "You didn't?"

"No," he said. "Warren did."

"What?"

"Yes," he continued. "He knew you were working on it and he asked me to fax him a draft when it made its rounds."

"I don't understand. He didn't mention anything about it to me. How did he—?"

Ethan shrugged. "Well, he knew about it and he read it."

I pursed my lips. "And I take it he didn't like it."

Ethan nodded. "You'll have to take it up with him, I'm afraid. He is still the editor in chief emeritus, after all."

"I will," I said, standing up.

"He's home from the hospital, you know," he said. "Still weak, but making a good recovery."

I nodded, noticing a suitcase near his desk. His jacket lay draped across the bag, signaling his imminent departure.

I shook my head in confusion. "Where are you going?"

"Oh, that," he said, his eyes meeting mine. "I thought I'd stay on the island for a while—until we sort things out."

I gulped.

"I thought we could use . . . the time apart." He searched my eyes for approval. "We've been through so much this past year," he continued. "It'll be good for us. We could both use some time to . . . figure things out."

"Right," I said quickly. "Of course." My eyes burned. I walked around his desk and kissed his cheek. I knew I had to leave quickly or run the risk of sobbing in his office. I didn't want to plead with him to stay. I wanted him to *want* to stay. "Well," I said, feeling a lump in my throat, "then I guess this is . . . good-bye."

I didn't wait to see his face, nor did I hear what he mumbled as I walked out the door. I had to leave. The air inside those four walls felt thick and suffocating. Outside the door, I closed my eyes and thought of the little sailboat my grandmother gave me when I was a child. The memory, foggy at first, came rushing in so clear, I could feel the spray of the seawater on my face. I had played with the little boat lovingly each summer in the tide pools on the beach, until one July when I worked up the courage to take it into the ocean, an idea inspired solely by a children's book from the 1950s that I'd found in a chest in the spare bedroom, *Scuffy the Tugboat*. So I set the little boat on the shore, gave it a swift push, and immediately watched a wave wrap its tendrils around the tiny mast, sweeping it out to sea. It broke my heart to see it go, and I stared at the shore for a long time after that, scolding myself. I'd sent it away, just as I feared I'd pushed my husband away.

I couldn't bear to stay at the office any longer, so I collected my bag from my desk and walked outside. I looked up when I heard the screech of a car, inches from me, followed by the honk of an angry driver. "Watch where you're going!" shouted the man behind the wheel. "I nearly ran you over!"

I nodded and walked on, hardly affected by the exchange, across the street and to the parking lot, where Ethan's BMW waited. I stared at the shiny car for a moment, blinking back tears. It glimmered in the spring sun, so flashy, so sad. A symbol of our failed marriage. I shook my head, turned back to the street, and hailed a cab.

Warren lived in an older high-rise downtown. He'd purchased the penthouse suite with his late wife years ago. It was a grand place—or at least, it once was. The private rooftop deck, above the living room, used to be my favorite hideaway in Seattle. On warm nights, Ethan and I would join Warren for wine there, counting the stars overhead, taking in a panoramic view only birds were fortunate enough to have—from the Space Needle to Alki Beach. No one went up there anymore, though. The spiral staircase had become too difficult for Warren's weak knees, and Ethan had become too busy for wine and stargazing. I'd been on the roof a final time in the spring only to discover that it had become a nesting ground for a family of very messy pigeons.

Warren had let the housekeeper go just after Christmas. "I don't care if there's dust on my coffee table!" he had exclaimed to Glenda on a visit months ago as she eyed the stacks of disheveled magazines and books and dust-caked windowsills. Warren was the only Kensington who seemed to care less about keeping up with appearances, and I'd always loved him more for it. Still, there was no denying that he hadn't been himself of late. I'd blamed his illness, but I couldn't help but wonder if there was something more. I took a deep breath and buzzed his apartment number.

"Yes?"

"Warren, it's me, Claire."

"Yes," he said. "Come on up."

I took the elevator to the twenty-third floor, imagining what he'd say when I got there. He'd tell me I couldn't print the story because it would disgrace the family. He'd say that it would incriminate Josephine, rest her soul. He'd make me promise not to utter a word of it.

I knocked on the door.

"Come in," he called out from inside. "The door's open."

I walked inside, where Warren sat at the table eating a sandwich.

"I was expecting you," he said, dabbing a spot of mustard from the corner of his mouth with a napkin. "You're a sharp reporter, Claire." He indicated the pages in front of him.

I walked closer and recognized the headline. My article.

"You're even better than my private investigators."

The house was eerily quiet. The tick of the clock on the wall grated.

He clasped his hands together. "To think that military-trained investigators couldn't find the files at the Sharpe house, but you could." He shook his head at me in amazement. "Now *that's* skill."

My heart beat faster. *My God.* He knew of the break-in at Lillian's home. Worse, he seemed to be responsible for it.

I shook my head. "Warren, I don't understand."

"Come, sit down," he said, pointing to the chair beside him. "I've been trying to solve this mystery for many years," he continued. "It took me a great deal of time to find out what happened to Vera Ray. The case files were mysteriously lost in a fire at the police station. Too convenient, don't you think? Then I—"

My hand trembled. *What is he telling me? What does this all mean?* "Warren," I said, shaking my head, "I don't understand."

His smile put me at ease. "At first I thought it was because I wanted to protect my family, to seal away the truth in all of its ugliness. But it's more than that. It's a very personal story for me."

I covered my mouth, the wheels in my mind spinning so quickly I could hardly keep up. "Warren, are you telling me that you think you are . . . ?"

He nodded. "Yes. I killed the story because it needed a new ending. Thomas Kensington was not Daniel." His smile said everything. "I am. I wanted to tell you myself."

I gasped. "How did you find out? You were only a boy when—"

"Yes, the past is a blur, of course," he said. "I was only three when I was taken."

Taken.

I shook my head, processing the weight of the revelation. *I'm looking right at Daniel Ray. He's been here all along.*

"But a boy can sense things, even from a young age," he said. "Mother looked at me differently than the others."

"You mean Elaine?"

"Yes," he said. "At first I thought I must have been less lovable than my sister. But as I got older, I came to wonder if there was something else. One night after a party when Mother and Father had drunk too much wine, I heard them arguing in the parlor. Mother mentioned her name. *Vera.* She said it was all her fault that I was performing poorly in school. She blamed my grades on Vera's 'weak genes.' Of course, I didn't know what she was talking about or who Vera was. I didn't think about it again until Aunt Josephine had a stroke in the 1980s. The family gathered around her bed at the hospital. Father hadn't seen his sister in more than fifty years. He refused to speak to her after a falling-out they had when I was a boy. So when he showed up—when we all showed up—she was hysterical, trying to tell me how sorry she was for ruining my life, for taking me as a child, for taking me away from Vera. Mother and Father said it was only the illness speaking, that her mind wasn't right, but I knew that wasn't the case. What she said had to be rooted in truth, and when I began to look into my past, I learned they were protecting me from something very terrible. From what I have pieced together, Vera and my father were madly in love, but she was poor, and the family disapproved of her, but no one more than his sister, Josephine. Vera's mother worked as her nanny years before. Aunt Josie didn't like the woman, so she took her anger out on her daughter, Vera. She hated the thought of me, a Kensington, being raised by a commoner, so she took matters into her own hands."

"Did your father, Charles, know about this?"

"As far as I know, he, tragically, learned the truth from Josephine after Vera's death," he said. "I suspect that Josephine worried that being the good man that he was, he'd make sure I was reunited with my mother if she were still living. In her mind, she had to wait until Vera was out of the picture entirely."

I shuddered. "So what did your father say when you landed on his doorstep?"

"Josephine orchestrated it with the precision of a marionette," he said. "From what I can piece together from her mutterings at the hospital years ago, she didn't tell him who I really was, not at first. My father had a good heart. He was a man of charity. She said I needed a home, and my father took me in. Then, shortly after Thomas died, Josephine confessed her crime to Father—perhaps her own terrible loss made her realize just what she had taken from Vera and prompted her to come clean. She maintained that she did it only for my well-being, said that a Kensington should never be raised in poverty. He didn't speak to Josephine again after that, not for a long time to come."

"So he and his wife adopted you, and kept the secret all those years?"

"Yes," he said. "No one spoke about the past. It was all carefully shrouded, until it forced itself free. That's the thing about secrets— they always do find their way. Even if it takes a lifetime."

"Vera, your mother, died in a boat on the lake that night," I said. "Do you think she died at Josephine's hands?"

Warren sighed. "I think she had something to do with it. I think she may have directed Vera to that leaky boat, knowing she couldn't swim."

I nodded. "The thing that I don't quite understand is why the police didn't push the case harder, and why they were so quick to charge Ivanoff with Vera's murder."

"That's why I wanted to get my hands on those case files," he said. "I suspect Josephine, and others in the family, had something to do with that fire at the station. In any case, my family is well con-nected. If Josephine or anyone else needed a favor from the police, it happened. Ivanoff was the easy target. By going after him, they took the spotlight off of the family, and what really happened." He turned back to the draft of my article before him. "I couldn't have written it better myself."

"When you realized all of this, why didn't you go to the police? Why didn't you do something?"

"Do what? Report my family to the police? Have them arrest a dying woman?"

I saw his point.

"No," he continued. "What happened is in the past. Nothing I do can bring my mother back."

"You're right."

He paused, as if trying to remember something. "I was going through some of my father's old papers last year, and I found the ledger where his accountant kept records of his finances. I discovered something interesting inside."

"What?"

"You know the women's shelter on First Avenue?"

I nodded. "Hope House, right? I did a feature on the program last year. It's a wonderful place. They take in homeless mothers and pregnant women."

Warren looked out the window at the Seattle skyline. "My father founded it," he said.

I smiled with satisfaction. "Charles."

Warren's eyes filled with pride. "Mother could never understand why Father spent so much time on his charity work. I think poor people frightened her, but not Father."

"It all makes sense," I said. "He built Hope House in memory of Vera. Oh, Warren, you are your father's son. Now I know where your big heart comes from, your sense of humanity."

"I only wish I could have talked to him about this years ago," he said.

I pointed to the article in his hands. "And now that you have the whole story, do you feel peace?"

"Yes, in some ways," he said. "But still, there's something missing, something I'm hoping you can help me with."

I nodded. "Yes, anything."

"My old home," he said wistfully. "The apartment I shared with Vera. You've been there, haven't you?"

"Yes."

He sighed. "It's the one piece of the puzzle I wasn't able to solve. It's funny, I can remember the strangest details, like the way the lamppost flickered outside the window, and the grating sound of the women doing the wash in basins in the alley. But for the life of me, I can't remember the location of the apartment. I used to go out walking late at night, hoping I'd recall the address, wishing some storefront or old building would call to me, but all these years, the place has eluded me." His eyes, pleading and misty, stared into mine. "Can you take me there, Claire?"

"I would love nothing more," I said. "How about tomorrow afternoon?"

He closed his eyes for a moment, then opened them with new strength. "Thank you, dear."

I leaned in to kiss his cheek. "Is it weird that I want to call you Daniel now? It must sound so strange to hear the name."

"No," he said. "It doesn't. It's the name that's always been in my heart."

Chapter 20

The next morning, I sat up in bed and stretched my arms. Ethan was gone, yes, leaving a vacant spot in my heart, but I tried not to think about it. I put a bowl of instant oatmeal in the microwave and watched out the window as a ferry streamed into the bay. Ethan and I used to love to sit and watch the ferries come in and out. We had pet names for them. Edgar. Duncan. Maude. I smiled, recalling the day he'd named one Horace.

The phone rang from the kitchen, and I ran to pick it up. "Hello?"

"Claire, it's Eva."

"Hi," I said. "It's good to hear from you again." I couldn't wait to tell her about Warren.

"I was wondering if you might be able to stop by today," she said. "There's something that occurred to me and . . . well, we can talk when you get here. Are you free?"

"Yes," I said, thinking of my afternoon plans with Warren. We could stop by Eva's place first. I could reunite two old friends. "Would noon be all right?"

"Fine," she said.

"Oh, and Eva, I'll be bringing along a friend. Someone I'd like you to meet."

"Wonderful," she said. "The more the merrier."

I finished my oatmeal, then pulled my hair into a ponytail. Without thinking about what I was doing, I lifted a pair of shorts and a T-shirt from my dresser, and stood in front of the floor-length mirror in my bedroom. My legs were not what they were. Once toned and strong, they looked soft and doughy. I wasn't a runner anymore. *Could I ever be again?*

I turned to the closet, which looked bare without Ethan's clothes inside. I looked away, and a flash of blue caught my attention on the lower shoe rack. My running shoes. They sat there unassumingly, no longer taunting me the way they had in previous months. Now they only waited patiently, quietly. I walked to them and picked them up, sitting on the bed as I slowly sank my feet into their soft soles. I liked the way they felt, snug and sure. I laced them up, tying the bow into a double knot. My heart beat faster as I took a sip of water and tucked my cell phone and keys into my pocket, rituals I had done hundreds of times before going on jogs in the past.

Gene didn't say anything as I stepped off the elevator and walked through the lobby. It was a moment unworthy of conversation. Besides, my mind was churning and my heart heavy. It had been a year since I'd last set out for a jog. A life-changing year. He simply held the door open for me as I walked out onto the street, nodding as I crossed the threshold. I'd run many races over the years. But this one, even if it only turned out to be three blocks, felt like the race of my life. And it was.

At first I walked. *One foot in front of the other.* Once strong and solid, my legs felt like popsicle sticks under me. I shook my head. *No, I can't do this.* A gap in the sidewalk sent my heart racing. I remembered the car jetting toward me. The way I'd tripped. The impact, followed by the snap in my abdomen. *One foot in front of the other.* I picked up my pace, cautiously. *Breathe.* The sun shone down on my cheeks, warm and approving. A woman looked up at me from a nearby café and smiled. *Breathe.* Birds chirped from their perch on the electrical lines overhead. Before I knew it, I was running again, really running.

I zigzagged through the blocks by the apartment, then decided to make the hike up past Café Lavanto. I wouldn't go in, not after Dominic's revelation the other night. But I longed to run past it, to imagine Warren playing outside as a boy. Sweaty and out of breath, I reached the top of the hill and doubled over with a side ache. I clutched my side and took several deep breaths, then looked up at the café on the block ahead. The building was partitioned off with orange cones. Men in hardhats holding clipboards buzzed around the entrance, pointing to the structure. Yellow caution tape forbade anyone from coming in for a latte. Or a hot chocolate. *Surely they aren't starting demolition yet?* I pulled my cell phone out of my pocket and dialed Dominic's number, but after three rings, his voice mail picked up. "Dominic," I said loudly over the noise of a large truck backing up in front of the café. "You said you were selling it, but I didn't think this was happening so soon. I . . ."

Speechless, I hung up my phone, inching closer to the caution tape, and waved at a man wearing a yellow hard hat. "Excuse me!" I shouted.

He walked over with the look of someone who did not want to be bothered.

"What's going on here?"

"The building's going to come down," he said. "Well, not today. We're just getting ready."

"No!" I cried. "It can't be."

The man shrugged. "Well, it is." He flipped his clipboard around to display the architectural drawings for what looked like a new condo building. In the renderings, a Starbucks café occupied the bottom floor. "We got permits pushed through quickly on this one. Boss wants the new building up before the one across the street is finished.

I shook my head.

"Hard to believe an old place like this stuck around as long as it did," he said, glancing at the sign on the window. "What a dump."

"This *dump*," I said, "happens to be a very special place. It's where—"

The man shouted something at a worker in the distance and walked away.

"It's where Vera and Daniel lived," I continued, even if I was the only one listening. "You can't tear it down. You just can't."

I watched for a while as the construction crew milled about. They swarmed like termites gathering to devour a rotted piece of wood. I wanted to fling myself at the building and hold my arms out to protect it, the way hard-core environmentalists chain themselves to trees. I felt sick thinking of all the memories, all the secrets, that would come toppling down when the wrecking ball tore through it. *I hated to think that I might have missed something, but most important was making sure Warren got the chance to see it one more time.*

I willed myself to walk away, picking up my pace to a jog as soon as I rounded the corner. As my breath quickened, my mind turned to Ethan again. The memories caused my feet to push harder, my heart to pound louder. Before I knew it, I'd sprinted past Pacific Place and up to Broad Street, where the Space Needle gleamed overhead. That's when it hit me. *It isn't Ethan's forgiveness I'm looking for; it's my own.*

My phone rang inside my pocket and I slowed my pace. When I saw Ethan's number on the screen, my first instinct was to let the call go to voice mail. I thought about letting *him* go. I reached inside my pocket and clutched the phone as it rang a second time and then a third. I pulled it out. We had lost a baby. We had lost part of ourselves. We had been through so much. Too much. But it didn't mean we had to lose each other.

I clicked the green button.

"Hi," I said into the phone.

"Hi," he said. "I want to come home—that is, if you'll let me."

"But I thought you said—"

"Claire, I don't know what I said, and I can honestly say I don't know how to fix us. All I know is that I want to."

"Oh, Ethan," I cried. "I want that too."

"I'll be on the next ferry."

I ran another mile, then slowed to a walk once I was a block away from the apartment. Heart pounding. Face unable to stop smiling. I reached for my cell phone in my pocket and dialed Elliott Bay Jewelers.

"Yes, this is Claire Aldridge. I purchased a watch for my husband a while ago, and, well, I've decided on the engraving."

"Yes," the woman said, "what will it be?"

"Can you just print 'Sonnet 43'?"

"That's it?" the woman asked. "Nothing else?"

"No," I said. "It sums up everything I need to say."

I hung up the phone just as I reached the apartment building. Gene held the door open for me, sweat streaming down my face. "You're back," he said with a proud smile.

"I'm back," I said, stepping into the elevator. This time, the words finally rang true.

I looked up from the couch as Ethan walked into the apartment. He set his bag down by the door, and it toppled over, spilling a file folder out onto the rug, but he didn't stop to retrieve it. "Claire, I'm so sorry," he said with a cautious smile, "for the way I've behaved."

"Me too," I said quietly.

He walked to me and knelt down so that his face was directly in front of mine. "You're running again," he said quietly.

"Yeah," I replied. "Finally." I ran my fingers through his hair. A kiss of gray appeared at his temples, reminding me how much I longed to grow old with this man.

"A funny thing happened," he said. "On the ferry over to the island, I saw a couple with a little boy." He wiped a tear from his eye. "He was about the age our son would have been. One. Just barely walking."

I clasped both hands behind Ethan's neck and began to cry. "Our *son?*"

He nodded. "We had a son."

"Ethan," I cried, letting the revelation sink in and pierce my heart.

"He was a beautiful boy," he said through tears. "He had your nose. I love your nose."

I buried my face in his chest as he rocked me slowly. "I started to think about what life would be like without you, Claire, without us. Honey, I don't want that life."

"I don't either," I said, feeling a lump in my throat.

"What did the grief counselor say? That when you lose a child, you're twice as likely to end up divorced?"

I nodded. "Something like that."

"Let's beat that statistic," he said, wrapping his arm around my waist. "Let's start over.

I nodded. "Daniel," I said softly under my breath.

Ethan looked confused. "Daniel?"

"Yes," I said, smiling. "Our baby. I want to call him Daniel."

"Yes," he said, his voice shaking with emotion. "Daniel. A perfect name for our first son."

I smiled. "You talk as if we'll have another."

He grinned. "I'd like it if we did. If you're ready . . ."

"I'm getting there," I said, nuzzling my cheek against his neck.

"I'm sorry I wasn't there for you," he said softly. "Can you ever forgive me?"

I weaved my fingers through his. "Can you ever forgive *me*?"

"I already have," he said, looking out the window at the Sound and then back at me. "Hey, let's forget about work today and go somewhere, right now, to celebrate our new beginning."

I looked at the clock. "I can't," I said. "Not just yet. I already have a date."

Ethan looked confused.

"With your grandfather," I said, pressing my face against his chest, breathing in the scent of his crisp white shirt. My heart sank when I remembered the café's proposed demolition. We were too late, but not too late for a final glance. Maybe that's all

Warren needed, anyway. "I'd love it if you came with us," I said, looking up at Ethan. "It's a big moment for him." I paused. "And for me."

His keys jingled when he pulled them from his pocket, the sound of two people moving forward—together. "I'll drive you."

Ethan parked the car on the street in front of Eva's building and Warren turned to me with a confused look. "But I thought we were going to—"

I looked at my watch, conscious of every minute passing. Even if the building wasn't going to come down today, just knowing that it was so close to demolition made me increasingly anxious for Warren to see it one last time. But I'd promised Eva. "I wanted to make a stop first," I said. "Just for a minute. There's someone I'd like you to meet."

Warren and Ethan followed as I led them to the elevator up to Eva's floor. I knocked when we got to her door.

"Claire," Eva said cheerfully, welcoming us inside. "And you brought friends! Let's see, this must be your husband?" she said, turning to Ethan.

"Yes, ma'am," Ethan said, slipping an arm around my waist. I loved the warmth of his embrace, but it wasn't our moment; it was theirs.

"Eva," I said quietly, "this is Warren Kensington, but you know him by another name."

She looked at me and then at Warren, searching his face.

"Eva," Warren said. Remembrance flickered in his eyes as he extended a hand to her. "It's so good to see you again. You may remember me as Daniel. Daniel Ray."

"My God," Eva gasped. "Am I dreaming?" She sat down in a chair by the window. "It's a miracle," she continued, turning to me. "How did you . . . ? Where did you . . . ?"

"He's my grandfather," Ethan said.

Eva looked at me and then at Warren, astonished.

Warren nodded. "And this fine reporter here cracked the case."

Eva looked shaken. "You mean, you've been alive this whole time?"

Warren sat down beside her and smiled. "Well, this old ticker's still beating, so I guess so."

Eva reached her hand out to Warren's arm. "I can hardly believe you're here," she said. "Your mother missed you so."

"I can only imagine," he said.

"Do you remember, Daniel?"

"I think so. I have moments when I believe I can remember that life. When I close my eyes, I can see her face."

Eva smiled. "Vera's face?"

"Yes," he said quietly.

I knelt down beside Warren's chair. "I found her grave site," I said.

Warren looked deeply moved. "How?"

"Eva told me."

"My God," he said. "I've been looking for her for so long, I . . ."

"Would you like me to take you there today, after we visit the old apartment building?"

"Yes," Warren said, shifting in his chair. As he lifted his leg, he knocked a magazine from the coffee table. I reached to pick it up and my bracelet slid down to the base of my wrist. The sapphires sparkled in the afternoon sun streaming through the windows.

Eva sat up in her chair. "Claire, that bracelet," she said. "It's what I wanted to talk to you about. I noticed it on your wrist the other day. May I ask where you got it?"

I turned to Ethan, who waited quietly near the door, leaning against the doorframe. "My husband gave it to me," I said proudly. "It was a gift."

"Let me see it," she said, extending her hand.

I held my wrist out to her and she studied the gold chain for a long time. "Yes," she said.

"What is it?"

"Vera's bracelet. The one Charles gave to her as a gift when he was courting her."

"It can't be," I said.

"She's right," Warren said with certainty. "Father gave it to me when I was a young man. He said to give it to a very special woman because it had belonged to someone he once loved. I gave it to my wife, and when she died, I passed it on to Ethan to give to you."

I shook my head in disbelief. "All this time, I've been wearing her bracelet."

Ethan knelt beside me and I squeezed his hand. "I remember now," I said, recalling my research. "The autopsy report. Charles Kensington"—I turned to Warren—"your father picked up her personal effects. This must have been after Josephine told him the truth about you, after he found out that Vera had died searching for her son."

I clutched the bracelet with new appreciation. It had clung to Vera's wrist the night she took her last breath and had found its way to my arm some eighty years later.

"My late wife always loved that bracelet," Warren said. "If only she could have known the real story. We'll meet again," he said, looking up toward the sky with a wink. "And I'll have quite a story to tell her."

"Will you ever," Eva said.

I stood up. "I'm sure you two could reminisce forever, but Warren has one more stop to make—that is, if you're ready."

"Yes," he said, standing. "I am."

Eva followed us to the door. "I can't tell you how good it is to see you," she said to Warren. "I feel like Mother's soul can rest now."

"Aunt Caroline?" he said, as if extracting a memory long buried in his mind.

"Yes. My mother. It was her dying wish to find you."

"I hope she's smiling down now," he said.

"I know she is," Eva replied. "With Vera."

My heart pounded as Ethan drove toward Café Lavanto. He pulled the car into a load-and-unload zone at the foot of the hill leading up to the café. "Doesn't look like there's any parking on the street," he said, squinting ahead. "I'll just drop you off here."

I unfastened my seat belt in the backseat and inched closer to Warren in the passenger seat. "It may be the last chance to see the old building," I said. "They're going to tear it down."

"What a shame," he said, trying to get a look at the scene ahead. "Why?"

"Condo buildings," I said.

"Doesn't this city have enough of those?"

I shrugged. "Seattle seems to have an insatiable appetite for condos and Starbucks." I looked out at the café. "It's a shame, really. The owner is a good man. He's selling it to support his mother. She's been ill for a long time and she can't pay her medical bills."

I wasn't sure if Warren was listening. His gaze remained fixed on the street.

"Are you coming in?" I asked Ethan, before stepping out onto the sidewalk. The afternoon sun beamed in through the windshield and made his green eyes sparkle.

He glanced at his grandfather and then at me. "You go ahead, Claire," he said with a smile. "It's your story to finish."

"Thank you," I whispered.

"I'll be back to pick you up in a half hour," he said, his eyes filled with the love I'd missed so much. "Think that will be enough time?"

I nodded and gave Warren's hand a squeeze as we stepped out of the car and onto the sidewalk, inching toward the café cautiously, quietly. "Are you ready?" I asked.

He nodded, and we walked slowly up the steep block, pausing many times so Warren could catch his breath. A construction zone was no place for someone recently released from the hospital, and for a moment I felt guilty about taking him there. But then I remembered that it had been his idea, his wish.

"Claire!" I looked up to see Dominic rushing toward us. "I'm so glad you're here. I've been trying to call you back all afternoon, but your phone must be off."

I reached into my bag and realized that I'd accidently turned the ringer off. "Listen," I said, "I don't blame you."

He clutched a manila envelope. "I'm signing the papers this afternoon," he said apologetically. "It will be a day or two before they start demolition." He rubbed his brow. "Claire, I really hate that I have to do this, but it's the only way I know how to provide for my mother."

I held up my hand. "Please, don't apologize. I understand."

"You do?"

"Yes," I said. "I just wish there was another way. I'm sick about seeing this old place go."

"My brother and sister offered to chip in," he said. "We started a fund in her name to get community support. A bank back home has offered to match donations dollar for dollar. But we haven't raised near enough."

Warren stood next to me, half-listening to the exchange without taking his eyes off the door to the café. The trim, a burnt red, was in dire need of paint, particularly the upper right edge, which exposed the bare wood underneath the chipped topcoat. I wondered what color the doorframe had been in the 1930s.

Dominic gave me a knowing look and nodded toward the café, just as another truck pulled up to the street. "It's OK," he whispered. "I'll ask them not to go in until you two are done. Take all the time you need."

I looked at Dominic curiously. "How do you even know who . . . ?"

He smiled. "Daniel, right?"

I nodded. "But how did you . . . ?"

"I knew you'd find him," he said, grinning.

We took a step closer, and Warren looked at me for reassurance. "I've been waiting for this moment for a long time," he said, staring at the door, then turning to face me with misty eyes.

I worried about his heart, both the physical and the emotional toll. But he needed this. His life was like a tragic novel missing the final chapter, a beautiful one. We'd found it, dusted it off, and now it was time to read it. "Thank you, Claire," he said.

Dominic held the door open and we walked inside. The old La Marzocco espresso machine had been moved from its spot on the bar. A dark shadow of coffee stains remained in its place. The tables and chairs had been pushed to the side wall, lined up and ready to be carted out. The beautiful fireplace looked lonely on the far wall. I took a deep breath. Those beautiful tiles by Ivanoff the mason. They'd be destroyed along with everything else.

"Warren?" I said.

He didn't answer.

I reached for his hand. "Warren, are you all right?"

"I remember," he said, his eyes big and his body still. "This hallway. There were men here. Drunken men. Mother used to hurry me inside and we'd run past them, up the stairs."

He walked a few paces, slowly, toward the back of the café. "May I?" he asked, turning back to Dominic.

"Please," Dominic said.

I followed Warren through the door that led to the back room and up the staircase. The stairs creaked underfoot, and I offered my arm to steady him, but he shook his head.

He stood on the little landing and ran his hand along the baluster. "All these years," he said, reaching into the pocket of his coat, "I have dreamt about this place." He paused to pull out a handkerchief and dab the corner of his eye. "And to be here . . . it's just as I remember it."

I reached for his hand. "Do you remember her? Vera?"

He nodded. "I do. Well, I suppose it's less of a memory, and more of a . . . *feeling*." He closed his eyes and took a deep breath. "An instinct. Your heart never forgets your mother."

I blinked back a tear, watching his eyes search the wall by the stairs. He walked closer, operating on instinct, patting his hand along the base of the trim.

I approached the wall. "What is it?"

He stepped back and sighed. "It's nothing," he said. "I thought I remembered something, but . . ."

"It must be difficult," I said, "to be here again."

His eyes glimmered. "It must have destroyed her, losing me the way she did. It would have destroyed my wife to lose one of our children. She would have never been the same."

"To have searched for you the way she did, she must have loved you very much," I said.

Warren nodded, before starting his descent down the stairs. I followed, keeping my hand near his elbow to help steady him.

"I'll take you back now," I said. "You must be tired."

He didn't seem to hear me. He looked right, then left, as if he could sense something, *feel* something.

"Warren?" I asked. "Are you OK?"

He walked back to the stairs in silence, then stopped in front of a few boxes nestled against the wall. He knelt down and pushed them aside, exposing the paneling along the crumbling lath and plaster. Dominic and I watched as he traced the grooves in the wall, as if operating on muscle memory. Moments later, we heard the creak of a hinge, and Warren pried open a tiny door. *A secret compartment.* My heart beat faster.

He pushed his hand inside the little space in the wall. I knelt beside him and watched as he pulled out a feather caked in dust. He twisted it between his fingers and smiled to himself before setting it on the hardwood floor. Beside it, he set an apricot-colored pebble, a penny, three white shells, and a tattered ace of hearts. "I found it downstairs," he said, marveling at the card. "Mama let me keep it."

Mama.

I watched as he reached inside the wall again, this time pulling out an envelope. He held it up to me with a trembling hand. In faded ink were the words "To Daniel." He turned to me. "Claire, could you please read it to me?"

I nodded, lifting the edge of the yellowed envelope. I pulled out the delicate page inside and unfolded it, looking at Warren before casting my gaze on the first line:

> *My dearest Daniel,*
>
> *My world ended the day you disappeared, my sweet son. Whoever took you away also stole my heart, my life. I lived to see you smile, to hear you laugh, to share your joy. And the world seems less beautiful without you. I know you are near. I feel it in my heart; I believe you will come back to this place. Our special place. And when you do, I want you to know how much I love you, even though I may not be here to tell you so.*
>
> *One day we will be reunited, my child. One day I will sing to you again and hold you in my arms. Until then, I will be loving you, and dreaming of you.*
>
> *Your loving mother,*
>
> *Vera*

Here was little Daniel before me. I could see him as Vera once had. Soft, plump cheeks where wrinkles were. Blond curls instead of white wisps. Bright blue eyes unclouded by age.

Warren looked up to me. "The café," he said. "It's being destroyed?"

I nodded. "I'm so sorry, Warren. Dominic is selling. He has to—"

"How much is the offer?"

"I'm sorry?"

"The developer who wants to buy it, how much have they offered?"

I shook my head. "I don't know. Dominic didn't say."

"I'll double it."

I couldn't contain my smile. "Really, Warren? You'd do that?"

He smiled. "I can't let them tear down my childhood home, now, can I? And didn't he say that his family needed the funds? Might as well put this old Kensington money to good use." He looked around the little room. "Yes, that fine young man can keep things just as they are. I won't change anything." His eyes looked misty. "Well, except *one* thing."

"And what's that?"

"The name," he said. "I will change it to Vera's Café."

"Oh, Warren!" I exclaimed, hugging him tightly. "She'd be so proud."

I glanced at Vera's letter a final time, and a sentence at the bottom of the page caught my eye. A postscript. I'd overlooked it somehow.

"Wait," I said. "There's something I missed."

P.S. Daniel, don't forget Max. I found him in the snow. He's missed you.

I shook my head in confusion. "Max?"

Warren looked astonished. He reached inside the wall again, a little deeper this time. A moment later, he retrieved a child's teddy bear, ragged, with a tattered blue velvet bow.

"Max," Warren said, adjusting the dusty bow. "I dropped him, the night she came for me." His chin quivered. "She wouldn't let me go back to get him."

"Josephine?"

"Yes," he said. "All I could think about was how cold he'd be in the snow. It was so cold."

I put my hand on his shoulder. "Your mother found him and saved him for you," I said. "She knew you'd come home."

Warren rose to his feet, cradling the little bear in his arms. He pressed his face against the bear's, tucking his finger under the frayed ribbon, the way he might have done as a boy. It was only fabric, thread, and stuffing, crudely sewn. But to Warren this stuffed creature might have been worth every dollar of his fortune.

"I'll be out front," I whispered, offering him the moment of solitude I felt he needed. "We can leave when you're ready."

He nodded, and I walked out to the front of the café. Dominic tucked his hands in his pockets and looked at me sheepishly. "I'm so sorry for—"

"Please don't apologize," I said. "Everything worked out the way it was supposed to." I looked back at Warren. "When he's ready, he has something he'd like to talk to you about."

Dominic looked at me quizzically. "He does?"

I smiled and walked to the door without pausing to see the regret in his eyes.

"Good-bye, Dominic," I said, pushing the door open and stepping out to the street. Ethan would be there soon. We were beginning a new chapter—a better one—and every part of me felt lighter because of it. The sun filtered through the trees, and I noticed a barrel-chested robin pecking around near my feet. Bold and unscathed by my presence, she stared up at me with her head cocked to the right. It took a moment before I noticed her nest a few feet away, lying in a mangled pile of loose twigs and swaths of moss on the sidewalk. A single blue egg with a jagged crack along the center lay on the cement, its yolky center spilling out onto the curb.

Poor thing. She lost her baby, just as Vera had lost hers—I took a deep breath—and just as I had lost mine. It was unfair. It was tragic. But it was life.

The bird circled the nest, pecking in vain at a twig, before retreating a few feet away on the curb. I could almost feel the moment when she realized her efforts were futile. The moment she *let go.* She flew into the air, stopping briefly on a branch of the cherry tree overhead as if to memorize the scene, to say a final good-bye.

I felt the tug in my belly just then, the old ache. I wrapped my arms around the abdomen that had carried and lost a baby. *Good-bye, my Daniel.* "I will always love you," I whispered.

The wind picked up just then, rustling the branches of the cottonwood tree overhead, disturbing its fluffy seedlings and sending them flying through the air. *Just like snow.* I caught one in my hand and smiled, looking up to the sky as the robin flapped her wings, circled overhead, and then flew away.

Acknowledgments

A heartfelt thank you to my dear literary agent, Elisabeth Weed, for her encouragement, guidance, and kindness, always. Elisabeth, working with you is such a pleasure and a privilege. Also, much gratitude and a double-shot latte to Stephanie Sun, whose feedback always make my stories stronger. (Wait, make that a triple!) And, a huge thanks to Jenny Meyer for sharing my books with readers in so many countries—from Germany to Italy, Spain to Turkey, and more (wow!)—and Dana Borowitz at UTA, for representing my books so proficiently in the world of film.

To my friends at Plume, beginning with my extraordinary editor, Denise Roy, who was immediately enthusiastic about this story, from the title to its characters, reading the first draft late into the night so she could give me quick feedback—you are, in a word, amazing, and I adore working with you. To Phil Budnick, Kym Surridge, Milena Brown, Liz Keenan, Ashley Pattison, the incredible Plume sales force, and the many, many others at Penguin who work hard to make my novels successful, I am so grateful for your support and partnership.

This novel may have never been written had I not heard the haunting song "Blackberry Winter" on the radio by the gifted singer and pianist Hilary Kole (see Author's Note for the full story).

And I may have never heard the song had it not been aired on the truly fantastic Sirius Satellite Radio station Siriusly Sinatra, which always makes me want to write a novel about Frank Sinatra.

Thank you to the friends who have cheered me on—especially those who are mothers. Big hugs to you, Sally Farhat Kassab, Camille Noe Pagán, the lovely PEPS gals, and so many others. I also want to mention two very special friends who have rebounded from disappointment and loss in recent years—both have been a tremendous inspiration to me as women and mothers: Lisa Bach, your great strength and resilience amazes and inspires me. And Wendi Parriera, you have taught me so much about faith and hope in the face of the unthinkable.

To my parents, for too many reasons to list here, but especially to my mom, Karen Mitchell, for her blackberry pies and making life lovely for her children and her grandchildren; and to my dad, Terry Mitchell, for his dedication to his children, for our jogs together, and for all those long walks to that old cemetery where childhood curiosity blossomed into literary inspiration. To my brothers Josh and Josiah, and my sister, Jessica, my dearest friend who is a profound inspiration to me in motherhood and life—love to you all.

My beloved sons—Carson, Russell, and Colby—this book is for you.

Finally, to my readers: Thank you for welcoming my stories into your lives, for reading them with your book clubs, and for telling your friends and families about them. I have many more to come—some in progress, others just little glimmers in my mind—and I can hardly wait for you to read them.

Author's Note

One morning, while in the car with my husband and our young sons, an intriguing song came on the radio. I had never heard it before, but I was instantly transfixed by the melody, and the singer's haunting voice. I turned to my husband, who was driving: "This is a *beautiful* song!" I exclaimed. "Do you know it?" He shook his head. I glanced at the radio, and the screen read, "Blackberry Winter by Hilary Kole." The title made my heart flutter. As a lifelong Northwesterner, blackberries are special to me. I get nostalgic when I think about the after-dinner walks I took with my parents and siblings during the summers of my childhood. We'd all take bowls and tromp through the woods near our home, scouting for blackberries. My sister and I would eat the majority of them, and the rest would find their way into one of mom's famous pies or cobblers. Summer just wasn't summer without berry-stained fingers.

That day in the car, I pulled out my phone (which, ahem, happens to be a BlackBerry) and e-mailed myself the name of the song and its artist. I wanted to read the lyrics, but mostly, I wanted to know the origins of the title. *What is a blackberry winter?* Later, at home, I sat down at my desk to do some research. I learned that the term is old-fashioned weather jargon for a late-season cold snap—think of plunging temperatures and snowfall in May, just when the delicate white flowers are beginning to appear on the blackberry vines.

I couldn't get the words "blackberry winter" out of my head, and that night, I began to sketch out the concept for this novel. The story came to me quickly and vividly: Vera and Daniel and the little apartment they shared in the 1930s; his beloved teddy bear lying face-down in the cold snow; Claire and her curious reporter's mind and her own deep pain and grief; snowflakes falling on the spring cherry blossoms.

For the next many months, I lived and breathed *Blackberry Winter.* At the heart of this story, for me, were the raw emotions of motherhood. I began writing the novel when I was pregnant with my third son, and I channeled Vera and Claire's pain and often heartbreaking experiences. I thought a lot about how it would feel to lose a child, and what I would do. Then, in a heartbreaking turn of events, shortly before I finished the book, one of my dearest friends, Wendi Parriera, lost her two-year-old son to a rare form of brain cancer. It broke my heart to watch her say good-bye to her precious boy, and I wept with her on the phone as she held her son against her chest in the final hours of his life. But, I also saw her strength, and the light in her eye—the one that told me how thankful she is to have been the mother of this beautiful child, and how excited she is to know, with certainty, that she'll be seeing him again, in heaven. Wendi reminds me, always, that motherhood— life—no matter how short, is a gift.

While my characters' challenges are great and their stories tragic, like my dear friend, I like to think that they found their own sense of peace and truth—swirling in a late-season snowstorm and hidden among the protective thorns of the blackberry vines.

Thank you for reading. I hope this novel touches your heart in the same way it touched mine.

Turn the page for a sneak peek of

THE VIOLETS OF
MARCH

Sarah Jio's heartbreaking novel of love,
hope and second chances

**Publishing in paperback and ebook
March 2020**

Chapter 1

"I guess this is it," Joel said, leaning into the doorway of our apartment. His eyes darted as if he was trying to memorize every detail of the turn-of-the-century New York two-story, the one we'd bought together five years ago and renovated—in happier times. It was a sight: the entryway with its delicate arch, the old mantel we'd found at an antique store in Connecticut and carted home like treasure, and the richness of the dining room walls. We'd agonized about the paint color but finally settled on Morocco Red, a shade that was both wistful and jarring, a little like our marriage. Once it was on the walls, he thought it was too orange. I thought it was just right.

Our eyes met for a second, but I quickly looked down at the dispenser in my hands and robotically pried off the last piece of packing tape, hastily plastering it on the final box of Joel's belongings that he'd come over that morning to retrieve. "Wait," I said, recalling a fleck of a blue leather-bound hardback I'd seen in the now-sealed box. I looked up at him accusatorily. "Did you take my copy of *Years of Grace*?"

I had read the novel on our honeymoon in Tahiti six years

prior, though it wasn't the memory of our trip I wanted to eulogize with its tattered pages. Looking back, I'll never know how the 1931 Pulitzer Prize winner by the late Margaret Ayer Barnes ended up in a dusty stack of complimentary books in the resort's lobby, but as I pulled it out of the bin and cracked open its brittle spine, I felt my heart contract with a deep familiarity that I could not explain. The moving story told in its pages, of love and loss and acceptance, of secret passions and the weight of private thoughts, forever changed the way I viewed my own writing. It may have even been the reason why I *stopped* writing. Joel had never read the book, and I was glad of it. It was too intimate to share. It read to me like the pages of my unwritten diary.

Joel watched as I peeled the tape back and opened the box, digging around until I found the old novel. When I did I let out a sigh of emotional exhaustion.

"Sorry," he said awkwardly. "I didn't realize you—"

He didn't realize a lot of things about me. I grasped the book tightly, then nodded and re-taped the box. "I guess that's everything," I said, standing up.

He glanced cautiously toward me, and I returned his gaze this time. For another few hours, at least until I signed the divorce papers later that afternoon, he would still be my husband. Yet it was difficult to look into those dark brown eyes knowing that the man I had married was leaving me, for someone else. *How did we get here?*

The scene of our demise played out in my mind like a tragic movie, the way it had a million times since we'd been separated. It opened on a rainy Monday morning in November. I was making scrambled eggs smothered in Tabasco, his favorite, when he told me about Stephanie. The way she made him laugh. The way she understood him. The way they *connected*. I pictured the image of two Lego pieces fusing together, and I shuddered. It's funny; when I think back to that morning, I can actually smell burned eggs and Tabasco. Had I known that this is what the end of my marriage would smell like, I would have made pancakes.

I looked once again into Joel's face. His eyes were sad and unsure. I knew that if I rose to my feet and threw myself into his arms, he might embrace me with the love of an apologetic husband who wouldn't leave, wouldn't end our marriage. But, no, I told myself. The damage had been done. Our fate had been decided. "Good-bye, Joel," I said. My heart may have wanted to linger, but my brain knew better. He needed to go.

Joel looked wounded. "Emily, I—"

Was he looking for forgiveness? A second chance? I didn't know. I extended my hand as if to stop him from going on. "Good-bye," I said, mustering all my strength.

He nodded solemnly, then turned to the door. I closed my eyes and listened as he shut it quietly behind him. He locked it from the outside, a gesture that made my heart seize. *He still cares.* . . . About my safety, at least. I shook my head and reminded myself to get the locks changed, then listened as his footsteps became quieter, until they were completely swallowed up by the street noise.

My phone rang sometime later, and when I stood up to get it, I realized that I'd been sitting on the floor engrossed in *Years of Grace* ever since Joel left. Had a minute passed? An hour?

"Are you coming?" It was Annabelle, my best friend. "You promised me you wouldn't sign your divorce papers alone."

Disoriented, I looked at the clock. "Sorry, Annie," I said,

fumbling for my keys and the dreaded manila envelope in my bag. I was supposed to meet her at the restaurant forty-five minutes ago. "I'm on my way."

"Good," she said. "I'll order you a drink."

The Calumet, our favorite lunch spot, was four blocks from my apartment, and when I arrived ten minutes later, Annabelle greeted me with a hug.

"Are you hungry?" she asked after we sat down.

I sighed. "No."

Annabelle frowned. "Carbs," she said, passing me the bread basket. "You need carbs. Now, where are those papers? Let's get this over with."

I pulled the envelope out of my bag and set it on the table, staring at it with the sort of caution one might reserve for dynamite.

"You realize this is all your fault," Annabelle said, half-smiling.

I gave her a dirty look. "What do you mean, my fault?"

"You don't *marry* men named Joel," she continued with that *tsk-tsk* sound in her voice. "Nobody marries Joels. You date Joels, you let them buy you drinks and pretty little things from Tiffany, but you don't marry them."

Annabelle was working on her PhD in social anthropology. In her two years of research, she had analyzed marriage and divorce data in an unconventional way. According to her findings, a marriage's success rate can be accurately predicted by the man's name.

Marry an Eli and you're likely to enjoy wedded bliss for about 12.3 years. Brad? 6.4. Steves peter out after just four. And as far as Annabelle is concerned, don't ever—*ever*—marry a Preston.

"So what does the data say about Joel again?"

"Seven point two years," she said in a matter-of-fact tone.

I nodded. We had been married for six years and two weeks.

"You need to find yourself a Trent," she continued.

I made a displeased face. "I hate the name Trent."

"OK, then an Edward or a Bill, or—no, a Bruce," she said. "These are names with marital longevity."

"Right," I said sarcastically. "Maybe you should take me husband-shopping at a retirement home."

Annabelle is tall and thin and beautiful—Julia Roberts beautiful, with her long, wavy dark hair, porcelain skin, and intense dark eyes. At thirty-three she had never been married. The reason, she'd tell you, was jazz. She couldn't find a man who liked Miles Davis and Herbie Hancock as much as she did.

She waved for the waiter. "We'll take two more, please." He whisked away my martini glass, leaving a water ring on the envelope.

"It's time," she said softly.

My hand trembled a little as I reached into the envelope and pulled out a stack of papers about a half-inch thick. My lawyer's assistant had flagged three pages with hot pink "sign here" sticky notes.

I reached into my bag for a pen and felt a lump in my throat as I signed my name on the first page, and then the next, and then the next. Emily Wilson, with an elongated *y* and a pronounced *n*. It was the exact way I'd signed my name since the fifth grade. Then I scrawled out the date, February 28, 2005, the day our marriage was laid to rest.

"Good girl," Annabelle said, inching a fresh martini closer to me. "So are you going to write about Joel?" Because I am a writer, Annabelle, like everyone else I knew, believed that writing about my relationship with Joel as a thinly veiled novel would be the best revenge.

"You could build a whole story around him, except change his name slightly," she continued. "Maybe call him Joe, and make him look like a total jerk." She took a bite and nearly choked on her food, laughing, before saying, "No, a jerk with *erectile dysfunction*."

The only problem is that even if I had wanted to write a revenge novel about Joel, which I didn't, it would have been a terrible book. Anything I got down on paper, if I could get anything down on paper, would have lacked imagination. I know this because I had woken up every day for the past eight years, sat at my desk, and stared at a blank screen. Sometimes I'd crank out a great line, or a few solid pages, but then I'd get stuck. And once I was frozen, there was no melting the ice.

My therapist, Bonnie, called it clinical (as in terminal) writer's block. My muse had taken ill, and her prognosis didn't look good.

Eight years ago I wrote a best-selling novel. Eight years ago I was on top of the world. I was skinny—not that I'm fat now (well, OK, so the thighs, yes, maybe a little)—and on the *New York Times* best seller list. And if there were such a thing as the *New York Times* best life list, I would have been on that, too.

After my book, *Calling Ali Larson*, was published, my agent encouraged me to write a follow-up. Readers wanted a sequel, she told me. And my publisher had already offered to double my advance for a second book. But as hard as I tried, I had nothing more to write, nothing more to say. And eventually, my agent stopped calling. Publishers stopped wondering. Readers stopped caring. The only evidence that my former life wasn't just a figment was the royalty checks that came in the mail every so often and an occasional letter I received from a somewhat deranged reader by the name of Lester McCain, who believed he was in love with Ali, my book's main character.

I still remember the rush I felt when Joel walked up to me at my book release party at the Madison Park Hotel. He was at some cocktail party in an adjoining room when he saw me standing in the doorway. I was wearing a Betsey Johnson dress, which in 1997 was *the ultimate*: a black strapless number that I'd spent an embarrassing amount of money on. But, oh yes, it was worth *every penny*. It was still in my closet, but I suddenly had the urge to go home and burn it.

"You look stunning," he had said, rather boldly, before even introducing himself. I remember how I felt when I heard him utter those words. It could have been his trademark pick-up line, and let's be real, it probably was. But it made me feel like a million bucks. It was so Joel.

A few months prior to that, *GQ* had done a big spread on the most eligible "regular-guy" bachelors in America—no, not the list that every two years always features George Clooney; the one that listed a surfer in San Diego, a dentist in Pennsylvania, a teacher in Detroit, and, yes, an attorney in New York, Joel. He had made the Top 10. And somehow, *I* had snagged him.

And lost him.

Annabelle was waving her hands in front of me. "Earth to Emily," she said.

"Sorry," I replied, shuddering a little. "No, I won't be writing about Joel." I shook my head and tucked the papers back into the envelope, then put it in my bag. "If I write anything again, it will be different than any story I've ever tried to write."

Annabelle shot me a confused look. "What about the follow-up to your last book? Aren't you going to finish that?"

"Not anymore," I said, folding a paper napkin in half and then in half again.

"Why not?"

I sighed. "I can't do it anymore. I can't force myself to churn out 85,000 mediocre words, even if it means a book deal. Even if it means thousands of readers with my book in their hands on beach vacations. No, if I ever write anything again—if I ever write again—it will be different."

Annabelle looked as if she wanted to stand up and applaud. "Look at you," she said, smiling. "You're having a breakthrough."

"No I'm not," I said stubbornly.

"Sure you are," she countered. "Let's analyze this some more." She clasped her hands together. "You said you want to write something *different*, but what I think you mean is that your heart wasn't in your last book."

"You could say that, yes," I said, shrugging.

Annabelle retrieved an olive from her martini glass and popped it into her mouth. "Why don't you write about something you actually *care* about?" she said a moment later. "Like a place, or a person that inspired you."

I nodded. "Isn't that what every writer tries to do?"

"Yeah," she said, shooing away the waiter with a "we're fine, and no we would not like the bill yet" look, then turning back to me with intense eyes. "But have you actually *tried* it? I mean, your book was fantastic—it really was, Em—but was there anything in it that was, well, *you*?"

She was right. It was a fine story. It was a best seller, for crying out loud. So why couldn't I feel proud of it? Why didn't I feel *connected* to it?

"I've known you a long time," she continued, "and I know that it wasn't a story that grew out of your life, your experiences."

It wasn't. But what in my life could I draw from? I thought about my parents and grandparents, and then shook my head.

"That's the problem," I said. "Other writers have plenty to mine from—bad mothers, abuse, adventurous childhoods. My life has been so vanilla. No deaths. No trauma. Not even a dead pet. Mom's cat, Oscar, is twenty-two years old. There's nothing there that warrants storytelling, believe me; I've thought about it."

"I don't think you're giving yourself enough credit," she said. "There must be something. Some spark."

This time I permitted my mind to wander, and when it did, I immediately thought of my great-aunt Bee, my mother's aunt, and her home on Bainbridge Island, in Washington State. I missed her as much as I missed the island. How had I let so many years pass since my last visit? Bee, who was eighty-five going on twenty-nine, had never had children, so my sister and I, by default, became her surrogate grandchildren. She sent us birthday cards with crisp fifty-dollar bills inside, Christmas gifts that were actually cool, and Valentine's Day candy, and when we'd visit in the summers from our home in Portland, Oregon, she'd sneak chocolate under our pillows before our mother could scream, "No, they just brushed their teeth!"

Bee was unconventional, indeed. But there was also something a little *off* about her. The way she talked too much. Or talked too little. The way she was simultaneously welcoming and petulant, giving and selfish. And then there were her secrets. I loved her for having them.

My mother always said that when people live alone for the better part of their lives they become immune to their own quirks. I wasn't sure if I bought into the theory or not, partly because I was worried about a lifetime of spinsterhood myself. I contented myself with watching for signs.

Bee. I could picture her immediately at her Bainbridge Island kitchen table. For every day I have known her, she has eaten the same breakfast: sourdough toast with butter and whipped honey. She slices the golden brown toasted bread into four small squares and places them on a paper towel she has folded in half. A generous smear of softened butter goes on each piece, as thick as frosting on a cupcake, and each is then topped by a good-size dollop of whipped honey. As a child, I watched her do this hundreds of times, and now, when I'm sick, sourdough toast with butter and honey is like medicine.

Bee isn't a beautiful woman. She towers above most men, with a face that is somehow too wide, shoulders too large, teeth too big. Yet the black-and-white photos of her youth reveal a spark of something, a certain prettiness that all women have in their twenties.

I used to love a particular photo of her at just that age, which hung in a seashell-covered frame high on the wall in the hallway of my childhood home, hardly in a place of honor, as one had to stand on a step stool to see it clearly. The old, scalloped-edge photo depicted a Bee I'd never known. Seated with a group of friends on a beach blanket, she appeared carefree and was smiling seductively. Another woman leaned in close to her, whispering in her ear. *A secret.* Bee clutched a string of pearls dangling from her neck and gazed at the camera in a way I'd never witnessed her look at Uncle Bill. I wondered who stood behind the lens that day so many years ago.

"What did she say?" I asked my mother one day as a child, peering up at the photograph.

Mom didn't look up from the laundry she was wrestling with in the hallway. "What did *who* say?"

I pointed to the woman next to Bee. "The pretty lady whispering in Aunt Bee's ear."

Mom immediately stood up and walked to my side. She reached up and wiped away the dust on the glass frame with the edge of her sweater. "We'll never know," she said, her regret palpable as she regarded the photo.

My mother's late uncle, Bill, was a handsome World War II hero. Everybody said he had married Bee for her money, but it's a theory that didn't hold weight with me. I had seen the way he kissed her, the way he wrapped his arms around her waist during those summers of my childhood. He had loved her; there was no doubt of that.

Even so, I knew by the way my mother talked that she disapproved of their relationship, that she believed Bill could have done better for himself. Bee, in her mind, was too unconventional, too unladylike, too brash, too *everything*.

Yet we kept coming to visit Bee, summer after summer. Even after Uncle Bill died when I was nine. The place was kind of ethereal, with the seagulls flying overhead, the sprawling gardens, the smell of the Puget Sound, the big kitchen with its windows facing out onto the gray water, the haunting hum of the waves crashing on the shore. My sister and I loved it, and despite my mother's feelings about Bee, I know she loved the place too. It had a tranquilizing effect on all of us.

Annabelle gave me a knowing look. "You *do* have a story in there, don't you?"

I sighed. "Maybe," I said noncommittally.

"Why don't you take a trip?" she suggested. "You need to get away, to clear your head for a while."

I scrunched up my nose at the idea. "Where would I go?"

"Somewhere far away from here."

She was right. The Big Apple is a fair-weather friend. The city loves you when you're flying high and kicks you when you're down.

"Will you come with me?" I imagined the two of us on a tropical beach, with umbrella cocktails.

She shook her head. "No."

"Why not?" I felt like a puppy—a scared, lost puppy who just wanted someone to put her collar on and show her where to go, what to do, how to be.

"I can't go with you because you need to do this on your own." Her words jarred me. She looked me straight in the eye, as if I needed to absorb every drop of what she was about to say. "Em, your marriage has ended and, well, it's just that you haven't shed a single tear."

On the walk back to my apartment I thought about what Annabelle had said, and my thoughts, once again, turned to my aunt Bee. *How have I let so many years pass without visiting her?*

I heard a shrill, shrieking sound above my head, the unmistakable sound of metal on metal, and looked up. A copper duck weather vane, weathered to a rich gray-green patina, stood at attention on the roof of a nearby café. It twirled noisily in the wind.

My heart pounded as I took in the familiar sight. Where had I seen it before? Then it hit me. *The painting. Bee's painting.* Until that moment, I had forgotten about the five-by-seven canvas she'd given me when I was a child. She used to paint, and I remember the great sense of honor I felt when she chose me to be the caretaker of the artwork. I had called it a masterpiece, and my words made her smile.

I closed my eyes and could see the oil-painted seascape perfectly: the duck weather vane perched atop that old beach cottage, and the couple, hand in hand, on the shore.

I felt overcome with guilt. Where was the painting? I'd packed it away after Joel and I moved into the apartment—he didn't think it matched our decor. Just like I'd distanced myself from the island I'd loved as a child, I had packed away the relics of my past in boxes. *Why? For what?*

I picked up my pace until it turned into a full-fledged jog. I thought of *Years of Grace. Did the painting accidentally end up in a box of Joel's things too? Or worse, did I mistakenly pack it in a box of books and clothes for the Goodwill pickup?* I reached the door to the apartment and jammed my key into the lock, then sprinted up the stairs to the bedroom and flung open the closet door. There, on the top shelf, were two boxes. I pulled one down and rummaged through its contents: a few stuffed animals from childhood, a box of old Polaroids, and several notebooks' worth of clippings from my two-year stint writing for the college newspaper. Still, no painting.

I reached for the second box, and looked inside to find a Raggedy Ann doll, a box of notes from junior high crushes, and my beloved Strawberry Shortcake diary from elementary school. That was it.

How could I have lost it? How could I have been so careless? I stood up, giving the closet a final once-over. A plastic bag shoved far into the back corner suddenly caught my eye. My heart raced with anticipation as I pulled it out into the light.

Inside the bag, wrapped in a turquoise and pink beach towel, was the painting. Something deep inside me ached as I clutched it in my hands. The weather vane. The beach. The old cottage. They were all as I remembered them. But not the couple. No, something was different. I had always imagined the subjects to be Bee and Uncle Bill. The woman was most certainly Bee, with her long legs and trademark baby blue capri pants. Her "summer pants," she'd called them. But the man wasn't Uncle Bill. No. How could I have missed this? Bill had light hair, sandy blond. But this man had thick, wavy dark hair. *Who was he? And why did Bee paint herself with him?*

I left the mess on the floor and walked, with the painting, downstairs to my address book. I punched the familiar numbers into the phone and took a long, deep breath, listening to the chime of the first ring and then the second.

"Hello?" Her voice was the same—deep and strong, with soft edges.

"Bee, it's me, Emily," I said, my voice cracking a little. "I'm sorry it's been so long. It's just that I—"

"Nonsense, dear," she said. "No apologies necessary. Did you get my postcard?"

"Your postcard?"

"Yes, I sent it last week after I heard your news."

"You heard?" I hadn't told very many people about Joel. Not my parents in Portland—not yet, anyway. Not my sister in Los Angeles, with her perfect children, doting husband, and organic vegetable garden. Not even my therapist. Even so, I wasn't surprised that the news had made its way to Bainbridge Island.

"Yes," she said. "And I wondered if you'd come for a visit." She paused. "This island is a marvelous place to heal."

I ran my finger along the edge of the painting. I wanted to be there just then—on Bainbridge Island, in Bee's big, warm kitchen.

"When are you coming?" Bee never wastes words.

"Is tomorrow too soon?"

"Tomorrow," she said, "is the first of March, the month the sound is at its best, dear. It's absolutely *alive*."

I knew what she meant when she said it. The churning gray water. The kelp and the seaweed and barnacles. I could almost taste the salty air. Bee believed that the Puget Sound was the great healer. And I knew that when I arrived, she would encourage me to take my shoes off and go wading, even if it was one o'clock in the morning—even if it was forty-three degrees, which it probably would be.

"And, Emily?"

"Yes?"

"There's something important that we need to talk about."

"What is it?"

"Not now. Not over the phone. When you get here, dear."

After I hung up, I walked downstairs to the mailbox to find a credit card bill, a Victoria's Secret catalog—addressed to Joel—and a large square envelope. I recognized the return address, and it only took me a moment to remember where I'd seen it: on the divorce papers. There was also the fact that I'd Googled it the week before. It was Joel's new town house on Fifty-seventh—the one he was sharing with Stephanie.

The adrenaline started pumping when I considered the fact that Joel could have been reaching out to me. Maybe he was sending me a letter, a card—no, a romantic beginning to a scavenger hunt: an invitation to meet him somewhere in the city, where there'd be another clue, and then after four more, there he'd be, standing in front of the hotel where we met so many years ago. And he'd be holding a rose—no, a sign, and it would read, I'M SORRY. I LOVE YOU. FORGIVE ME. Exactly like that. It could be the perfect ending to a tragic romance. *Give us a happy ending, Joel*, I found myself whispering as I ran my finger along the envelope. *He still loves me. He still feels something.*

But when I lifted the edge of the envelope and carefully pulled out the gold-tinged card inside, the fantasy came to a crashing halt. All I could do was stare.

The thick card stock. The fancy calligraphy. It was a wedding invitation. *His* wedding invitation. Six p.m. Dinner. Dancing. A celebration of love. Beef or chicken. Accepts with pleasure. Declines with regret. I walked to the kitchen, calmly bypassing the recycle bin, and instead set the little stack of gold stationery right into the kitchen trash, on top of a take-out box of moldy chicken chow mein.

Fumbling with the rest of the mail, I dropped a magazine, and when I reached down to pick it up, I saw the postcard from Bee, which had been hiding in the pages of *The New Yorker*. The front featured a ferry boat, white with green trim, coming into Eagle Harbor. I flipped it over and read:

> Emily,
>
> The island has a way of calling one back when it's time. Come home. I have missed you, dear.
>
> All my love,
>
> Bee

I pressed the postcard to my chest and exhaled deeply.

One mother's desperate hope for survival.
One woman's search for the truth ...

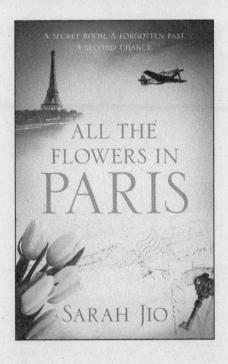

1943: In occupied Paris, Celine creates bespoke bouquets at her father's flower shop on rue Cler, whilst trying to shield her young daughter from the brutal reality of war. But when an SS officer takes an interest in Celine and her family, all their lives are put in jeopardy.

2009: Caroline wakes in Paris with no memory of her previous life. Hunting for clues to her identity in her apartment on the rue Cler, she discovers a bundle of letters written by a young widow during the Second World War. As she peels back the layers of the past, Caroline finds new purpose – but Celine's story is unfinished. Desperate to find out the truth, Caroline digs deeper, uncovering dark and dangerous secrets ...

Can learning the truth about Celine help
Caroline unlock the mystery of her past?